HORROR IN THE BIZARRE HANDS OF JOE R. LANSDALE

We are trapped in the drive-in. On the screen, a young girl tries to flee her mother, father, and older brother. They explain that, as the youngest member of the family, it's only right that she provide sustenance. A chill runs up my back. Not because it's a horrible thing they suggest. Because I too am hungry, and they seem to make good sense.

HELL THROUGH A WINDSHIELD

Calhoun had killed four bounty hunters so far. The last had been Pink Lady McGuire—one mean mama—three hundred pounds of rolling, ugly meat that carried a twelve-gauge Remington pump and a bad attitude. Calhoun cut her throat and, as a joke, did her before she bled to death. This not only proved that he was a dangerous sonofabitch, it also proved he had bad taste.

ON THE FAR SIDE OF THE CADILLAC DESERT WITH DEAD FOLKS

"SHORT STORIES BY ONE OF THE BIGGEST NAMES IN HORROR AND ONE OF MY FAVORITE AUTHORS ... NOT FOR THE SQUEAMISH OR EASILY OFFENDED."
Denver Rocky Mountain News

S0-BYG-239

BY BIZARRE HANDS

JOE R. LANSDALE

Introduction by Lewis Shiner

AVON BOOKS ◆ NEW YORK

AVON BOOKS
A division of
The Hearst Corporation
1350 Avenue of the Americas
New York, New York 10019

Copyright © 1989 by Joe R. Lansdale
Introduction copyright © 1989 by Lewis Shiner
Cover art copyright © 1989 by J. K. Potter
Published by arrangement with Mark V. Zeising
Library of Congress Catalog Card Number: 91-91794
ISBN: 0-380-71205-9

First Avon Books Printing: September 1991

AVON TRADEMARK REG. U.S. PAT. OFF. AND IN OTHER COUNTRIES, MARCA
REGISTRADA, HECHO EN U.S.A.

Printed in the U.S.A.

RA 10 9 8 7 6 5 4 3 2 1

This book is dedicated with love and respect
to Ardath Mayhar
who read most of these before anyone else
and was always there
with encouragement or a wise suggestion.

AUTHOR'S PREFACE

A number of these stories have been slightly revised due to editorial meddling or my not liking what I put down in the first place. I've tried to keep that sort of thing to a minimum, however, so that the stories will reflect the energy they were born with and not suffer after the fact dissection and beautification.

"Hell Through a Windshield" appears here in its entirety for the first time, as it was originally cut for space considerations, and two stories, "The Fat Man and the Elephant" and "The Steel Valentine" appear here for the first time anywhere. "I Tell You It's Love," "By Bizarre Hands," "Letter From the South, Two Moons West of Nacogdoches," appeared in small magazines and will be new to most readers. "Boys Will Be Boys" appeared in a small magazine, but became part of my novel *The Nightrunners*, and "The Windstorm Passes" became part of *The Magic Wagon*.

Lastly, I'd like to thank John Skipp and Craig Spector for allowing me to print "On the Far Side of the Cadillac Desert With Dead Folks" so close to its appearance in their anthology, *Book of the Dead*.

And so you can be specific about the stories, see from what team they were drafted, here's your program:

"Fish Night," 1982. From *Specter!*, edited by Bill Pronzini, Arbor House Books.

"The Pit," 1987. From *The Black Lizard Anthology of Crime Fiction*, edited by Edward Gorman, Black Lizard Books.

"Duck Hunt," 1986. From *After Midnight*, edited by Charles L. Grant, Tor Books.

"By Bizarre Hands," Winter/Spring 1988. From *Hardboiled* No. 9.

"The Steel Valentine" appears here for the first time.

"I Tell You It's Love," 1983. From *Modern Stories*.

"Letter from the South, Two Moons West of Nacogdoches," Winter 1986. From *Last Wave* No. 5.

"Boys Will Be Boys," Winter 1985/86. From *Hardboiled* No. 3.

"The Fat Man and the Elephant" appears here for the first time.

"Hell Through a Windshield," April 1985. From *Rod Serling's The Twilight Zone Magazine*.

"Down by the Sea Near the Great Big Rock," 1984. From *Masks*, edited by J.N. Williamson, Maclay & Associates.

"Trains Not Taken," Spring 1987. From *RE:AL* (Stephen F. Austin State University, Nacogdoches, Texas).

"Tight Little Stitches in a Dead Man's Back," 1986. From *Nukes*, edited by John Maclay, Maclay & Associates.

"The Windstorm Passes," Spring 1986. From *Pulpsmith*.

"Night They Missed the Horror Show," 1988. From *Silver Scream*, edited by David Schow, Dark Harvest Press.

"On the Far Side of the Cadillac Desert with Dead Folks," 1989. From *Book of the Dead*, edited by John Skipp and Craig Spector, Bantam Books.

CONTENTS

INTRODUCTION

by Lewis Shiner

Joe Lansdale scares the living shit out of some people.

I'm talking about his work here, of course. Joe himself is a sweetheart: modest, funny, easygoing, quick to make friends. He's even as gentle and peace-loving as you could hope for in a six-foot, 180-pound former karate instructor with more black belts than he has shoes.

No, the problem comes from these stories he keeps writing. They get great rejection letters from top editors in the field. People love his writing, his dialogue, his sense of place, but they can't quite bring themselves to publish him. They invite him into anthologies and then when they read what he sends them, they ask him to leave quietly and please not break anything on the way out.

I know how they feel. I bought a story from Joe myself, "I Tell You It's Love," and it didn't scare me, exactly, but it made me very damned uncomfortable.

So what is it about these stories? What kind of stories *are* they, exactly?

People have been trying for years to explain what kind of writer Joe is. They've compared him to Clive Barker, which I don't really see. Barker is best known for the explicit violence of his work, and yes, Joe's done that. But Joe has never spilled a quart of blood without good and sufficient reason. The violence in Joe's stories is not there for its own sake, but as a natural outgrowth of the characters.

He's been compared to Barry Hannah, a master of voice and atmosphere. Joe does that too, with the best of them, but he hooks that voice and atmosphere to a story engine that just won't quit.

He's been compared to Mark Twain, which comes closer than any of the others. Twain was a stylist, a storyteller, and a social critic. He wrote for literature professors as well as the barely literate. Even so, Twain never disappeared from his work as thoroughly as Joe does, leaving only the naked voice of another, infinitely strange human mind.

If we can't pin Joe down as a writer, how about putting the stories themselves into categories? After all he is one of the brightest lights of modern horror fiction, part of this new "splatterpunk" business we keep hearing about. Right?

Wrong. Joe at his best, as he is in this book, doesn't properly fit in anywhere. "Night They Missed the Horror Show" reads like a horror story, but there's nothing supernatural about it. Likewise "The Steel Valentine" (one of two stories original to this anthology) and "The Pit." "Duck Hunt" is a similar exercise in realistic horror, except its most obvious inspiration is the animated cartoon.

"Tight Little Stitches in a Dead Man's Back" is neither quite S/F nor quite fantasy; "Trains Not Taken" is not quite a western; and "Hell Through a Windshield" is not quite a memoir. "The Fat Man and the Elephant" (the other original, and perhaps my favorite in the collection) most resembles a mainstream story of character, but unlike any you will ever see in *The New Yorker*.

Joe's life would have been easier if he'd been willing to blunt these stories in order to fit them into the conventional categories. Publishers would be able to slap a label on him that would stick; his audience would already be defined; people writing introductions to his short story collections could say, "If you like [fill in the blank] you'll love Joe Lansdale."

But Joe doesn't walk that line, and he's not the first. For example there's Don DeLillo and William Goldman and Graham Greene, writers who have become categories unto themselves. It takes longer for these writers to build an audience, longer to find a publisher who'll put up with their departures. They demand readers who think for themselves, who want more than just one more fix of the same old thing.

There's not a lot of incentive for these writers. The pressure to go rogue this way, to jump off the interstate and cut your own roads, has to come from inside. It takes ambition and determination, patience and courage. Much the same qualities it took for Joe to drag himself, by his bootstraps, out of the East Texas swamps of Gladewater, Texas (immortalized as "Mud Creek" in many of his stories) and off to the relative metropolis of Nacogdoches.

Once those new roads are cut, however, everybody else is rushing to get on them.

Joe has as much drive to write as anybody I've ever seen. He's never met a writing challenge he couldn't solve with his one-size-fits-all advice, "Put ass to chair in front of typewriter." He spends every available minute working. There was a stretch after his son Keith was born when that meant typing with an infant on his lap. (Which made, by the way, for some weird intrusions in his letters.)

Joe writes from his heart, and he lives the same way. I've gotten letters from him that tore my work to shreds, and then awkwardly apologized for his honesty. The thing is, I don't believe there was a choice involved. If Joe couldn't tell me what he really thought, I don't think he would have been able to write at all.

Which brings us back to the stories in this collection. Every one of them is the truth the way Joe saw it at the time. Joe doesn't especially enjoy frightening or disturbing or embarrassing his readers. But if that's the price of honesty, it's a price he's willing to pay.

This is Joe's first short story collection. I think it's a triumph in its own small way. Here is an individual whose vision was strong enough to overpower the faint-hearted, to confound the restrictions of genres, to outlast poverty, tragedy, and obscurity. Here is a vision that is finally coming into its own.

This book documents Joe's vision in technicolor and 3-D. It's an express mail package from hell, full of black humor, crawling horror, outrageous and telling satire, memorable characters, and above all a sense of personal integrity. And if the truth makes you a little uncomfortable, or maybe just flat scares the shit out of you, then you'd better leave the lights on while you read it.

FISH NIGHT

For Bill Pronzini

It was a bleached-bone afternoon with a cloudless sky and a monstrous sun. The air trembled like a mass of gelatinous ectoplasm. No wind blew.

Through the swelter came a worn, black Plymouth, coughing and belching white smoke from beneath its hood. It wheezed twice, backfired loudly, died by the side of the road.

The driver got out and went around to the hood. He was a man in the hard winter years of life, with dead brown hair and a heavy belly riding his hips. His shirt was open to the navel, the sleeves rolled up past his elbows. The hair on his chest and arms was gray.

A younger man climbed out on the passenger side, went around front too. Yellow sweat-explosions stained the pits of his white shirt. An unfastened, striped tie was draped over his neck like a pet snake that had died in its sleep.

"Well?" the younger man said.

The old man said nothing. He opened the hood. A calliope note of steam blew out from the radiator in a white puff, rose to the sky, turned clear.

"Damn," the old man said, and he kicked the bumper of the Plymouth as if he were kicking a foe in the teeth. He got little satisfaction out of the action, just a nasty scuff on his brown wingtip and a jar to his ankle that hurt like hell.

"Well?" the young man repeated.

"Well what? What do you think? Dead as the can opener

trade this week. Deader. The radiator's chickenpocked with holes."

"Maybe someone will come by and give us a hand."

"Sure."

"A ride anyway."

"Keep thinking that, college boy."

"Someone is bound to come along," the young man said.

"Maybe. Maybe not. Who else takes these cutoffs? The main highway, that's where everyone is. Not this little no account shortcut." He finished by glaring at the young man.

"I didn't make you take it," the young man snapped. "It was on the map. I told you about it, that's all. You chose it. You're the one that decided to take it. It's not my fault. Besides, who'd have expected the car to die?"

"I did tell you to check the water in the radiator, didn't I? Wasn't that back as far as El Paso?"

"I checked. It had water then. I tell you, it's not my fault. You're the one that's done all the Arizona driving."

"Yeah, yeah," the old man said, as if this were something he didn't want to hear. He turned to look up the highway.

No cars. No trucks. Just heat waves and miles of empty concrete in sight.

They seated themselves on the hot ground with their backs to the car. That way it provided some shade—but not much. They sipped on a jug of lukewarm water from the Plymouth and spoke little until the sun fell down. By then they had both mellowed a bit. The heat had vacated the sands and the desert chill had settled in. Where the warmth had made the pair snappy, the cold drew them together.

The old man buttoned his shirt and rolled down his sleeves while the young man rummaged a sweater out of the backseat. He put the sweater on, sat back down. "I'm sorry about this," he said suddenly.

"Wasn't your fault. Wasn't anyone's fault. I just get to yelling sometime, taking out the can-opener trade on everything but the can-openers and myself. The days of the door-to-door salesman are gone, son.''

"And I thought I was going to have an easy summer job,'' the young man said.

The old man laughed. "Bet you did. They talk a good line, don't they?''

"I'll say!''

"Make it sound like found money, but there ain't no found money, boy. Ain't nothing simple in this world. The company is the only one ever makes any money. We just get tireder and older with more holes in our shoes. If I had any sense I'd have quit years ago. All you got to make is this summer—''

"Maybe not that long.''

"Well, this is all I know. Just town after town, motel after motel, house after house, looking at people through screen wire while they shake their heads No. Even the cockroaches at the sleazy motels begin to look like little fellows you've seen before, like maybe they're door-to-door peddlers that have to rent rooms too.''

The young man chuckled. "You might have something there.''

They sat quietly for a moment, welded in silence. Night had full grip on the desert now. A mammoth gold moon and billions of stars cast a whitish glow from eons away.

The wind picked up. The sand shifted, found new places to lie down. The undulations of it, slow and easy, were reminiscent of the midnight sea. The young man, who had crossed the Atlantic by ship once, said as much.

"The sea?'' the old man replied. "Yes, yes, exactly like that. I was thinking the same. That's part of the reason it bothers me. Part of why I was stirred up this afternoon. Wasn't just the heat doing it. There are memories of mine out here,'' he nodded at the desert, "and they're visiting me again.''

The young man made a face. "I don't understand.''

"You wouldn't. You shouldn't. You'd think I'm crazy.''

"I already think you're crazy. So tell me.''

The old man smiled. "All right, but don't you laugh.''

"I won't.''

A moment of silence moved in between them. Finally the old man said, "It's fish night, boy. Tonight's the full moon and this is the right part of the desert if memory serves me, and the feel is right—I mean, doesn't the night feel like it's made up of some fabric, that it's different from other nights, that it's like being inside a big dark bag, the sides sprinkled with glitter, a spotlight at the top, at the open mouth, to serve as a moon?"

"You lost me."

The old man sighed. "But it feels different. Right? You can feel it too, can't you?"

"I suppose. Sort of thought it was just the desert air. I've never camped out in the desert before, and I guess it is different."

"Different, all right. You see, this is the road I got stranded on twenty years back. I didn't know it at first, least not consciously. But down deep in my gut I must have known all along I was taking this road, tempting fate, offering it, as the football people say, an instant replay."

"I still don't understand about fish night. What do you mean, you were here before?"

"Not this exact spot, somewhere along in here. This was even less of a road back then than it is now. The Navajos were about the only ones who traveled it. My car conked out like this one today, and I started walking instead of waiting. As I walked the fish came out. Swimming along in the starlight pretty as you please. Lots of them. All the colors of the rainbow. Small ones, big ones, thick ones, thin ones. Swam right up to me . . . *right through me!* Fish just as far as you could see. High up and low down to the ground.

"Hold on boy. Don't start looking at me like that. Listen: You're a college boy, you know what was here before we were, before we crawled out of the sea and changed enough to call ourselves men. Weren't we once just slimy things, brothers to the things that swim?"

"I guess, but—"

"Millions and millions of years ago this desert was a sea bottom. Maybe even the birthplace of man. Who knows? I read that in some science books. And I got to thinking this: If the ghosts of people who have lived can haunt houses, why can't the ghosts of creatures long dead haunt where they once lived, float about in a ghostly sea?''

"Fish with a soul?''

"Don't go small-mind on me, boy. Look here: Some of the Indians I've talked to up North tell me about a thing they call the manitou. That's a spirit. They believe everything has one. Rocks, trees, you name it. Even if the rock wears to dust or the tree gets cut to lumber, the manitou of it is still around.''

"Then why can't you see these fish all the time?''

"Why can't we see ghosts all the time? Why do some of us never see them? Time's not right, that's why. It's a precious situation, and I figure it's like some fancy time lock—like the banks use. The lock clicks open at the bank, and there's the money. Here it ticks open and we get the fish of a world long gone.''

"Well, it's something to think about," the young man managed.

The old man grinned at him. "I don't blame you for thinking what you're thinking. But this happened to me twenty years ago and I've never forgotten it. I saw those fish for a good hour before they disappeared. A Navajo came along in an old pickup right after and I bummed a ride into town with him. I told him what I'd seen. He just looked at me and grunted. But I could tell he knew what I was talking about. He'd seen it too, and probably not for the first time.

"I've heard that Navajos don't eat fish for some reason or another, and I bet it's the fish in the desert that keep them from it. Maybe they hold them sacred. And why not? It was like being in the presence of the Creator; like crawling around in the liquids with no cares in the world.''

"I don't know. That sounds sort of . . .''

"Fishy?'' The old man laughed. "It does, it does. So this Navajo drove me to town. Next day I got my car fixed and went on. I've never taken that cutoff again—until today, and I think that was more than accident. My subconscious was driving me. That night scared me, boy, and I don't mind admitting it. But it was wonderful too, and I've never been able to get it out of my mind.''

The young man didn't know what to say.

The old man looked at him and smiled. ''I don't blame you,'' he said. ''Not even a little bit. Maybe I am crazy.''

They sat awhile longer with the desert night, and the old man took his false teeth out and poured some of the warm water on them to clean them of coffee and cigarette residue.

''I hope we don't need that water,'' the young man said.

''You're right. Stupid of me! We'll sleep awhile, start walking before daylight. It's not far to the next town. Ten miles at best.'' He put his teeth back in. ''We'll be just fine.''

The young man nodded.

No fish came. They did not discuss it. They crawled inside the car, the young man in the front seat, the old man in the back. They used their spare clothes to bundle under, to pad out the cold fingers of the night.

Near midnight the old man came awake suddenly and lay with his hands behind his head and looked up and out the window opposite him, studied the crisp desert sky.

And a fish swam by.

Long and lean and speckled with all the colors of the world, flicking its tail as if in good-bye. Then it was gone.

The old man sat up. Outside, all about, were the fish— all sizes, colors, and shapes.

''Hey, boy, wake up!''

The younger man moaned.

''Wake up!''

The young man, who had been resting face down on his arms, rolled over. ''What's the matter? Time to go?''

''The fish.''

''Not again.''

''Look!''

The young man sat up. His mouth fell open. His eyes bloated. Around and around the car, faster and faster in whirls of dark color, swam all manner of fish.

''Well, I'll be . . . *How?*''

"I told you, I told you."

The old man reached for the door handle, but before he could pull it a fish swam lazily through the back window glass, swirled about the car, once, twice, passed through the old man's chest, whipped up and went out through the roof.

The old man cackled, jerked open the door. He bounced around beside the road. Leaped up to swat his hands through the spectral fish. "Like soap bubbles," he said. "No. Like smoke!"

The young man, his mouth still agape, opened his door and got out. Even high up he could see the fish. Strange fish, like nothing he'd ever seen pictures of or imagined. They flitted and skirted about like flashes of light.

As he looked up, he saw, nearing the moon, a big dark cloud. The only cloud in the sky. That cloud tied him to reality suddenly, and he thanked the heavens for it. Normal things still happened. The whole world had not gone insane.

After a moment the old man quit hopping among the fish and came out to lean on the car and hold his hand to his fluttering chest.

"Feel it, boy? Feel the presence of the sea? Doesn't it feel like the beating of your own mother's heart while you float inside the womb?"

And the younger man had to admit that he felt it, that inner rolling rhythm that is the tide of life and the pulsating heart of the sea.

"How?" the young man said. "Why?"

"The time lock, boy. The locks clicked open and the fish are free. Fish from a time before man was man. Before civilization started weighing us down. I know it's true. The truth's been in me all the time. It's in us all."

"It's like time travel," the young man said. "From the past to the future, they've come all that way."

"Yes, yes, that's it . . . Why, if they can come to our world, why can't we go to theirs? Release that spirit inside of us, tune into their time?"

"Now wait a minute . . ."

"My God, that's it! They're pure, boy, pure. Clean and

free of civilization's trappings. That must be it! They're pure and we're not. We're weighted down with technology. These clothes. That car.''

The old man started removing his clothes.

"Hey!" the young man said. "You'll freeze."

"If you're pure, if you're completely pure," the old man mumbled, "that's it . . . yeah, that's the key."

"You've gone crazy."

"I won't look at the car," the old man yelled, running across the sand, trailing the last of his clothes behind him. He bounced about the desert like a jack-rabbit. "God, God, nothing is happening, nothing," he moaned. "This isn't my world. I'm of that world. I want to float free—in the belly of the sea, away from can openers and cars and—"

The young man called the old man's name. The old man did not seem to hear.

"I want to leave here!" the old man yelled. Suddenly he was springing about again. "The teeth!" he yelled. "It's the teeth. Dentist, science, foo!" He punched a hand into his mouth, plucked the teeth free, tossed them over his shoulder.

Even as the teeth fell the old man rose. He began to stroke. To swim up and up and up, moving like a pale pink seal among the fish.

In the light of the moon the young man could see the pooched jaws of the old man, holding the last of the future's air. Up went the old man, up, up, up, swimming strong in the long-lost waters of a time gone by.

The young man began to strip off his own clothes. Maybe he could nab him, pull him down, put the clothes on him. Something . . . God, something . . . but, what if *he* couldn't come back? And there were the fillings in his teeth, the metal rod in his back from a motorcycle accident. No, unlike the old man, this was his world and he was tied to it. There was nothing he could do.

A great shadow weaved in front of the moon, made a wriggling slat of darkness that caused the young man to let go of his shirt buttons and look up.

A black rocket of a shape moved through the invisible

sea: a shark, the granddaddy of all sharks, the seed for all of man's fears of the deep.

And it caught the old man in its mouth, began swimming upward toward the golden light of the moon. The old man dangled from the creature's mouth like a ragged rat from a house cat's jaws. Blood blossomed out of him, coiled darkly in the invisible sea.

The young man trembled. "Oh God," he said once.

Then along came that thick dark cloud, rolling across the face of the moon.

Momentary darkness.

And when the cloud passed there was light once again, and an empty sky.

No fish.

No shark.

And no old man.

Just the night, the moon and the stars.

THE PIT

For Ed Gorman

Six months earlier they had captured him. Tonight Harry went into the pit. He and Big George, right after the bull terriers got through tearing the guts out of one another. When that was over, he and George would go down and do their business. The loser would stay there and be fed to the dogs, each of which had been starved for the occasion.

When the dogs finished eating, the loser's head would go up on a pole. Already a dozen poles circled the pit. On each rested a head, or skull, depending on how long it had been exposed to the elements, ambitious pole-climbing ants and hungry birds. And of course how much flesh the terriers ripped off before it was erected.

Twelve poles. Twelve heads.

Tonight a new pole and a new head went up.

Harry looked about at the congregation. All sixty or so of them. They were a sight. Like mad creatures out of Lewis Carroll. Only they didn't have long rabbit ears or tall silly hats. They were just backwoods rednecks, not too unlike himself. With one major difference. They were as loony as waltzing mice. Or maybe they weren't crazy and he was. Sometimes he felt as if he had stepped into an alternate universe where the old laws of nature and what was right and wrong did not apply. Just like Alice plunging down the rabbit hole into Wonderland.

The crowd about the pit had been mumbling and talking, but now they grew silent. Out into the glow of the neon lamps stepped a man dressed in a black suit and hat.

A massive rattlesnake was coiled about his right arm. It was wriggling from shoulder to wrist. About his left wrist a smaller snake was wrapped, a copperhead. The man held a Bible in his right hand. He was called Preacher.

Draping the monstrous rattlesnake around his neck, Preacher let it hang there. It dangled that way as if drugged. Its tongue would flash out from time to time. It gave Harry the willies. He hated snakes. They always seemed to be smiling. Nothing was that fucking funny, not all the time.

Preacher opened the Bible and read:

"Behold, I give unto you the power to tread on serpents and scorpions, and over all the power of the enemy: and nothing will by any means hurt you."

Preacher paused and looked at the sky. "So God," he said, "we want to thank you for a pretty good potato crop, though you've done better, and we want to thank you for the terriers, even though we had to raise and feed them ourselves, and we want to thank you for sending these outsiders our way, thank you for Harry Joe Stinton and Big George, the nigger."

Preacher paused and looked about the congregation. He lifted the hand with the copperhead in it high above his head. Slowly he lowered it and pointed the snake-filled fist at George. "Three times this here nigger has gone into the pit, and three times he has come out victorious. Couple times against whites, once against another nigger. Some of us think he's cheating.

"Tonight, we bring you another white feller, one of your chosen people, though you might not know it on account of the way you been letting the nigger win here, and we're hoping for a good fight with the nigger being killed at the end. We hope this here business pleases you. We worship you and the snakes in the way we ought to. Amen."

Big George looked over at Harry. "Be ready, sucker. I'm gonna take you apart like a gingerbread man."

Harry didn't say anything. He couldn't understand it. George was a prisoner just as he was. A man degraded and made to lift huge rocks and pull carts and jog mile on miles every day. And just so they could get in shape for this—to go down into that pit and try and beat each other to death for the amusement of these crazies.

And it had to be worse for George. Being black, he was seldom called anything other than ''nigger'' by these psychos. Furthermore, no secret had been made of the fact that they wanted George to lose, and for him to win. The idea of a black pit champion was eating their little honky hearts out.

Yet, Big George had developed a sort of perverse pride in being the longest lived pit fighter yet.

''It's something I can do right,'' George had once said. ''On the outside I wasn't nothing but a nigger, an uneducated nigger working in rose fields, mowing big lawns for rich white folks. Here I'm still the nigger, but I'm THE NIGGER, the bad-ass nigger, and no matter what these peckerwoods call me, they know it, and they know I'm the best at what I do. I'm the king here. And they may hate me for it, keep me in a cell and make me run and lift stuff, but for that time in the pit, they know I'm the one that can do what they can't do, and they're afraid of me. I like it.''

Glancing at George, Harry saw that the big man was not nervous. Or at least not showing it. He looked as if he were ready to go on vacation. Nothing to it. He was about to go down into that pit and try and beat a man to death with his fists and it was nothing. All in a day's work. A job well done for an odd sort of respect that beat what he had had on the outside.

The outside. It was strange how much he and Big George used that term. *The outside.* As if they were enclosed in some small bubble-like cosmos that perched on the edge of the world they had known; a cosmos invisible to *the outsiders*, a spectral place with new mathematics and nebulous laws of mind and physics.

Maybe he was in hell. Perhaps he had been wiped out on the highway and had gone to the dark place. Just maybe his memory of how he had arrived here was a false dream inspired by demonic powers. The whole thing about him taking a wrong turn through Big Thicket country and having his truck break down just outside of Morganstown was an illusion, and stepping onto the Main Street of Morganstown, population sixty-six, was his crossing the River Styx and landing smack dab in the middle of a hell designed for good old boys.

God, had it been six months ago?

He had been on his way to visit his mother in Woodville, and he had taken a shortcut through the Thicket. Or so he thought. But he soon realized that he had looked at the map wrong. The shortcut listed on the paper was not the one he had taken. He had mistaken that road for the one he wanted. This one had not been marked. And then he reached Morganstown and his truck had broken down. He had been forced into six month's hard labor alongside George, the champion pit fighter, and now the moment for which he had been groomed arrived.

They were bringing the terriers out now. One, the champion, was named Old Codger. He was getting on in years. He had won many a pit fight. Tonight, win or lose, this would be his last battle. The other dog, Muncher, was young and inexperienced, but he was strong and eager for blood.

A ramp was lowered into the pit. Preacher and two men, the owners of the dogs, went down into the pit with Codger and Muncher. When they reached the bottom a dozen bright spot lights were thrown on them. They seemed to wade through the light.

The bleachers arranged about the pit began to fill. People mumbled and passed popcorn. Bets were placed and a little, fat man wearing a bowler hat copied them down in a note pad as fast as they were shouted. The ramp was removed.

In the pit, the men took hold of their dogs by the scruff of the neck and removed their collars. They turned the dogs so they were facing the walls of the pit and could not see one another. The terriers were about six feet apart, butts facing.

Preacher said, "A living dog is better than a dead lion."

Harry wasn't quite sure what that had to do with anything.

"Ready yourselves," Preacher said. "Gentlemen, face your dogs."

The owners slapped their dogs across the muzzle and whirled them to face one another. They immediately began to leap and strain at their masters' grips.

"Gentlemen, release your dogs."

The dogs did not bark. For some reason, that was what Harry noted the most. They did not even growl. They were quick little engines of silence.

Their first lunge was a miss and they snapped air. But the second time they hit head on with the impact of .45 slugs. Codger was knocked on his back and Muncher dove for his throat. But the experienced dog popped up its head and grabbed Muncher by the nose. Codger's teeth met through Muncher's flesh.

Bets were called from the bleachers.

The little man in the bowler was writing furiously.

Muncher, the challenger, was dragging Codger, the champion, around the pit, trying to make the old dog let go of his nose. Finally, by shaking his head violently and relinquishing a hunk of his muzzle, he succeeded.

Codger rolled to his feet and jumped Muncher. Muncher turned his head just out of the path of Codger's jaws. The older dog's teeth snapped together like a spring-loaded bear trap, saliva popped out of his mouth in a fine spray.

Muncher grabbed Codger by the right ear. The grip was strong and Codger was shook like a used condom about to be tied and tossed. Muncher bit the champ's ear completely off.

Harry felt sick. He thought he was going to throw up. He saw that Big George was looking at him. "You think this is bad, motherfucker," George said, "this ain't nothing but a cake walk. Wait till I get you in that pit."

"You sure run hot and cold, don't you?" Harry said.

"Nothing personal," George said sharply and turned back to look at the fight in the pit.

Nothing personal, Harry thought. God, what could be more personal? Just yesterday, as they trained, jogged along together, a pickup loaded with gun-bearing crazies driving alongside of them, he had felt close to George.

They had shared many personal things these six months, and he knew that George liked him. But when it came to the pit, George was a different man. The concept of friendship became alien to him. When Harry had tried to talk to him about it yesterday, he had said much the same thing. "Ain't nothing personal, Harry my man, but when we get in that pit don't look to me for nothing besides pain, cause I got plenty of that to give you, a lifetime of it, and I'll just keep it coming."

Down in the pit Codger screamed. It could be described no other way. Muncher had him on his back and was biting him on the belly. Codger was trying to double forward and get hold of Muncher's head, but his tired jaws kept slipping off of the sweaty neck fur. Blood was starting to pump out of Codger's belly.

"Bite him, boy," someone yelled from the bleachers, "tear his ass up, son."

Harry noted that every man, woman and child was leaning forward in their seat, straining for a view. Their faces full of lust, like lovers approaching a vicious climax. For a few moments they were in that pit and they were the dogs. Vicarious thrills without the pains.

Codger's legs began to flap.

"Kill him! Kill him!" the crowd began to chant.

Codger had quit moving. Muncher was burrowing his muzzle deeper into the old dog's guts. Preacher called for a pickup. Muncher's owner pried the dog's jaw loose of Codger's guts. Muncher's muzzle looked as if it had been dipped in red ink.

"This sonofabitch is still alive," Muncher's owner said of Codger.

Codger's owner walked over to the dog and said, "You little fucker!" He pulled a Saturday Night Special from his coat pocket and shot Codger twice in the head. Codger didn't even kick. He just evacuated his bowels right there.

Muncher came over and sniffed Codger's corpse, then, lifting his leg, he took a leak on the dead dog's head. The stream of piss was bright red.

* * *

The ramp was lowered. The dead dog was dragged out and tossed behind the bleachers. Muncher walked up the ramp beside his owner. The little dog strutted like he had just been crowned King of Creation. Codger's owner walked out last. He was not a happy man. Preacher stayed in the pit. A big man known as Sheriff Jimmy went down the ramp to join him. Sheriff Jimmy had a big pistol on his hip and a toy badge on his chest. The badge looked like the sort of thing that had come in a plastic bag with a capgun and whistle. But it was his sign of office and his word was iron.

A man next to Harry prodded him with the barrel of a shotgun. Walking close behind George, Harry went down the ramp and into the pit. The man with the shotgun went back up. In the bleachers the betting had started again, the little, fat man with the bowler was busy.

Preacher's rattlesnake was still lying serenely about his neck, and the little copperhead had been placed in Preacher's coat pocket. It poked its head out from time to time and looked around.

Harry glanced up. The heads and skulls on the poles—in spite of the fact they were all eyeless, and due to the strong light nothing but bulbous shapes on shafts—seemed to look down, taking as much amusement in the situation as the crowd on the bleachers.

Preacher had his Bible out again. He was reading a verse. ". . . when thou walkest through the fire, thou shalt not be burned; neither shall the flame kindle upon thee . . ."

Harry had no idea what that or the snakes had to do with anything. Certainly he could not see the relationship with the pit. These people's minds seemed to click and grind to a different set of internal gears than those on *the outside*.

The reality of the situation settled on Harry like a heavy, woolen coat. He was about to kill or be killed, right here in this dog-smelling pit, and there was nothing he could do that would change that.

He thought perhaps his life should flash before his eyes or something, but it did not. Maybe he should try to think of something wonderful, a last fine thought of what used to be. First he summoned up the image of his wife. That did nothing for him. Though his wife had once been pretty and bright, he could not remember her that way. The image that came to mind was quite different. A dumpy, lazy woman with constant back pains and her hair pulled up into an eternal topknot of greasy, brown hair. There was never a smile on her face or a word of encouragement for him. He always felt that she expected him to entertain her and that he was not doing a very good job of it. There was not even a moment of sexual ecstasy that he could recall. After their daughter had been born she had given up screwing as a wasted exercise. Why waste energy on sex when she could spend it complaining.

He flipped his mental card file to his daughter. What he saw was an ugly, potato-nosed girl of twelve. She had no personality. Her mother was Miss Congeniality compared to her. Potato Nose spent all of her time pining over thin, blond heartthrobs on television. It wasn't bad enough that they glared at Harry via the tube, they were also pinned to her walls and hiding in magazines she had cast throughout the house.

These were the last thoughts of a man about to face death?

There was just nothing there.

His job had sucked. His wife hadn't.

He clutched at straws. There had been Melva, a fine looking little cheerleader from high school. She had the brain of a dried black-eyed pea, but God-All-Mighty, did she know how to hide a weenie. And there had always been that strange smell about her, like bananas. It was especially strong about her thatch, which was thick enough for a bald eagle to nest in.

But thinking about her didn't provide much pleasure either. She had gotten hit by a drunk in a Mack truck while parked alongside a dark road with that Pulver boy.

Damn that Pulver. At least he had died in ecstasy. Had never known what hit him. When that Mack went up his ass he probably thought for a split second he was having the greatest orgasm of his life.

Damn that Melva. What had she seen in Pulver anyway?

He was skinny and stupid and had a face like a peanut pattie.

God, he was beat at every turn. Frustrated at every corner. No good thoughts or beautiful visions before the moment of truth. Only blackness, a life of dull, planned movements as consistent and boring as a bran-conscious geriatric's bowel movement. For a moment he thought he might cry.

Sheriff Jimmy took out his revolver. Unlike the badge it was not a toy. "Find your corner, boys."

George turned and strode to one side of the pit, took off his shirt and leaned against the wall. His body shined like wet licorice in the spot lights.

After a moment, Harry made his legs work. He walked to a place opposite George and took off his shirt. He could feel the months of hard work rippling through his flesh. His mind was suddenly blank. There wasn't even a god he believed in. No one to pray to. Nothing to do but the inevitable.

Sheriff Jimmy walked to the middle of the pit. He yelled out for the crowd to shut up.

Silence reigned.

"In this corner," he said, waving the revolver at Harry, "we have Harry Joe Stinton, a family man and pretty good feller for an outsider. He's six two and weighs two hundred and thirty-eight pounds, give or take a pound since my bathroom scales ain't exactly on the money."

A cheer went up.

"Over here," Sheriff Jimmy said, waving the revolver at George, "standing six four tall and weighing two hundred and forty-two pounds, we got the nigger, present champion of this here sport."

No one cheered. Someone made a loud sound with his mouth that sounded like a fart, the greasy kind that goes on and on and on.

George appeared unfazed. He looked like a statue. He knew who he was and what he was. The Champion Of The Pit.

"First off," Sheriff Jimmy said, "you boys come forward and show your hands."

Harry and George walked to the center of the pit, held out their hands, fingers spread wide apart, so that the crowd could see they were empty.

"Turn and walk to your corners and don't turn around," Sheriff Jimmy said.

George and Harry did as they were told. Sheriff Jimmy followed Harry and put an arm around his shoulders. "I got four hogs riding on you," he said. "And I'll tell you what, you beat the nigger and I'll do you a favor. Elvira, who works over at the cafe has already agreed. You win and you can have her. How's that sound?"

Harry was too numb with the insanity of it all to answer. Sheriff Jimmy was offering him a piece of ass if he won, as if this would be greater incentive than coming out of the pit alive. With this bunch there was just no way to anticipate what might come next. Nothing was static.

"She can do more tricks with a six inch dick than a monkey can with a hundred foot of grapevine, boy. When the going gets rough in there, you remember that. Okay?"

Harry didn't answer. He just looked at the pit wall.

"You ain't gonna get nowhere in life being sullen like that," Sheriff Jimmy said. "Now, you go get him and plow a rut in his black ass."

Sheriff Jimmy grabbed Harry by the shoulders and whirled him around, slapped him hard across the face in the same way the dogs had been slapped. George had been done the same way by the preacher. Now George and Harry were facing one another. Harry thought George looked like an ebony gargoyle fresh escaped from hell. His bald, bullet-like head gleamed in the harsh lights and his body looked as rough and ragged as stone.

Harry and George raised their hands in classic boxer stance and began to circle one another.

From above someone yelled, "Don't hit the nigger in the head, it'll break your hand. Go for the lips, they got soft lips."

The smell of sweat, dog blood and Old Codger's shit

was thick in the air. The lust of the crowd seemed to have an aroma as well. Harry even thought he could smell Preacher's snakes. Once, when a boy, he had been fishing down by the creek bed and had smelled an odor like that, and a water moccasin had wriggled out beneath his legs and splashed in the water. It was as if everything he feared in the world had been put in this pit. The idea of being put deep in the ground. Irrational people for whom logic did not exist. Rotting skulls on poles about the pit. Living skulls attached to hunched-forward bodies that yelled for blood. Snakes. The stench of death—blood and shit. And every white man's fear, racist or not—a big, black man with a lifetime of hatred in his eyes.

The circle tightened. They could almost touch one another now.

Suddenly George's lip began to tremble. His eyes poked out of his head, seemed to be looking at something just behind and to the right of Harry.

"Sss . . . snake!" George screamed.

God, thought Harry, one of Preacher's snakes has escaped. Harry jerked his head for a look.

And George stepped in and knocked him on his ass and kicked him full in the chest. Harry began scuttling along the ground on his hands and knees, George following along kicking him in the ribs. Harry thought he felt something snap inside, a cracked rib maybe. He finally scuttled to his feet and bicycled around the pit. Goddamn, he thought, I fell for the oldest trick in the book. Here I am fighting for my life and I fell for it.

"Way to go, stupid fuck!" A voice screamed from the bleachers. "Hey nigger, why don't you try, 'hey, your shoe's untied,' he'll go for it."

"Get off the goddamned bicycle," someone else yelled. "Fight."

"You better run," George said. "I catch you I'm gonna punch you so hard in the mouth, gonna knock your fucking teeth out your asshole . . ."

Harry felt dizzy. His head was like a yo-yo doing the Around the World trick. Blood ran down his forehead, dribbled off the tip of his nose and gathered on his upper lip. George was closing the gap again.

I'm going to die right here in this pit, thought Harry. I'm going to die just because my truck broke down outside of town and no one knows where I am. That's why I'm going to die. It's as simple as that.

Popcorn rained down on Harry and a tossed cup of ice hit him in the back. "Wanted to see a fucking foot race," a voice called, "I'd have gone to the fucking track."

"Ten on the nigger," another voice said.

"Five bucks the nigger kills him in five minutes."

When Harry back-pedaled past Preacher, the snake man leaned forward and snapped, "You asshole, I got a sawbuck riding on you."

Preacher was holding the big rattler again. He had the snake gripped just below the head, and he was so upset over how the fight had gone so far, he was unconsciously squeezing the snake in a vice-like grip. The rattler was squirming and twisting and flapping about, but Preacher didn't seem to notice. The snake's forked tongue was outside its mouth and it was really working, slapping about like a thin strip of rubber come loose on a whirling tire. The copperhead in Preacher's pocket was still looking out, as if along with Preacher he might have a bet on the outcome of the fight as well. As Harry danced away the rattler opened its mouth so wide its jaws came unhinged. It looked as if it were trying to yell for help.

Harry and George came together again in the center of the pit. Fists like black ball bearings slammed the sides of Harry's head. The pit was like a whirlpool, the walls threatening to close in and suck Harry down into oblivion.

Kneeing with all his might, Harry caught George solidly in the groin. George grunted, stumbled back, half-bent over.

The crowd went wild.

Harry brought cupped hands down on George's neck, knocked him to his knees. Harry used the opportunity to knock out one of the big man's teeth with the toe of his shoe.

He was about to kick him again when George reached

up and clutched the crotch of Harry's khakis, taking a crushing grip on Harry's testicles.

"Got you by the balls," George growled.

Harry bellowed and began to hammer wildly on top of George's head with both fists. He realized with horror that George was pulling him forward. *By God, George was going to bite him on the balls.*

Jerking up his knee he caught George in the nose and broke his grip. He bounded free, skipped and whooped about the pit like an Indian dancing for rain.

He skipped and whooped by Preacher. Preacher's rattler had quit twisting. It hung loosely from Preacher's tight fist. Its eyes were bulging out of its head like the humped backs of grub worms. Its mouth was closed and its forked tongue hung limply from the edge of it.

The copperhead was still watching the show from the safety of Preacher's pocket, its tongue zipping out from time to time to taste the air. The little snake didn't seem to have a care in the world.

George was on his feet again, and Harry could tell that already he was feeling better. Feeling good enough to make Harry feel real bad.

Preacher abruptly realized that his rattler had gone limp. "No, God no!" he cried. He stretched the huge rattler between his hands. "Baby, baby," he bawled, "breathe for me, Sapphire, breathe for me." Preacher shook the snake viciously, trying to jar some life into it, but the snake did not move.

The pain in Harry's groin had subsided and he could think again. George was moving in on him, and there just didn't seem any reason to run. George would catch him, and when he did, it would just be worse because he would be even more tired from all that running. It had to be done. The mating dance was over, now all that was left was the intercourse of violence.

A black fist turned the flesh and cartilage of Harry's nose into smouldering putty. Harry ducked his head and caught another blow to the chin. The stars he had not been able to see above him because of the lights, he could now see below him, spinning constellations on the floor of the pit.

It came to him again, the fact that he was going to die right here without one good, last thought. But then maybe there was one. He envisioned his wife, dumpy and sullen and denying him sex. George became her and she became George and Harry did what he had wanted to do for so long, he hit her in the mouth. Not once, but twice and a third time. He battered her nose and he pounded her ribs. And by God, but she could hit back. He felt something crack in the center of his chest and his left cheekbone collapsed into his face. But Harry did not stop battering her. He looped and punched and pounded her dumpy face until it was George's black face and George's black face turned back to her face and he thought of her now on the bed, naked, on her back, battered, and he was naked mounting her, and the blows of his fists were the sexual thrusts of his cock and he was pounding her until—

George screamed. He had fallen to his knees. His right eye was hanging out on the tendons. One of Harry's straight rights had struck George's cheekbone with such power it had shattered it and pressured the eye out of its socket.

Blood ran down Harry's knuckles. Some of it was George's. Much of it was his own. His knuckle bones showed through the rent flesh of his hands, but they did not hurt. They were past hurting.

George wobbled to his feet. The two men stood facing one another, neither moving. The crowd was silent. The only sound in the pit was the harsh breathing of the two fighters, and Preacher who had stretched Sapphire out on the ground on her back and was trying to blow air into her mouth. Occasionally he'd lift his head and say in tearful supplication, "Breathe for me, Sapphire, breathe for me."

Each time Preacher blew a blast into the snake, its white underbelly would swell and then settle down, like a leaky balloon that just wouldn't hold air.

George and Harry came together. Softly. They had their

arms on each others shoulders and they leaned against one another, breathed each others breath.

Above, the silence of the crowd was broken when a heckler yelled, "Start some music, the fuckers want to dance."

"It's nothing personal," George said.

"Not at all," Harry said.

They managed to separate, reluctantly, like two lovers who had just copulated to the greatest orgasm of their lives.

George bent slightly and put up his hands. The eye dangling on his cheek looked like some tentacled creature trying to crawl up and into the socket. Harry knew that he would have to work on that eye.

Preacher screamed. Harry afforded him a sideways glance. Sapphire was awake. And now she was dangling from Preacher's face. She had bitten through his top lip and was hung there by her fangs. Preacher was saying something about the power to tread on serpents and stumbling about the pit. Finally his back struck the pit wall and he slid down to his butt and just sat there, legs sticking out in front of him, Sapphire dangling off his lip like some sort of malignant growth. Gradually, building momentum, the snake began to thrash.

Harry and George met again in the center of the pit. A second wind had washed in on them and they were ready. Harry hurt wonderfully. He was no longer afraid. Both men were smiling, showing the teeth they had left. They began to hit each other.

Harry worked on the eye. Twice he felt it beneath his fists, a grape-like thing that cushioned his knuckles and made them wet. Harry's entire body felt on fire—twin fires, ecstasy and pain.

George and Harry leaned together, held each other, waltzed about.

"You done good," George said, "make it quick."

The black man's legs went out from under him and he fell to his knees, head bent. Harry took the man's head in his hands and kneed him in the face with all his might. George went limp. Harry grasped George's chin and the back of his head and gave a violent twist. The neck bone snapped and George fell back, dead.

The copperhead, which had been poking its head out of Preacher's pocket, took this moment to slither away into a crack in the pit's wall.

Out of nowhere came weakness. Harry fell to his knees. He touched George's ruined face with his fingers.

Suddenly hands had him. The ramp was lowered. The crowd cheered. Preacher—Sapphire dislodged from his lip—came forward to help Sheriff Jimmy with him. They lifted him up.

Harry looked at Preacher. His lip was greenish. His head looked like a sun-swollen watermelon, yet, he seemed well enough. Sapphire was wrapped around his neck again. They were still buddies. The snake looked tired. Harry no longer felt afraid of it. He reached out and touched its head. It did not try to bite him. He felt its feathery tongue brush his bloody hand.

They carried him up the ramp and the crowd took him, lifted him high above their heads. He could see the moon and the stars now. For some odd reason they did not look familiar. Even the nature of the sky seemed different.

He turned and looked down. The terriers were being herded into the pit. They ran down the ramp like rats. Below, he could hear them begin to feed, to fight for choice morsels. But there were so many dogs, and they were so hungry, this only went on for a few minutes. After a while they came back up the ramp followed by Sheriff Jimmy closing a big lock-bladed knife and by Preacher who held George's head in his outstretched hands. George's eyes were gone. Little of the face remained. Only that slick, bald pate had been left undamaged by the terriers.

A pole came out of the crowd and the head was pushed onto its sharpened end and the pole was dropped into a deep hole in the ground. The pole, like a long neck, rocked its trophy for a moment, then went still. Dirt was kicked into the hole and George joined the others, all those beautiful, wonderful heads and skulls.

They began to carry Harry away. Tomorrow he would have Elvira, who could do more tricks with a six inch dick than a monkey could with a hundred foot of grapevine, then he would heal and a new outsider would come through and they would train together and then they would mate in blood and sweat in the depths of the pit.

The crowd was moving toward the forest trail, toward town. The smell of pines was sweet in the air. And as they carried him away, Harry turned his head so he could look back and see the pit, its maw closing in shadow as the lights were cut, and just before the last one went out Harry saw the heads on the poles and, dead center of his vision, was the shiny bald pate of his good friend George.

DUCK HUNT

For Marylois Dunn

There were three hunters and three dogs. The hunters had shiny shotguns, warm clothes and plenty of ammo. The dogs were each covered in big blue spots and were sleek and glossy and ready to run. No duck was safe.

The hunters were Clyde Barrow, James Clover and little Freddie Clover who was only fifteen and very excited to be asked along. However, Freddie did not really want to see a duck, let alone shoot one. He had never killed anything but a sparrow with his BB gun and that had made him sick. But he was nine then. Now he was ready to be a man. His father told him so.

With this hunt he felt he had become part of a secret organization. One that smelled of tobacco smoke and whiskey breath; sounded of swear words, talk about how good certain women were, the range and velocity of rifles and shotguns, the edges of hunting knives, the best caps and earflaps for winter hunting.

In Mud Creek the hunt made the man.

Since Freddie was nine he had watched with more than casual interest, how when a boy turned fifteen in Mud Creek, he would be invited to The Hunting Club for a talk with the men. Next step was a hunt, and when the boy returned he was a boy no longer. He talked deep, walked sure, had whiskers bristling on his chin and could take up with the assurance of not being laughed at, cussing, smoking and watching women's butts as a matter of course.

Freddie wanted to be a man too. He had pimples, no pubic hair to speak of (he always showered quickly at

27

school to escape derisive remarks about the size of his equipment and the thickness of his foliage), scrawny legs and little, gray, watery eyes that looked like ugly planets spinning in white space.

And truth was, Freddie preferred a book to a gun.

But came the day when Freddie turned fifteen and his father came home from the Club, smoke and whiskey smell clinging to him like a hungry tick, his face slightly dark with beard and tired-looking from all-night poker.

He came into Freddie's room, marched over to the bed where Freddie was reading *THOR*, clutched the comic from his son's hands, sent it fluttering across the room with a rainbow of comic panels.

"Nose out of the book," his father said. "Time to join the Club."

Freddie went to the Club, heard the men talk ducks, guns, the way the smoke and blood smelled on cool morning breezes. They told him the kill was the measure of a man. They showed him heads on the wall. They told him to go home with his father and come back tomorrow bright and early, ready for his first hunt.

His father took Freddie downtown and bought a flannel shirt (black and red), a thick jacket (fleece lined), a cap (with ear flaps) and boots (waterproof). He took Freddie home and took a shotgun down from the rack, gave him a box of ammo, walked him out back to the firing range and made him practice while he told his son about hunts and the war and about how men and ducks died much the same.

Next morning before the sun was up, Freddie and his father had breakfast. Freddie's mother did not eat with them. Freddie did not ask why. They met Clyde over at the Club and rode in his jeep down dirt roads, clay roads and trails, through brush and briars until they came to a mass of reeds and cattails that grew thick and tall as Japanese bamboo.

They got out and walked. As they walked, pushing aside the reeds and cattails, the ground beneath their feet turned marshy. The dogs ran ahead.

When the sun was two hours up, they came to a bit of

a clearing in the reeds, and beyond them Freddie could see the break-your-heart-blue of a shiny lake. Above the lake, coasting down, he saw a duck. He watched it sail out of sight.

"Well boy?" Freddie's father said.

"It's beautiful," Freddie said.

"Beautiful, hell, are you ready?"

"Yes, sir."

On they walked, the dogs way ahead now, and finally they stood within ten feet of the lake. Freddie was about to squat down into hiding as he had heard of others doing, when a flock of ducks burst up from a mass of reeds in the lake and Freddie, fighting off the sinking feeling in his stomach, tracked them with the barrel of the shotgun, knowing what he must do to be a man.

His father's hand clamped over the barrel and pushed it down. "Not yet," he said.

"Huh?" said Freddie.

"It's not the ducks that do it," Clyde said.

Freddie watched as Clyde and his father turned their heads to the right, to where the dogs were pointing—noses forward, paws upraised—to a thatch of underbrush. Clyde and his father made quick commands to the dogs to stay, then they led Freddie into the brush, through a twisting maze of briars and out into a clearing where all the members of The Hunting Club were waiting.

In the center of the clearing was a gigantic duck decoy. It looked ancient and there were symbols carved all over it. Freddie could not tell if it were made of clay, iron or wood. The back of it was scooped out, gravy-bowl-like, and there was a pole in the center of the indention; tied to the pole was a skinny man. His head had been caked over with red mud and there were duck feathers sticking in it, making it look like some kind of funny cap. There was a ridiculous, wooden duck bill held to his head by thick elastic straps. Stuck to his butt was a duster of duck feathers. There was a sign around his neck that read DUCK.

The man's eyes were wide with fright and he was trying to say or scream something, but the bill had been fastened in such a way he couldn't make any more than a mumble.

Freddie felt his father's hand on his shoulder. "Do it," he said. "He ain't nobody to anybody we know. Be a man."

"Do it! Do it! Do it!" came the cry from The Hunting Club.

Freddie felt the cold air turn into a hard ball in his throat. His scrawny legs shook. He looked at his father and The Hunting Club. They all looked tough, hard and masculine.

"Want to be a titty baby all your life?" his father said.

That put steel in Freddie's bones. He cleared his eyes with the back of his sleeve and steadied the barrel on the derelict's duck's head.

"Do it!" came the cry. "Do it! Do it! Do it!"

At that instant he pulled the trigger. A cheer went up from The Hunting Club, and out of the clear, cold sky, a dark blue norther blew in and with it came a flock of ducks. The ducks lit on the great idol and on the derelict. Some of them dipped their bills in the derelict's wetness.

When the decoy and the derelict were covered in ducks, all The Hunting Club lifted their guns and began to fire.

The air became full of smoke, pellets, blood and floating feathers.

When the gunfire died down and the ducks died out, The Hunting Club went forward and bent over the decoy, did what they had to do. Their smiles were red when they lifted their heads. They wiped their mouths gruffly on the backs of their sleeves and gathered ducks into hunting bags until they bulged. There were still many carcasses lying about.

"Good shooting, son," Fred's father said and clapped him manfully on the back.

"Yeah," said Fred, scratching his crotch, "got that sonofabitch right between the eyes, pretty as a picture."

They all laughed.

The sky went lighter, and the blue norther that was rustling the reeds and whipping feathers about blew up and out and away in an instant. As the men walked away from there, talking deep, walking sure, whiskers bristling on all their chins, they promised that tonight they would get Fred a woman.

BY BIZARRE HANDS

For Scott Cupp

When the traveling preacher heard about the Widow Case and her retarded girl, he set out in his black Dodge to get over there before Halloween night.

Preacher Judd, as he called himself—though his name was really Billy Fred Williams—had this thing for retarded girls, due to the fact that his sister had been simple-headed, and his mama always said it was a shame she was probably going to burn in hell like a pan of biscuits forgot in the oven, just on account of not having a full set of brains.

This was a thing he had thought on considerable, and this considerable thinking made it so he couldn't pass up the idea of baptizing and giving some God-training to female retards. It was something he wanted to do in the worst way, though he had to admit there wasn't any burning desire in him to do the same for boys or men or women that were half-wits, but due to his sister having been one, he certainly had this thing for girl simples.

And he had this thing for Halloween, because that was the night the Lord took his sister to hell, and he might have taken her to glory had she had any bible-learning or God-sense. But she didn't have a drop, and it was partly his own fault, because he knew about God and could sing some hymns pretty good. But he'd never turned a word of benediction or gospel music in her direction. Not one word. Nor had his mama, and his papa wasn't around to do squat.

The old man ran off with a bucktoothed laundry woman that used to go house to house taking in wash and bringing

31

it back the next day, but when she took in their wash, she took in Papa too, and she never brought either of them back. And if that wasn't bad enough, the laundry contained everything they had in the way of decent clothes, including a couple of pairs of nice dress pants and some pin-striped shirts like niggers wear to funerals. This left him with one old pair of faded overalls that he used to wear to slop the hogs before the critters killed and ate Granny and they had to get rid of them because they didn't want to eat nothing that had eaten somebody they knew. So, it wasn't bad enough Papa ran off with a beaver-toothed wash woman and his sister was a drooling retard, he now had only the one pair of ugly, old overalls to wear to school, and this gave the other kids three things to tease him about, and they never missed a chance to do it. Well, four things. He was kind of ugly too.

It got tiresome.

Preacher Judd could remember nights waking up with his sister crawled up in the bed alongside him, lying on her back, eyes wide open, her face bathed in cool moonlight, picking her nose and eating what she found, while he rested on one elbow and tried to figure out why she was that way.

He finally gave up figuring, decided that she ought to have some fun, and he could have some fun too. Come Halloween, he got him a bar of soap for marking up windows and a few rocks for knocking out some, and he made his sister and himself ghost-suits out of old sheets in which he cut mouth and eye holes.

This was her fifteenth year and she had never been trick-or-treating. He had designs that she should go this time, and they did, and later after they'd done it, he walked her back home, and later yet, they found her out back of the house in her ghost-suit, only the sheet had turned red because her head was bashed in with something and she had bled out like an ankle-hung hog. And someone had turned her trick-or-treat sack—the handle of which was still clutched in her fat grip—inside out and taken every bit of candy she'd gotten from the neighbors.

The sheriff came out, pulled up the sheet and saw that she was naked under it, and he looked her over and said that she looked raped to him, and that she had been killed by bizarre hands.

Bizarre hands never did make sense to Preacher Judd, but he loved the sound of it, and never did let it slip away, and when he would tell about his poor sister, naked under the sheets, her brains smashed out and her trick-or-treat bag turned inside out, he'd never miss ending the story with the sheriff's line about her having died by bizarre hands.

It had a kind of ring to it.

He parked his Dodge by the roadside, got out and walked up to the Widow Case's, sipping on a Frosty Root Beer. But even though it was late October, the Southern sun was as hot as Satan's ass and the root beer was anything but frosty.

Preacher Judd was decked out in his black suit, white shirt and black loafers with black and white checked socks, and he had on his black hat, which was short-brimmed and made him look, he thought, exactly like a traveling preacher ought to look.

Widow Case was out at the well, cranking a bucket of water, and nearby, running hell out of a hill of ants with a stick she was waggling, was the retarded girl, and Preacher Judd thought she looked remarkably like his sister.

He came up, took off his hat and held it over his chest as though he were pressing his heart into proper place, and smiled at the widow with all his gold-backed teeth.

Widow Case put one hand on a bony hip, used the other to prop the bucket of water on the well-curbing. She looked like a shaved weasel, Preacher Judd thought, though her ankles weren't shaved a bit and were perfectly weasel-like. The hair there was thick and black enough to be mistaken for thin socks at a distance.

"Reckon you've come far enough," she said. "You look like one of them Jehovah Witnesses or such. Or one of them kind that run around with snakes in their teeth and hop to nigger music.''

''No ma'm, I don't hop to nothing, and last snake I seen I run over with my car.''

''You here to take up money for missionaries to give to them starving African niggers? If you are, forget it. I don't give to the niggers around here, sure ain't giving to no hungry foreign niggers that can't even speak English.''

''Ain't collecting money for nobody. Not even myself.''

''Well, I ain't seen you around here before, and I don't know you from white rice. You might be one of them mash murderers for all I know.''

''No ma'm, I ain't a mash murderer, and I ain't from around here. I'm from East Texas.''

She gave him a hard look. ''Lots of niggers there.''

''Place is rotten with them. Can't throw a dog tick without you've hit a burr-head in the noggin'. That's one of the reasons I'm traveling through here, so I can talk to white folks about God. Talking to niggers is like,'' and he lifted a hand to point, ''talking to that well-curbing there, only that well-curbing is smarter and a lot less likely to sass, since it ain't expecting no civil rights or a chance to crowd up with our young'ns in schools. It knows its place and it stays there, and that's something for that well-curbing, if it ain't nothing for niggers.''

''Amen.''

Preacher Judd was feeling pretty good now. He could see she was starting to eat out of his hand. He put on his hat and looked at the girl. She was on her elbows now, her head down and her butt up. The dress she was wearing was way too short and had broken open in back from her having outgrown it. Her panties were dirt-stained and there was gravel, like little b.b.s hanging off of them. He thought she had legs that looked strong enough to wrap around an alligator's neck and choke it to death.

''Cindereller there,'' the widow said, noticing he was watching, ''ain't gonna have to worry about going to school with niggers. She ain't got the sense of a nigger. She ain't got no sense at all. A dead rabbit knows more than she knows. All she does is play around all day, eat bugs and such and drool. In case you haven't noticed, she's simple.''

"Yes ma'm, I noticed. Had a sister the same way. She got killed on a Halloween night, was raped and murdered and had her trick-or-treat candy stolen, and it was done, the sheriff said, by bizarre hands.''

"No kiddin'?''

Preacher Judd held up a hand. "No kiddin'. She went on to hell, I reckon, 'cause she didn't have any God talk in her. And retard or not, she deserved some so she wouldn't have to cook for eternity. I mean, think on it. How hot it must be down there, her boiling in her own sweat, and she didn't do nothing, and it's mostly my fault 'cause I didn't teach her a thing about The Lord Jesus and his daddy, God.''

Widow Case thought that over. "Took her Halloween candy too, huh?''

"Whole kitandkaboodle. Rape, murder and candy theft, one fatal swoop. That's why I hate to see a young'n like yours who might not have no Word of God in her . . . Is she without training?''

"She ain't even toilet trained. You couldn't perch her on the outdoor convenience if she was sick and her manage to hit the hole. She can't do nothing that don't make a mess. You can't teach her a thing. Half the time she don't even know her name.'' As if to prove this, Widow Case called, "Cindereller.''

Cinderella had one eye against the ant hill now and was trying to look down the hole. Her butt was way up and she was rocking forward on her knees.

"See,'' said Widow Case, throwing up her hands. "She's worse than any little ole baby, and it ain't no easy row to hoe with her here and me not having a man around to do the heavy work.''

"I can see that . . . By the way, call me Preacher Judd . . . And can I help you tote that bucket up to the house there?''

"Well now,'' said Widow Case, looking all the more like a weasel, "I'd appreciate that kindly.''

* * *

He got the bucket and they walked up to the house. Cinderella followed, and pretty soon she was circling around him like she was a shark closing in for the kill, the circles each time getting a mite smaller. She did this by running with her back bent and her knuckles almost touching the ground. Ropes of saliva dripped out of her mouth.

Watching her, Preacher Judd got a sort of warm feeling all over. She certainly reminded him of his sister. Only she had liked to scoop up dirt, dog mess and stuff as she ran, and toss it at him. It wasn't a thing he thought he'd missed until just that moment, but now the truth was out and he felt a little teary-eyed. He half-hoped Cinderella would pick up something and throw it on him.

The house was a big, drafty thing circled by a wide flower bed that didn't look to have been worked in years. A narrow porch ran half-way around it, and the front porch had man-tall windows on either side of the door.

Inside, Preacher Judd hung his hat on one of the foil wrapped rabbit ears perched on top of an old Sylvania tv set, and followed the widow and her child into the kitchen.

The kitchen had big iron frying pans hanging on wall pegs, and there was a framed embroidery that read GOD WATCHES OVER THIS HOUSE. It had been faded by sunlight coming through the window over the sink.

Preacher Judd sat the bucket on the ice box—the old sort that used real ice—then they all went back to the living room. Widow Case told him to sit down and asked him if he'd like some ice-tea.

"Yes, this bottle of Frosty ain't so good." He took the bottle out of his coat pocket and gave it to her.

Widow Case held it up and squinted at the little line of liquid in the bottom. "You gonna want this?"

"No ma'm, just pour what's left out and you can have the deposit." He took his Bible from his other pocket and opened it. "You don't mind if I try and read a verse or two to your Cindy, do you?"

"You make an effort on that while I fix us some tea. And I'll bring some things for ham sandwiches, too."

"That would be right nice. I could use a bite."

Widow Case went to the kitchen and Preacher Judd

smiled at Cinderella. "You know tonight's Halloween, Cindy?"

Cinderella pulled up her dress, picked a stray ant off her knee and ate it.

"Halloween is my favorite time of the year," he continued. "That may be strange for a preacher to say, considering it's a devil thing, but I've always loved it. It just does something to my blood. It's like a tonic for me, you know?"

She didn't know. Cinderella went over to the tv and turned it on.

Preacher Judd got up, turned it off. "Let's don't run the Sylvania right now, baby child," he said. "Let's you and me talk about God."

Cinderella squatted down in front of the set, not seeming to notice it had been cut off. She watched the dark screen like the White Rabbit considering a plunge down the rabbit hole.

Glancing out the window, Preacher Judd saw that the sun looked like a dropped cherry snowcone melting into the clay road that led out to Highway 80, and already the tumble bug of night was rolling in blue-black and heavy. A feeling of frustration went over him, because he knew he was losing time and he knew what he had to do.

Opening his Bible, he read a verse and Cinderella didn't so much as look up until he finished and said a prayer and ended it with "Amen."

"Uhman," she said suddenly.

Preacher Judd jumped with surprise, slammed the Bible shut and dunked it in his pocket. "Well, well now," he said with delight, "that does it. She's got some Bible training."

Widow Case came in with the tray of fixings. "What's that?"

"She said some of a prayer," Preacher Judd said. "That cinches it. God don't expect much from retards, and that ought to do for keeping her from burning in hell." He practically skipped over to the woman and her tray, stuck two fingers in a glass of tea, whirled and sprinkled the drops on Cinderella's head. Cinderella held out a hand as if checking for rain.

Preacher Judd bellowed out, "I pronounce you baptized. In the name of God, The Son, and The Holy Ghost. Amen."

"Well, I'll swan," the widow said. "That there tea works for baptizing?" She sat the tray on the coffee table.

"It ain't the tea water, it's what's said and who says it that makes it take . . . Consider that gal legal baptized . . . Now, she ought to have some fun too, don't you think? Not having a full head of brains don't mean she shouldn't have some fun."

"She likes what she does with them ants," Widow Case said.

"I know, but I'm talking about something special. It's Halloween. Time for young folks to have fun, even if they are retards. In fact, retards like it better than anyone else. They love this stuff . . . A thing my sister enjoyed was dressing up like a ghost."

"Ghost?" Widow Case was seated on the couch, making the sandwiches. She had a big butcher knife and she was using it to spread mustard on bread and cut ham slices.

"We took this old sheet, you see, cut some mouth and eye holes in it, then we wore them and went trick-or-treating."

"I don't know that I've got an old sheet. And there ain't a house close enough for trick-or-treatin' at."

"I could take her around in my car. That would be fun, I think. I'd like to see her have fun, wouldn't you? She'd be real scary too under that sheet, big as she is and liking to run stooped down with her knuckles dragging."

To make his point, he bent forward, humped his back, let his hands dangle and made a face he thought was an imitation of Cinderella.

"She would be scary, I admit that," Widow Case said. "Though that sheet over her head would take some away from it. Sometimes she scares me when I don't got my mind on her, you know? Like if I'm napping in there on the bed, and I sorta open my eyes, *and there she is*, looking at me like she looks at them ants. I declare, she looks like she'd like to take a stick and whirl it around on me."

"You need a sheet, a white one, for a ghost-suit."

"Now maybe it would be nice for Cindereller to go out and have some fun." She finished making the sandwiches and stood up. "I'll see what I can find."

"Good, good," Preacher Judd said rubbing his hands together. "You can let me make the outfit. I'm real good at it."

While Widow Case went to look for a sheet, Preacher Judd ate one of the sandwiches, took one and handed it down to Cinderella. Cinderella promptly took the bread off of it, ate the meat, and laid the mustard sides down on her knees.

When the meat was chewed, she took to the mustard bread, cramming it into her mouth and smacking her lips loudly.

"Is that good, sugar?" Preacher Judd asked.

Cinderella smiled some mustard bread at him, and he couldn't help but think the mustard looked a lot like baby shit, and he had to turn his head away.

"This do?" Widow Case said, coming into the room with a slightly yellowed sheet and a pair of scissors.

"That's the thing," Preacher Judd said, taking a swig from his ice tea. He set the tea down and called to Cinderella.

"Come on, sugar, let's you and me go in the bedroom there and get you fixed up and surprise your mama."

It took a bit of coaxing, but he finally got her up and took her into the bedroom with the sheet and scissors. He half-closed the bedroom door and called out to the widow, "You're going to like this."

After a moment, Widow Case heard the scissors snipping away and Cinderella grunting like a hog to trough. When the scissor sound stopped, she heard Preacher Judd talking in a low voice, trying to coach Cinderella on something, but as she wanted it to be a surprise, she quit trying to hear. She went over to the couch and fiddled with a sandwich, but she didn't eat it. As soon as she'd gotten out of eyesight of Preacher Judd, she'd upended the last of his root beer and it was as bad as he said. It sort of made her stomach sick and didn't encourage her to add any food to it.

Suddenly the bedroom door was knocked back, and Cinderella, having a big time of it, charged into the room with her arms held out in front of her yelling, "Woooo, woooo, goats."

Widow Case let out a laugh. Cinderella ran around the room yelling, "Woooo, woooo, goats," until she tripped over the coffee table and sent the sandwich makings and herself flying.

Preacher Judd, who'd followed her in after a second, went over and helped her up. The Widow Case, who had curled up on the couch in natural defense against the flying food and retarded girl, now uncurled when she saw something dangling on Preacher Judd's arm. She knew what it was, but she asked anyway. "What's that?"

"One of your piller cases. For a trick-or-treat sack."

"Oh," Widow Case said stiffly, and she went to straightening up the coffee table and picking the ham and makings off the floor.

Preacher Judd saw that the sun was no longer visible. He walked over to a window and looked out. The tumble bug of night was even more blue-black now and the moon was out, big as a dinner plate, and looking like it had gravy stains on it.

"I think we've got to go now," he said. "We'll be back in a few hours, just long enough to run the houses around here."

"Whoa, whoa," Widow Case said. "Trick-or-treatin' I can go for, but I can't let my daughter go off with no strange man."

"I ain't strange. I'm a preacher."

"You strike me as an all right fella that wants to do things right, but I still can't let you take my daughter off without me going. People would talk."

Preacher Judd started to sweat. "I'll pay you some money to let me take her on."

Widow Case stared at him. She had moved up close

now and he could smell root beer on her breath. Right then he knew what she'd done and he didn't like it any. It wasn't that he'd wanted it, but somehow it seemed dishonest to him that she swigged it without asking him. He thought she was going to pour it out. He started to say as much when she spoke up.

"I don't like the sound of that none, you offering me money."

"I just want her for the night," he said, pulling Cinderella close to him. "She'd have fun."

"I don't like the sound of that no better. Maybe you ain't as right thinking as I thought."

Widow Case took a step back and reached the butcher knife off the table and pushed it at him. "I reckon you better just let go of her and run on out to that car of yours and take your ownself trick-or-treatin'. And without my piller case."

"No ma'm, can't do that. I've come for Cindy and that's the thing God expects of me, and I'm going to do it. I got to do it. I didn't do my sister right and she's burning in hell. I'm doing Cindy right. She said some of a prayer and she's baptized. Anything happened to her, wouldn't be on my conscience."

Widow Case trembled a bit. Cinderella lifted up her ghost-suit with her free hand to look at herself, and Widow Case saw that she was naked as a jay-bird underneath.

"You let go of her arm right now, you pervert. And drop that piller case . . . Toss it on the couch would be better. It's clean."

He didn't do either.

Widow Case's teeth went together like a bear trap and made about as much noise, and she slashed at him with the knife.

He stepped back out of the way and let go of Cinderella, who suddenly let out a screech, broke and ran, started around the room yelling, "Wooooo, wooooo, goats."

Preacher Judd hadn't moved quick enough, and the knife had cut through the pillow case, his coat and shirt sleeve, but hadn't broke the skin.

When Widow Case saw her slashed pillow case fall to

the floor, a fire went through her. The same fire that went through Preacher Judd when he realized his J.C. Penney's suit coat which had cost him, with the pants, $39.95 on sale, was ruined.

They started circling one another, arms outstretched like wrestlers ready for the runtogether, and Widow Case had the advantage on account of having the knife.

But she fell for Preacher Judd holding up his left hand and wiggling two fingers like mule ears, and while she was looking at that, he hit her with a right cross and floored her. Her head hit the coffee table and the ham and fixings flew up again.

Preacher Judd jumped on top of her and held her knife hand down with one of his, while he picked up the ham with the other and hit her in the face with it, but the ham was so greasy it kept sliding off and he couldn't get a good blow in.

Finally he tossed the ham down and started wrestling the knife away from her with both hands while she chewed on one of his forearms until he screamed.

Cinderella was still running about, going, "Wooooo, wooooo, goats," and when she ran by the Sylvania, her arm hit the foil-wrapped rabbit ears and sent them flying.

Preacher Judd finally got the knife away from Widow Case, cutting his hand slightly in the process, and that made him mad. He stabbed her in the back as she rolled out from under him and tried to run off on all fours. He got on top of her again, knocking her flat, and he tried to pull the knife out. He pulled and tugged, but it wouldn't come free. She was as strong as a cow and was crawling across the floor and pulling him along as he hung tight to the thick, wooden butcher knife handle. Blood was boiling all over the place.

Out of the corner of his eye, Preacher Judd saw that his retard was going wild, flapping around in her ghost-suit like a fat dove, bouncing off walls and tumbling over furniture. She wasn't making the ghost sounds now. She knew something was up and she didn't like it.

"Now, now," he called to her as Widow Case dragged

him across the floor, yelling all the while, "Bloody murder, I'm being kilt, bloody murder, bloody murder!"

"Shut up, goddamnit!" he yelled. Then, reflecting on his words, he turned his face heavenward. "Forgive me my language, God." Then he said sweetly to Cinderella, who was in complete bouncing distress, "Take it easy, honey. Ain't nothing wrong, not a thing."

"Oh Lordy mercy, I'm being kilt!" Widow Case yelled.

"Die, you stupid old cow."

But she didn't die. He couldn't believe it, but she was starting to stand. The knife he was clinging to pulled him to his feet, and when she was up, she whipped an elbow around, whacked him in the ribs and sent him flying.

About that time, Cinderella broke through a window, tumbled onto the porch, over the edge and into the empty flower bed.

Preacher Judd got up and ran at Widow Case, hitting her just above the knees and knocking her down, cracking her head a loud one on the Sylvania, but it still didn't send her out. She was strong enough to grab him by the throat with both hands and throttle him.

As she did, he turned his head slightly away from her digging fingers, and through the broken window he could see his retarded ghost. She was doing a kind of two step, first to the left, then to the right, going, "Unhhh, unhhhh," and it reminded Preacher Judd of one of them dances sinners do in them places with lots of blinking lights and girls up on pedestals doing lashes with their hips.

He made a fist and hit the widow a couple of times, and she let go of him and rolled away. She got up, staggered a second, that started running toward the kitchen, the knife still in her back, only deeper from having fallen on it.

He ran after her and she staggered into the wall, her hands hitting out and knocking one of the big iron frying pans off its peg and down on her head. It made a loud BONG, and Widow Case went down.

Preacher Judd let out a sigh. He was glad for that. He was tired. He grabbed up the pan and whammed her a few times, then, still carrying the pan, he found his hat in the living room and went out on the porch to look for Cinderella.

She wasn't in sight.

He ran out in the front yard calling her, and saw her making the rear corner of the house, running wildly, hands close to the ground, her butt flashing in the moonlight every time the sheet popped up. She was heading for the woods out back.

He ran after her, but she made the woods well ahead of him. He followed in, but didn't see her. "Cindy," he called. "It's me. Ole Preacher Judd. I come to read you some Bible verses. You'd like that wouldn't you?" Then he commenced to coo like he was talking to a baby, but still Cinderella did not appear.

He trucked around through the woods with his frying pan for half an hour, but didn't see a sign of her. For a half-wit, she was a good hider.

Preacher Judd was covered in sweat and the night was growing slightly cool and the old Halloween moon was climbing to the stars. He felt like just giving up. He sat down on the ground and started to cry.

Nothing ever seemed to work out right. That night he'd taken his sister out hadn't gone fully right. They'd gotten the candy and he'd brought her home, but later, when he tried to get her in bed with him for a little bit of the thing animals do without sin, she wouldn't go for it, and she always had before. Now she was uppity over having a ghost-suit and going trick-or-treating. Worse yet, her wearing that sheet with nothing under it did something for him. He didn't know what it was, but the idea of it made him kind of crazy.

But he couldn't talk or bribe her into a thing. She ran out back and he ran after her and tackled her, and when he started doing to her what he wanted to do, out beneath the Halloween moon, underneath the apple tree, she started screaming. She could scream real loud, and he'd had to choke her some and beat her in the head with a rock. After that, he felt he should make like some kind of theft was at the bottom of it all, so he took all her Halloween candy.

He was sick thinking back on that night. Her dying

without no God-training made him feel lousy. And he couldn't get those Tootsie Rolls out of his mind. There must have been three dozen of them. Later he got so sick from eating them all in one sitting that to this day he couldn't stand the smell of chocolate.

He was thinking on these misfortunes, when he saw through the limbs and brush a white sheet go by.

Preacher Judd poked his head up and saw Cinderella running down a little path going, "Wooooo, wooooo, goats."

She had already forgotten about him and had the ghost thing on her mind.

He got up and crept after her with his frying pan. Pretty soon she disappeared over a dip in the trail and he followed her down.

She was sitting at the bottom of the trail between two pines, and ahead of her was a clear lake with the moon shining its face in the water. Across the water the trees thinned, and he could see the glow of lights from a house. She was looking at those lights and the big moon in the water and was saying over and over, "Oh, priddy, priddy."

He walked up behind her and said, "It sure is, sugar," and he hit her in the head with the pan. It gave a real solid ring, kind of like the clap of a sweet church bell. He figured that one shot to the bean was sufficient, since it was a good overhand lick, but she was still sitting up and he didn't want to be no slacker about things, so he hit her a couple more times, and by the second time, her head didn't give a ring, just sort of a dull thump, like he was hitting a thick, rubber bag full of mud.

She fell over on what was left of her head and her butt cocked up in the air, exposed as the sheet fell down her back. He took a long look at it, but found he wasn't interested in doing what animals do without sin anymore. All that hitting on the Widow Case and Cinderella had tuckered him out.

He pulled his arm way back, tossed the frying pan with all his might toward the lake. It went in with a soft splash. He turned back toward the house and his car, and when he got out to the road, he cranked up the Dodge and drove away noticing that the Halloween sky was looking blacker. It was because the moon had slipped behind some dark clouds. He thought it looked like a suffering face behind a veil, and as he drove away from the Case's, he stuck his head out the window for a better look. By the time he made the hill that dipped down toward Highway 80, the clouds had passed along, and he'd come to see it more as a happy jack-o-lantern than a sad face, and he took that as a sign that he had done well.

THE STEEL VALENTINE

For Jeff Banks

Even before Morley told him, Dennis knew things were about to get ugly.

A man did not club you unconscious, bring you to his estate and tie you to a chair in an empty storage shed out back of the place if he merely intended to give you a valentine.

Morley had found out about him and Julie.

Dennis blinked his eyes several times as he came to, and each time he did, more of the dimly lit room came into view. It was the room where he and Julie had first made love. It was the only building on the estate that looked out of place; it was old, worn, and not even used for storage; it was a collector of dust, cobwebs, spiders and desiccated flies.

There was a table in front of Dennis, a kerosine lantern on it, and beyond, partially hidden in shadow, a man sitting in a chair smoking a cigarette. Dennis could see the red tip glowing in the dark and the smoke from it drifted against the lantern light and hung in the air like thin, suspended wads of cotton.

The man leaned out of shadow, and as Dennis expected, it was Morley. His shaved, bullet-shaped head was sweaty and reflected the light. He was smiling with his fine, white teeth, and the high cheekbones were round, flushed circles that looked like clown rouge. The tightness of his skin, the few wrinkles, made him look younger than his fifty-one years.

And in most ways he was younger than his age. He was

a man who took care of himself. Jogged eight miles every morning before breakfast, lifted weights three times a week and had only one bad habit—cigarettes. He smoked three packs a day. Dennis knew all that and he had only met the man twice. He had learned it from Julie, Morley's wife. She told him about Morley while they lay in bed. She liked to talk and she often talked about Morley; about how much she hated him.

"Good to see you," Morley said, and blew smoke across the table into Dennis's face. "Happy Valentine's Day, my good man. I was beginning to think I hit you too hard, put you in a coma."

"What is this, Morley?" Dennis found that the mere act of speaking sent nails of pain through his skull. Morley really had lowered the boom on him.

"Spare me the innocent act, lover boy. You've been laying the pipe to Julie, and I don't like it."

"This is silly, Morley. Let me loose."

"God, they do say stupid things like that in real life. It isn't just the movies . . . You think I brought you here just to let you go, lover boy?"

Dennis didn't answer. He tried to silently work the ropes loose that held his hands to the back of the chair. If he could get free, maybe he could grab the lantern, toss it in Morley's face. There would still be the strand holding his ankles to the chair, but maybe it wouldn't take too long to undo that. And even if it did, it was at least some kind of plan.

If he got the chance to go one on one with Morley, he might take him. He was twenty-five years younger and in good shape himself. Not as good as when he was playing pro basketball, but good shape nonetheless. He had height, reach, and he still had wind. He kept the latter with plenty of jogging and tossing the special-made, sixty-five pound medicine ball around with Raul at the gym.

Still, Morley was strong. Plenty strong. Dennis could testify to that. The pulsating knot on the side of his head was there to remind him.

He remembered the voice in the parking lot, turning toward it and seeing a fist. Nothing more, just a fist hurtling toward him like a comet. Next thing he knew, he was here, the outbuilding.

Last time he was here, circumstances were different, and better. He was with Julie. He met her for the first time at the club where he worked out, and they had spoken, and ended up playing racquetball together. Eventually she brought him here and they made love on an old mattress in the corner; lay there afterward in the June heat of a Mexican summer, holding each other in a warm, sweaty embrace.

After that, there had been many other times. In the great house; in cars; hotels. Always careful to arrange a tryst when Morley was out of town. Or so they thought. But somehow he had found out.

"This is where you first had her," Morley said suddenly. "And don't look so wide-eyed. I'm not a mind reader. She told me all the other times and places too. She spat at me when I told her I knew, but I made her tell me every little detail, even when I knew them. I wanted it to come from her lips. She got so she couldn't wait to tell me. She was begging to tell me. She asked me to forgive her and take her back. She no longer wanted to leave Mexico and go back to the States with you. She just wanted to live."

"You bastard. If you've hurt her—"

"You'll what? Shit your pants? That's the best you can do, Dennis. You see, it's me that has *you* tied to the chair. Not the other way around."

Morley leaned back into the shadows again, and his hands came to rest on the table, the perfectly manicured fingertips steepling together, twitching ever so gently.

"I think it would have been inconsiderate of her to have gone back to the States with you, Dennis. Very inconsiderate. She knows I'm a wanted man there, that I can't go back. She thought she'd be rid of me. Start a new life with her ex-basketball player. That hurt my feelings, Dennis. Right to the bone." Morley smiled. "But she wouldn't have been rid of me, lover boy. Not by a long shot. I've got connections in my business. I could have followed her anywhere . . . In fact, the idea that she thought I couldn't offended my sense of pride.''

''Where is she? What have you done with her, you bald-headed bastard?''

After a moment of silence, during which Morley examined Dennis's face, he said, ''Let me put it this way. Do you remember her dogs?''

Of course he remembered the dogs. Seven Dobermans. Attack dogs. They always frightened him. They were big mothers, too. Except for her favorite, a reddish, under-sized Doberman named Chum. He was about sixty pounds, and vicious. ''Light, but quick,'' Julie used to say. ''Light, but quick.''

Oh yeah, he remembered those goddamn dogs. Sometimes when they made love in an estate bedroom, the dogs would wander in, sit down around the bed and watch. Dennis felt they were considering the soft, rolling meat of his testicles, savoring the possibility. It made him feel like a mean kid teasing them with a treat he never intended to give. The idea of them taking that treat by force made his erection soften, and he finally convinced Julie, who found his nervousness hysterically funny, that the dogs should be banned from the bedroom, the door closed.

Except for Julie, those dogs hated everyone. Morley included. They obeyed him, but they did not like him. Julie felt that under the right circumstances, they might go nuts and tear him apart. Something she hoped for, but never happened.

''Sure,'' Morley continued. ''You remember her little pets. Especially Chum, her favorite. He'd growl at me when I tried to touch her. Can you imagine that? All I had to do was touch her, and that damn beast would growl. He was crazy about his mistress, just crazy about her.''

Dennis couldn't figure what Morley was leading up to, but he knew in some way he was being baited. And it was working. He was starting to sweat.

''Been what,'' Morley asked, ''a week since you've seen your precious sweetheart? Am I right?''

Dennis did not answer, but Morley was right. A week. He had gone back to the States for a while to settle some matters, get part of his inheritance out of legal bondage so he could come back, get Julie, and take her to the States for good. He was tired of the Mexican heat and tired of Morley owning the woman he loved.

It was Julie who had arranged for him to meet Morley in the first place, and probably even then the old bastard had suspected. She told Morley a partial truth. That she had met Dennis at the club, that they had played racquetball together, and that since he was an American, and supposedly a mean hand at chess, she thought Morley might enjoy the company. This way Julie had a chance to be with her lover, and let Dennis see exactly what kind of man Morley was.

And from the first moment Dennis met him, he knew he had to get Julie away from him. Even if he hadn't loved her and wanted her, he would have helped her leave Morley.

It wasn't that Morley was openly abusive—in fact, he was the perfect host all the while Dennis was there—but there was an obvious undercurrent of connubial dominance and menace that revealed itself like a shark fin everytime he looked at Julie.

Still, in a strange way, Dennis found Morley interesting, if not likeable. He was a bright and intriguing talker, and a wizard at chess. But when they played and Morley took a piece, he smirked over it in such a way as to make you feel he had actually vanquished an opponent.

The second and last time Dennis visited the house was the night before he left for the States. Morley had wiped him out in chess, and when finally Julie walked him to the door and called the dogs in from the yard so he could leave without being eaten, she whispered, "I can't take him much longer."

"I know," he whispered back. "See you in about a week. And it'll be all over."

Dennis looked over his shoulder, back into the house, and there was Morley leaning against the fireplace mantle drinking a martini. He lifted the glass to Dennis as if in salute and smiled. Dennis smiled back, called goodbye to Morley and went out to his car feeling uneasy. The smile

Morley had given him was exactly the same one he used when he took a chess piece from the board.

"Tonight. Valentine's Day," Morley said, "that's when you two planned to meet again, wasn't it? In the parking lot of your hotel. That's sweet. Really. Lovers planning to elope on Valentine's Day. It has a sort of poetry, don't you think?"

Morley held up a huge fist. "But what you met instead of your sweetheart was this . . . I beat a man to death with this once, lover boy. Enjoyed every second of it."

Morley moved swiftly around the table, came to stand behind Dennis. He put his hands on the sides of Dennis's face. "I could twist your head until your neck broke, lover boy. You believe that, don't you? Don't you? . . . Goddamnit, answer me."

"Yes," Dennis said, and the word was soft because his mouth was so dry.

"Good. That's good. Let me show you something, Dennis."

Morley picked up the chair from behind, carried Dennis effortlessly to the center of the room, then went back for the lantern and the other chair. He sat down across from Dennis and turned the wick of the lantern up. And even before Dennis saw the dog, he heard the growl.

The dog was straining at a large leather strap attached to the wall. He was muzzled and ragged looking. At his feet lay something red and white. "Chum," Morley said. "The light bothers him. You remember ole Chum, don't you? Julie's favorite pet . . . Ah, but I see you're wondering what that is at his feet. That sort of surprises me, Dennis. Really. As intimate as you and Julie were, I'd think you'd know her. Even without her makeup."

Now that Dennis knew what he was looking at, he could make out the white bone of her skull, a dark patch of matted hair still clinging to it. He also recognized what was left of the dress she had been wearing. It was a red and white tennis dress, the one she wore when they played racquetball. It was mostly red now. Her entire body had been gnawed savagely.

"Murderer!" Dennis rocked savagely in the chair, tried to pull free of his bonds. After a moment of useless struggle and useless epithets, he leaned forward and let the lava hot gorge in his stomach pour out.

"Oh, Dennis," Morley said. "That's going to be stinky. Just awful. Will you look at your shoes? And calling me a murderer. Now, I ask you, Dennis, is that nice? I didn't murder anyone. Chum did the dirty work. After four days without food and water he was ravenous and thirsty. Wouldn't you be? And he was a little crazy too. I burned his feet some. Not as bad as I burned Julie's, but enough to really piss him off. And I sprayed him with this."

Morley reached into his coat pocket, produced an aerosol canister and waved it at Dennis.

"This was invented by some business associate of mine. It came out of some chemical warfare research I'm conducting. I'm in, shall we say . . . espionage? I work for the highest bidder. I have plants here for arms and chemical warfare . . . If it's profitable and ugly, I'm involved. I'm a real stinker sometimes. I certainly am."

Morley was still waving the canister, as if trying to hypnotize Dennis with it. "We came up with this to train attack dogs. We found we could spray a padded up man with this and the dogs would go bonkers. Rip the pads right off of him. Sometimes the only way to stop the beggers was to shoot them. It was a failure actually. It activated the dogs, but it drove them out of their minds and they couldn't be controlled at all. And after a short time the odor faded, and the spray became quite the reverse. It made it so the dogs couldn't smell the spray at all. It made whoever was wearing it odorless. Still, I found a use for it. A very personal use.

"I let Chum go a few days without food and water while I worked on Julie . . . And she wasn't tough at all, Dennis. Not even a little bit. Spilled her guts. Now that isn't entirely correct. She didn't spill her guts until later, when Chum got hold of her . . . Anyway, she told me what I wanted to know about you two, then I sprayed that delicate thirty-six, twenty-four, thirty-six figure of hers with this. And with Chum so hungry, and me having burned his feet and done some mean things to him, he was not in the best of humor when I gave him Julie.

"It was disgusting, Dennis. Really. I had to come back when it was over and shoot Chum with a tranquilizer dart, get him tied and muzzled for your arrival."

Morley leaned forward, sprayed Dennis from head to foot with the canister. Dennis turned his head and closed his eyes, tried not to breathe the foul-smelling mist.

"He's probably not all that hungry now," Morley said, "but this will still drive him wild."

Already Chum had gotten a whiff and was leaping at his leash. Foam burst from between his lips and frothed on the leather bands of the muzzle.

"I suppose it isn't polite to lecture a captive audience, Dennis, but I thought you might like to know a few things about dogs. No need to take notes. You won't be around for a quiz later.

"But here's some things to tuck in the back of your mind while you and Chum are alone. Dogs are very strong, Dennis. Very. They look small compared to a man, even a big dog like a Doberman, but they can exert a lot of pressure with their bite. I've seen dogs like Chum here, especially when they're exposed to my little spray, bite through the thicker end of a baseball bat. And they're quick. You'd have a better chance against a black belt in karate than an attack dog."

"Morley," Dennis said softly, "you can't do this."

"I can't?" Morley seemed to consider. "No, Dennis, I believe I can. I give myself permission. But hey, Dennis, I'm going to give you a chance. This is the good part now, so listen up. You're a sporting man. Basketball. Racquetball. Chess. Another man's woman. So you'll like this. This will appeal to your sense of competition.

"Julie didn't give Chum a fight at all. She just couldn't believe her Chummy-whummy wanted to eat her. Just wouldn't. She held out her hand, trying to soothe the old boy, and he just bit it right off. Right off. Got half the palm and the fingers in one bite. That's when I left them alone. I had a feeling her Chummy-whummy might start on me next, and I wouldn't have wanted that. Oooohhh, those sharp teeth. Like nails being driven into you.''

"Morley listen—"

"Shut up! You, Mr. Cock Dog and Basketball Star, just might have a chance. Not much of one, but I know you'll fight. You're not a quitter. I can tell by the way you play chess. You still lose, but you're not a quitter. You hang in there to the bitter end.''

Morley took a deep breath, stood in the chair and hung the lantern on a low rafter. There was something else up there too. A coiled chain. Morley pulled it down and it clattered to the floor. At the sound of it Chum leaped against his leash and flecks of saliva flew from his mouth and Dennis felt them fall lightly on his hands and face.

Morley lifted one end of the chain toward Dennis. There was a thin, open collar attached to it.

"Once this closes it locks and can only be opened with this.'' Morley reached into his coat pocket and produced a key, held it up briefly and returned it. "There's a collar for Chum on the other end. Both are made out of good leather over strong, steel chain. See what I'm getting at here, Dennis?''

Morley leaned forward and snapped the collar around Dennis's neck.

"Oh, Dennis,'' Morley said, standing back to observe his handiwork. "It's you. Really. Great fit. And considering the day, just call this my valentine to you.''

"You bastard.''

"The biggest.''

Morley walked over to Chum. Chum lunged at him, but with the muzzle on he was relatively harmless. Still, his weight hit Morley's legs, almost knocked him down.

Turning to smile at Dennis, Morley said, "See how strong he is? Add teeth to this little engine, some maneuverability . . . it's going to be awesome, lover boy. Awesome.''

Morley slipped the collar under Chum's leash and snapped it into place even as the dog rushed against him, nearly knocking him down. But it wasn't Morley he wanted. He was trying to get at the smell. At Dennis.

Dennis felt as if the fluids in his body were running out of drains at the bottoms of his feet.

"Was a little poontang worth this, Dennis? I certainly hope you think so. I hope it was the best goddamn piece you ever got. Sincerely, I do. Because death by dog is slow and ugly, lover boy. They like the throat and balls. So, you watch those spots, hear?"

"Morley, for God's sake, don't do this!"

Morley pulled a revolver from his coat pocket and walked over to Dennis. "I'm going to untie you now, stud. I want you to be real good, or I'll shoot you. If I shoot you, I'll gut shoot you, then let the dog loose. You got no chance that way. At least my way you've got a sporting chance—slim to none."

He untied Dennis. "Now stand."

Dennis stood in front of the chair, his knees quivering. He was looking at Chum and Chum was looking at him, tugging wildly at the leash, which looked ready to snap. Saliva was thick as shaving cream over the front of Chum's muzzle.

Morley held the revolver on Dennis with one hand, and with the other he reproduced the aerosol can, sprayed Dennis once more. The stench made Dennis's head float.

"Last word of advice," Morley said. "He'll go straight for you."

"Morley . . ." Dennis started, but one look at the man and he knew he was better off saving the breath. He was going to need it.

Still holding the gun on Dennis, Morley eased behind the frantic dog, took hold of the muzzle with his free hand, and with a quick ripping motion, pulled it and the leash loose.

Chum sprang.

Dennis stepped back, caught the chair between his legs, lost his balance. Chum's leap carried him into Dennis's chest, and they both went flipping over the chair.

Chum kept rolling and the chain pulled across Dennis's face as the dog tumbled to its full length; the jerk of the sixty pound weight against Dennis's neck was like a blow.

The chain went slack, and Dennis knew Chum was coming. In that same instant he heard the door open, glimpsed a wedge of moonlight that came and went, heard the door lock and Morley laugh. Then he was rolling, coming to his knees, grabbing the chair, pointing it with the legs out.

And Chum hit him.

The chair took most of the impact, but it was like trying to block a cannonball. The chair's bottom cracked and a leg broke off, went skidding across the floor.

The truncated triangle of the Doberman's head appeared over the top of the chair, straining for Dennis's face. Dennis rammed the chair forward.

Chum dipped under it, grabbed Dennis's ankle. It was like stepping into a bear trap. The agony wasn't just in the ankle, it was a sizzling web of electricity that surged through his entire body.

The dog's teeth grated bone and Dennis let forth with a noise that was too wicked to be called a scream.

Blackness waved in and out, but the thought of Julie lying there in ragged display gave him new determination.

He brought the chair down on the dog's head with all his might.

Chum let out a yelp, and the dark head darted away.

Dennis stayed low, pulled his wounded leg back, attempted to keep the chair in front of him. But Chum was a black bullet. He shot under again, hit Dennis in the same leg, higher up this time. The impact slid Dennis back a foot. Still, he felt a certain relief. The dog's teeth had missed his balls by an inch.

Oddly there was little pain this time. It was as if he were being encased in dark amber; floating in limbo. Must be like this when a shark hits, he thought. So hard and fast and clean you don't really feel it at first. Just go numb. Look down for your leg and it's gone.

The dark amber was penetrated by a bright stab of pain. But Dennis was grateful for it. It meant that his brain was working again. He swiped at Chum with the chair, broke him loose.

Swiveling on one knee, Dennis again used the chair as

a shield. Chum launched forward, trying to go under it, but Dennis was ready this time and brought it down hard against the floor.

Chum hit the bottom of the chair with such an impact, his head broke through the thin slats. Teeth snapped in Dennis's face, but the dog couldn't squirm its shoulders completely through the hole and reach him.

Dennis let go of the chair with one hand, slugged the dog in the side of the head with the other. Chum twisted and the chair came loose from Dennis. The dog bounded away, leaping and whipping its body left and right, finally tossing off the wooden collar.

Grabbing the slack of the chain, Dennis used both hands to whip it into the dog's head, then swung it back and caught Chum's feet, knocking him on his side with a loud splat.

Even as Chum was scrambling to his feet, out of the corner of his eye Dennis spotted the leg that had broken off the chair. It was lying less than three feet away.

Chum rushed and Dennis dove for the leg, grabbed it, twisted and swatted at the Doberman. On the floor as he was, he couldn't get full power into the blow, but still it was a good one.

The dog skidded sideways on its belly and forelegs. When it came to a halt, it tried to raise its head, but didn't completely make it.

Dennis scrambled forward on his hands and knees, chopped the chair leg down on the Doberman's head with every ounce of muscle he could muster. The strike was solid, caught the dog right between the pointed ears and drove his head to the floor.

The dog whimpered. Dennis hit him again. And again.

Chum lay still.

Dennis took a deep breath, watched the dog and held his club cocked.

Chum did not move. He lay on the floor with his legs spread wide, his tongue sticking out of his foam-wet mouth.

Dennis was breathing heavily, and his wounded leg felt

THE STEEL VALENTINE 59

as if it were melting. He tried to stretch it out, alleviate some of the pain, but nothing helped.

He checked the dog again.

Still not moving.

He took hold of the chain and jerked it. Chum's head came up and smacked back down against the floor.

The dog was dead. He could see that.

He relaxed, closed his eyes and tried to make the spinning stop. He knew he had to bandage his leg somehow, stop the flow of blood. But at the moment he could hardly think.

And Chum, who was not dead, but stunned, lifted his head, and at the same moment, Dennis opened his eyes.

The Doberman's recovery was remarkable. It came off the floor with only the slightest wobble and jumped.

Dennis couldn't get the chair leg around in time and it deflected off of the animal's smooth back and slipped from his grasp.

He got Chum around the throat and tried to strangle him, but the collar was in the way and the dog's neck was too damn big.

Trying to get better traction, Dennis got his bad leg under him and made an effort to stand, lifting the dog with him. He used his good leg to knee Chum sharply in the chest, but the injured leg wasn't good for holding him up for another move like that. He kept trying to ease his thumbs beneath the collar and lock them behind the dog's windpipe.

Chum's hind legs were off the floor and scrambling, the toenails tearing at Dennis's lower abdomen and crotch.

Dennis couldn't believe how strong the dog was. Sixty pounds of pure muscle and energy, made more deadly by Morley's spray and tortures.

Sixty pounds of muscle.

The thought went through Dennis's head again.

Sixty pounds.

The medicine ball he tossed at the gym weighed more. It didn't have teeth, muscle and determination, but it did weigh more.

And as the realization soaked in, as his grip weakened

and Chum's rancid breath coated his face, Dennis lifted his eyes to a rafter just two feet above his head; considered there was another two feet of space between the rafter and the ceiling.

He quit trying to choke Chum, eased his left hand into the dog's collar, and grabbed a hind leg with his other. Slowly, he lifted Chum over his head. Teeth snapped at Dennis's hair, pulled loose a few tufts.

Dennis spread his legs slightly. The wounded leg wobbled like an old pipe cleaner, but held. The dog seemed to weigh a hundred pounds. Even the sweat on his face and the dense, hot air in the room seemed heavy.

Sixty pounds.

A basketball weighed little to nothing, and the dog weighed less than the huge medicine ball in the gym. Somewhere between the two was a happy medium; he had the strength to lift the dog, the skill to make the shot—the most important of his life.

Grunting, cocking the wiggling dog into position, he prepared to shoot. Chum nearly twisted free, but Dennis gritted his teeth, and with a wild scream, launched the dog into space.

Chum didn't go up straight, but he did go up. He hit the top of the rafter with his back, tried to twist in the direction he had come, couldn't, and went over the other side.

Dennis grabbed the chain as high up as possible, bracing as Chum's weight came down on the other side so violently it pulled him onto his toes.

The dog made a gurgling sound, spun on the end of the chain, legs thrashing.

It took a long fifteen minutes for Chum to strangle.

When Chum was dead, Dennis tried to pull him over the rafter. The dog's weight, Dennis's bad leg, and his now aching arms and back, made it a greater chore than he had anticipated. Chum's head kept slamming against the rafter. Dennis got hold of the unbroken chair, and used it as a stepladder. He managed the Doberman over, and Chum fell to the floor, his neck flopping loosely.

Dennis sat down on the floor beside the dog and patted it on the head. "Sorry," he said.

He took off his shirt, tore it into rags and bound his bad leg with it. It was still bleeding steadily, but not gushing; no major artery had been torn. His ankle wasn't bleeding as much, but in the dim lantern light he could see that Chum had bitten him to the bone. He used most of the shirt to wrap and strengthen the ankle.

When he finished, he managed to stand. The shirt binding had stopped the bleeding and the short rest had slightly rejuvenated him.

He found his eyes drawn to the mess in the corner that was Julie, and his first thought was to cover her, but there wasn't anything in the room sufficient for the job.

He closed his eyes and tried to remember how it had been before. When she was whole and the room had a mattress and they had made love all the long, sweet, Mexican afternoon. But the right images would not come. Even with his eyes closed, he could see her mauled body on the floor.

Ducking his head made some of the dizziness go away, and he was able to get Julie out of his mind by thinking of Morley. He wondered when he could come back. If he was waiting outside.

But no, that wouldn't be Morley's way. He wouldn't be anxious. He was cocksure of himself, he would go back to the estate for a drink and maybe play a game of chess against himself, gloat a long, sweet while before coming back to check on his handiwork. It would never occur to Morley to think he had survived. That would not cross his mind. Morley saw himself as Life's best chess master, and he did not make wrong moves; things went according to plan. Most likely, he wouldn't even check until morning.

The more Dennis thought about it, the madder he got and the stronger he felt. He moved the chair beneath the rafter where the lantern was hung, climbed up and got it down. He inspected the windows and doors. The door had a sound lock, but the windows were merely boarded. Barrier enough when he was busy with the dog, but not now.

He put the lantern on the floor, turned it up, found the chair leg he had used against Chum, and substituted it for a pry bar. It was hard work and by the time he had worked the boards off the window his hands were bleeding and full of splinters. His face looked demonic.

Pulling Chum to him, he tossed him out the window, climbed after him clutching the chair leg. He took up the chain's slack and hitched it around his forearm. He wondered about the other Dobermans. Wondered if Morley had killed them too, or if he was keeping them around. As he recalled, the Dobermans were usually loose on the yard at night. The rest of the time they had free run of the house, except Morley's study, his sanctuary. And hadn't Morley said that later on the spray killed a man's scent? That was worth something; it could be the edge he needed.

But it didn't really matter. Nothing mattered anymore. Six dogs. Six war elephants. He was going after Morley.

He began dragging the floppy-necked Chum toward the estate.

Morley was sitting at his desk playing a game of chess with himself, and both sides were doing quite well, he thought. He had a glass of brandy at his elbow, and from time to time he would drink from it, cock his head and consider his next move.

Outside the study door, in the hall, he could hear Julie's dogs padding nervously. They wanted out, and in the past they would have been on the yard long before now. But tonight he hadn't bothered. He hated those bastards, and just maybe he'd get rid of them. Shoot them and install a burglar alarm. Alarms didn't have to eat or be let out to shit, and they wouldn't turn on you. And he wouldn't have to listen to the sound of dog toenails clicking on the tile outside of his study door.

He considered letting the Dobermans out, but hesitated. Instead, he opened a box of special Cuban cigars, took one, rolled it between his fingers near his ear so he could hear the fresh crackle of good tobacco. He clipped the end off the cigar with a silver clipper, put it in his mouth and lit it with a desk lighter without actually putting the flame to it. He drew in a deep lungfull of smoke and relished it, let it out with a soft, contented sigh.

At the same moment he heard a sound, like something being dragged across the gravel drive. He sat motionless a moment, not batting an eye. It couldn't be lover boy, he thought. No way.

He walked across the room, pulled the curtain back from the huge glass door, unlocked it and slid it open.

A cool wind had come along and it was shaking the trees in the yard, but nothing else was moving. Morley searched the tree shadows for some tell-tale sign, but saw nothing.

Still, he was not one for imagination. He *had* heard something. He went back to the desk chair where his coat hung, reached the revolver from his pocket, turned.

And there was Dennis. Shirtless, one pants leg mostly ripped away. There were blood-stained bandages on his thigh and ankle. He had the chain partially coiled around one arm, and Chum, quite dead, was lying on the floor beside him. In his right hand Dennis held a chair leg, and at the same moment Morley noted this and raised the revolver, Dennis threw it.

The leg hit Morley squarely between the eyes, knocked him against his desk, and as he tried to right himself, Dennis took hold of the chain and used it to swing the dead dog. Chum struck Morley on the ankles and took him down like a scythe cutting fresh wheat. Morley's head slammed into the edge of the desk and blood dribbled into his eyes; everything seemed to be in a mixmaster, whirling so fast nothing was identifiable.

When the world came to rest, he saw Dennis standing over him with the revolver. Morley could not believe the man's appearance. His lips were split in a thin grin that barely showed his teeth. His face was drawn and his eyes were strange and savage. It was apparent he had found the key in the coat, because the collar was gone.

Out in the hall, bouncing against the door, Morley could hear Julie's dogs. They sensed the intruder and wanted at him. He wished now he had left the study door open, or put them out on the yard.

"I've got money," Morley said.

"Fuck your money," Dennis screamed. "I'm not selling anything here. Get up and get over here."

Morley followed the wave of the revolver to the front of his desk. Dennis swept the chess set and stuff aside with a swipe of his arm and bent Morley backwards over the desk. He put one of the collars around Morley's neck, pulled the chain around the desk a few times, pushed it under and fastened the other collar over Morley's ankles.

Tucking the revolver into the waistband of his pants, Dennis picked up Chum and tenderly placed him on the desk chair, half-curled. He tried to poke the dog's tongue back into his mouth, but that didn't work. He patted Chum on the head, said, "There, now."

Dennis went around and stood in front of Morley and looked at him, as if memorizing the moment.

At his back the Dobermans rattled the door.

"We can make a deal," Morley said. "I can give you a lot of money, and you can go away. We'll call it even."

Dennis unfastened Morley's pants, pulled them down to his knees. He pulled the underwear down. He went around and got the spray can out of Morley's coat and came back.

"This isn't sporting, Dennis. At least I gave you a fighting chance."

"I'm not a sport," Dennis said.

He sprayed Morley's testicles with the chemical. When he finished he tossed the canister aside, walked over to the door and listened to the Dobermans scuttling on the other side.

"Dennis!"

Dennis took hold of the doorknob.

"Screw you then," Morley said. "I'm not afraid. I won't scream. I won't give you the pleasure."

"You didn't even love her," Dennis said, and opened the door.

The Dobermans went straight for the stench of the spray, straight for Morley's testicles.

Dennis walked calmly out the back way, closed the glass

door. And as he limped down the drive, making for the gate, he began to laugh.

Morley had lied. He did too scream. In fact, he was still screaming.

I TELL YOU IT'S LOVE

For Lew Shiner

The beautiful woman had no eyes, just sparkles of light where they should have been—or so it seemed in the candlelight. Her lips, so warm and inviting, so wickedly wild and suggestive of strange pleasures, held yet a hint of disaster, as if they might be fat red things skillfully molded from dried blood.

"Hit me," she said.

That is my earliest memory of her; a doll for my beating, a doll for my love.

I laid it on her with that black silk whip, slapping it across her shoulders and back, listening to the whisper of it as it rode down, delighting in the flat pretty sound of it striking her flesh.

She did not bleed, which was a disappointment. The whip was too soft, too flexible, too difficult to strike hard with.

"Hurt me," she said softly. I went to where she kneeled. Her arms were outstretched, crucifixion style, and bound to the walls on either side with strong silk cord the color and texture of the whip in my hand.

I slapped her. "Like it?" I asked. She nodded and I slapped her again . . . and again. A one-two rhythm, slow and melodic, time and again.

"Like it?" I repeated, and she moaned, "Yeah, oh yeah."

Later, after she was untied and had tidied up the blood from her lips and nose, we made brutal love; me with my thumbs bending the flesh of her throat, she with her nails

66

entrenched in my back. She said to me when we were finished, "Let's do someone."

That's how we got started. Thinking back now, once again I say I'm glad for fate; glad for Gloria; glad for the memory of the crying sounds, the dripping blood and the long sharp knives that murmured through flesh like a lover's whisper cutting the dark.

Yeah, I like to think back to when I walked hands in pockets down the dark wharves in search of that special place where there were said to be special women with special pleasures for a special man like me.

I walked on until I met a sailor leaning up against a wall smoking a cigarette, and he says when I ask about the place, "Oh, yeah, I like that sort of pleasure myself. Two blocks down, turn right, there between the warehouses, down the far end. You'll see the light." And he pointed and I walked on, faster.

Finding it, paying for it, meeting Gloria was the goal of my dreams. I was more than a customer to that sassy, dark mamma with the sparkler eyes. I was the link to fit her link. We made two strong, solid bonds in a strange cosmic chain. You could feel the energy flowing through us; feel the iron of our wills. Ours was a mating made happily in hell.

So time went by and I hated the days and lived for the nights when I whipped her, slapped her, scratched her, and she did the same to me. Then one night she said, "It's not enough. Just not enough anymore. Your blood is sweet and your pain is fine, but I want to see death like you see a movie, taste it like licorice, smell it like flowers, touch it like cold, hard stone."

I laughed, saying, "I draw the line at dying for you." I took her by the throat, fastened my grip until her breathing was a whistle and her eyes protruded like bloated corpse bellies.

"That's not what I mean," she managed. And then came the statement that brings us back to what started it all, "Let's do someone."

I laughed and let her go.

"You know what I mean?" she said. "You know what I'm saying."

"I know what you said. I know what you mean." I smiled. "I know very well."

"You've done it before, haven't you?"

"Once," I said, "in a shipyard, not that long ago."

"Tell me about it. God, tell me about it."

"It was dark and I had come off ship after six months out, a long six months with the men, the ship and the sea. So I'm walking down this dark alley, enjoying the night like I do, looking for a place with the dark ways, our kind of ways, baby, and I came upon this old wino lying in a doorway, cuddling a bottle to his face as if it were a lady's loving hand."

"What did you do?"

"I kicked him," I said, and Gloria's smile was a beauty to behold.

"Go on," she said.

"God, how I kicked him. Kicked him in the face until there was no nose, no lips, no eyes. Only red mush dangling from shrapneled bone; looked like a melon that had been dropped from on high, down into a mass of broken white pottery chips. I touched his face and tasted it with my tongue and my lips."

"Ohh," she sighed, and her eyes half-closed. "Did he scream?"

"Once. Only once. I kicked him too hard, too fast, too soon. I hammered his head with the toes of my shoes, hammered until my cuffs were wet and sticking to my ankles."

"Oh God," she said, clinging to me, "let's do it, let's do it."

We did. First time was a drizzly night and we caught an old woman out. She was a lot of fun until we got the knives out and then she went quick. There was that crippled kid next, lured him from the theater downtown, and how we did that was a stroke of genius. You'll find his wheelchair not far from where you found the van and the other stuff.

But no matter. You know what we did, about the kinds

of tools we had, about how we hung that crippled kid on that meat hook in my van until the flies clustered around the doors thick as grapes.

And of course there was the little girl. It was a brilliant idea of Gloria's to get the kid's tricycle into the act. The things she did with those spokes. Ah, but that woman was a connoisseur of pain.

There were two others, each quite fine, but not as nice as the last. Then came the night Gloria looked at me and said, "It's not enough. Just won't do."

I smiled. "No way, baby. I still won't die for you."

"No," she gasped, and took my arm. "You miss my drift. It's the pain I need, not just the watching. I can't live through them, can't feel it in me. Don't you see, it would be the ultimate."

I looked at her, wondering did I have it right.

"Do you love me?"

"I do," I said.

"To know that I would spend the last of my life with you, that my last memories would be the pleasure of your face, the feelings of pain, the excitement, the thrill, the terror."

Then I understood, and understood good. Right there in the car I grabbed her, took her by the throat and cracked her head up against the windshield, pressed her back, choked, released, choked, made it linger. By this time I was quite a pro. She coughed, choked, smiled. Her eyes swung from fear to love. God it was wonderful and beautiful and the finest experience we had ever shared.

When she finally lay still there in the seat, I was trembling, happier than I had ever been. Gloria looked fine, her eyes rolled up, her lips stretched in a rictus smile.

I kept her like that at my place for days, kept her in my bed until the neighbors started to complain about the smell.

I've been talking to this guy and he's got some ideas. Says he thinks I'm one of the future generation, and the fact of that scares him all to hell. A social mutation, he says. Man's primitive nature at the height of the primal scream.

Dog shit, we're all the same, so don't look at me like I'm some kind of freak. What does he do come Monday night? He's watching the football game, or the races or boxing matches, waiting for a car to overturn or for some guy to be carried out of the ring with nothing but mush left for brains. Oh yeah, he and I are similar, quite alike. You see, it's in us all. A low pitch melody not often heard, but there just the same. In me it peaks and thuds, like drums and brass and strings. Don't fear it. Let it go. Give it the beat and amplify. I tell you it's love of the finest kind.

So I've said my piece and I'll just add this: when they fasten my arms and ankles down and tighten the cap, I hope I feel the pain and delight in it before my brain sizzles to bacon, and may I smell the frying of my very own flesh . . .

LETTER FROM THE SOUTH, TWO MOONS WEST OF NACOGDOCHES

For Mignon Glass

Dear Hawk:

Your letter stating that you can't believe I'm not a Baptist, due to the fact that my morals and yours are so similar, astonishes me. How can you think only Baptists are good people and lead happy lives? You've known me longer than that, even if most of our contact has been through letters and phone calls.

Well, I might ask you the same in reverse. How can you accept such a silly pagan religion? And if you must consider a religion, why not look back to your heritage, instead of taking on a Hebrew mythology.

And how in the world can you believe being a Baptist makes you happier than others?

I'm quite happy, thank you. I mean I have my ups and downs, but from your cards and letters, our occasional phone calls, so do you. Don't we all?

In answering your question about why I don't believe more fully, I might add that I've been a student, if not a scholar, of religions all my life, and I find nothing to recommend the Baptist over any other religion, no matter what the origin. Only the Aztec and their nasty custom of human sacrifice could be worse, and I'll tell you, though it's off the subject, I think the old Chief of this country is crazy as hell to sell them the makings for a nuclear reactor. I don't care what sort of diplomatic gesture it was

71

meant to be. Those heart-cutters get up here on us and it's the last pow-wow, buddy. With just sticks and stones, practically, they ran the Spaniards off, so I sure don't want to see them with the ability to make the big shitty boom machine, if you know what I mean. They're tougher than us, I admit it. I say let's let our technology be our muscle, and not let those mean pyramid builders have an equalizer, because with their attitude about war and sacrifice, they're going to be a whole hell of a lot more equal than we are.

But that's off the point, as usual.

On to why I'm not a Baptist. Well, first off, let's keep this simple. Consult history text if you don't believe me, though that won't keep you from twisting them around to suit you, or from picking just those that say what you want them to say (I remember our argument before on the civil war with the Japs, and I've got to add, though I shouldn't bring it up again, how you can side at all with those bastards after what they've done to our people on the West Coast is beyond me), so perhaps my asking you to examine historical text isn't sound advice on my part, and you're sure to take it as an insult.

But history does show, Hawk, that John the Baptist was not the only religious nut running around at this time, and it was only fate that gave him the honor (a dubious one in my book) of becoming the "Messiah." I mean a dramatic death like decapitation and having the head put on a silver (Does the text actually say silver? I can't remember and am too lazy to check.) platter, and then the fact that the execution was performed at the bidding of a dance hall floozy of the time, and the head presented to her as a gift, does have a certain element of showboating, and that's just the sort of thing people latch onto. High drama.

It always occurs to me that Jesus of Nazareth, mentioned briefly in your so-called "Holy Book," and I believe he was a cousin or something to John if memory serves me, was as likely a candidate for martyrdom as John. Except for fate, he might well have been the one your congregation worships.

He, however, in spite of his many similarities to John, had the misfortune to suffer less than a martyr's death. He was hit and killed by a runaway donkey cart and knocked up on the curbing with his, how was it put in the book . . . ? Can't remember, but something like "with his flanks exposed." Words to that effect.

I believe it was Jesus's inglorious death, more than anything else, that jockeyed him to a lowly position in the race toward Messiahism (did I make that word up?). He certainly had all the goods John did. Nice fanaticism, pie in the sky, promises of an afterlife, etc. But it seems to be in our natures to prefer bloody, dramatic demises such as decapitation to a relatively minor death by runaway donkey cart, the latter casualty being all the more jinxed by the fact that he ended up draped over some curb with his ass exposed, his little deep, brown eye winking at the world.

If we were more open-minded, a religion might have formed where Jesus was worshipped, and instead of the little bleeding head on a platter medallions many of your congregation wear, they might be adorning themselves with little buttocks with donkey cart tracks across them.

Just a thought. Don't get mad.

The other thing you mention is the Platter of Turin. And I admit to you that it is indeed mysterious and fascinating. But I've never seen nor read anything that convinces me that whatever is making itself manifest on the platter—and I also admit it does look like a head with a bleeding stump—is in fact, the likeness of John the Baptist. And even if it is his likeness, and somehow the trauma of his death caused it to be forever captured in the platter, that still does not mean he is the Messiah.

Consider the statue of Custer at the site of the Battle of The Little Big Horn. Many have reported (and I believe it has been filmed) that it bleeds from the nose, ears and mouth from time to time. To some, this was interpreted to mean that Custer was a Saint and that the statue could cure illnesses. I know from our letters in the past that you hardly believe Custer a Saint, quite the contrary.

What I'm saying is this: there are many mysteries in the world, Hawk, and there are many interpretations. You need only choose a mystery and an interpretation to suit you.

Well, got to cut this short. Got to get dressed. There's a meeting tonight. They're having another public execution, and it's about time. Bunch of niggers are going to be crucified along Caddo Street and I don't want to miss that. Those stupid black bastards thinking they're good as us makes me ill. I've had my hood and robes starched special for the occasion, and I'm actually getting to light one of the pitch-covered niggers placed at the end to provide light. I also get to lead the local Scout troops in a song. I'm excited.

Oh, almost forgot. If you haven't read about it, we finally got that trouble maker Martin Luther King, and he's the main feature tonight. I know from your letters that you have a sort of begrudging respect for him, and I must admit his guerilla activities conducted with only twenty-two men throughout the South have been brilliant for his kind. But after tonight he'll plague the South no more.

As I said, wish you could be here, but I know you've got a big pow-wow going up there and I wish I could see it. Like to see your tribe strip the skin off those White Eyes slow and easy. They're worse than our niggers, and I'm only glad the last of them (far as we know) have been eliminated down here.

Another thing just hit me about this Baptist business, and I'll go ahead and get it off my chest. Here we are getting rid of the whites and the niggers, and you and some others have adopted their silly religion. I admit that our own is pretty damned dumb (Great Heap Big Spirit, Ugh), but doesn't that kind of thing, accepting their religion, give the lowlifes a sort of existence through us? Think about it.

Guess while I'm badmouthing them, might as well admit I'm against the trend to drop all of their ways, as some of the traditional methods just don't translate as well. This two moons and two suns bit is ridiculous. With automobiles that method is no longer correct. What used to be a two day trip is now only a matter of hours. And this switch over from their language to ours, the use of Cherokee writing for all tribes, is going to be a pain. I mean we'll all be speaking our tribal languages, translating the writing to

Cherokee, and when we all get together how are we going to converse? Which language will we pick? Cherokee for writing, because of their good alphabet makes sense, but which will be the superior tribal language, and how's it going to go down with folks when one is chosen over all the others?

Oh to hell with it. This old gal is going to have to get to stepping or she isn't going to have time to get dressed and moving.

Best to you,
Running Fox

BOYS WILL BE BOYS

For Karen Lansdale

1

Not so long ago, about a year back, a very rotten kid named Clyde Edson walked the earth. He was street-mean and full of savvy and he knew what he wanted and got it any way he wanted.

He lived in a big, evil house on a dying, grey street in Galveston, Texas, and he collected to him, like an old lady who brings in cats half-starved and near-eaten with mange, the human refuse and the young discards of a sick society.

He molded them. He breathed life into them. He made them feel they belonged. They were his creations, but he did not love them. They were just things to be toyed with until the paint wore thin and the batteries ran down, then out they went.

And this is the way it was until he met Brian Blackwood.

Things got worse after that.

2

—guy had a black leather jacket and dark hair combed back virgin-ass tight, slicked down with enough grease to lube a bone-dry Buick; came down the hall walking slow, head up, ice-blue eyes working like acid on everyone in sight; had the hall nearly to himself, plenty of room for his slow-stroll-swagger. The other high school kids were shouldering the wall, shedding out of his path like frenzied snakes shedding out of their skins.

You could see this Clyde was bad news. Hung in time.
Fifties-looking. Out of step. But who's going to say, "Hey,
dude, you look funny?"

Tough, this guy. Hide like the jacket he wore. No books
under his arm, nothing at all. Just cool.

Brian was standing at the water fountain first time he
saw Clyde, and immediately he was attracted to him. Not
in a sexual way. He wasn't funny. But in the manner metal
shavings are attracted to a magnet—can't do a thing about
it, just got to go to it and cling.

Brian knew who Clyde was, but this was the first time
he'd ever been close enough to feel the heat. Before, the
guy'd been a tough greaser in a leather jacket who spent
most of his time expelled from school. Nothing more.

But now he saw for the first time that the guy had something; something that up close shone like a well-honed
razor in the noonday sun.

Cool. He had that.

Class. He had that.

Difference. He had that.

He was a walking power plant.

Name was Clyde. Ol', mean, weird, don't-fuck-with-
me Clyde.

"You looking at something?" Clyde growled.

Brian just stood there, one hand resting on the water
fountain.

After a while he said innocently: "You."

"That right?"

"Uh-huh."

"Staring at me?"

"I guess."

"I see."

And then Clyde was on Brian, had him by the hair,
jerking his head down, driving a knee into his face. Brian
went back seeing constellations. Got kicked in the ribs
then. Hit in the eye as he leaned forward from that. Clyde
was making a regular bop bag out of him.

He hit Clyde back, aimed a nose shot through a swirling
haze of colored dots.

And it hurt so good. Like when he made that fat pig

Betty Sue Flowers fingernail his back until he bled; thrust up her hips until his cock ached and the rotten-fish smell of her filled his brain . . . Only this hurt better. Ten times better.

Clyde wasn't expecting that. This guy was coming back like he liked it.

Clyde dug that.

He kicked Brian in the nuts, grabbed him by the hair and slammed his forehead against the kid's nose. Made him bleed good, but didn't get a good enough lick in to break it.

Brian went down, grabbed Clyde's ankle, bit it.

Clyde yowled, dragged Brian around the hall.

The students watched, fascinated. Some wanted to laugh at what was happening, but none dared.

Clyde used his free foot to kick Brian in the face. That made Brian let go . . . for a moment. He dove at Clyde, slammed the top of his head into Clyde's bread basket, carried him back against the wall crying loudly, "Motherfucker!"

Then the principal came, separated them, screamed at them, and Clyde hit the principal and the principal went down and now Clyde and Brian were both standing up, together, *kicking the goddamned shit out of the goddamned principal in the middle of the goddamned hall.* Side by side they stood. Kicking. One. Two. One. Two. Left leg. Right leg. Feet moving together like the legs of a scurrying centipede . . .

3

They got some heat slapped on them for that; juvenile court action. It was a bad scene.

Brian's mother sat at a long table with his lawyer and whined like a blender on whip.

Good old mom. She was actually good for something. She had told the judge: "He's a good boy, your honor. Never got in any trouble before. Probably wouldn't have gotten into this, but he's got no father at home to be an example . . . ," and so forth.

If it hadn't been to his advantage, he'd have been disgusted. As it was, he sat in his place with his nice clean suit and tried to look ashamed and a little surprised at what he had done. And in a way he was surprised.

He looked over at Clyde. He hadn't bothered with a suit. He had his jacket and jeans on. He was cleaning his fingernails with a fingernail clipper.

When Mrs. Blackwood finished, Judge Lowry yawned. It was going to be one of those days. He thought: the dockets are full, this Blackwood kid has no priors, looks clean-cut enough, and this other little shit has a bookfull . . . Yet, he is a kid, and I feel big-hearted. Or, to put this into perspective, there's enough of a backlog without adding this silly case to it.

If I let the Blackwood kid go, it'll look like favoritism because he's clean-cut and this is his first time—and that is good for something. Yet, if I don't let the Edson kid go too, then I'm saying the same crime is not as bad when it's committed by a clean-cut kid with a whining momma.

All right, he thought. We'll keep it simple. Let them both go, but give it all some window dressing.

And it was window dressing, nothing more. Brian was put on light probation, and Clyde, already on probation, was given the order to report to his probation officer more frequently, and that was the end of that.

Piece of cake.

The school expelled them for the rest of the term, but that was no mean thing. They were back on the streets before the day was out.

For the moment, Clyde went his way and Brian went his.

But the bond was formed.

4

A week later, mid-October.

Brian Blackwood sat in his room, his head full of pleasant but overwhelming emotions. He got a pen and loose-leaf notebook out of his desk drawer, began to write savagely.

I've never kept a journal before, and I don't know if I'll continue to keep one after tonight, but the stuff that's going on inside of me is boiling up something awful and I feel if I don't get it out I'm going to explode and there isn't going to be anything left of me but blood and shit stains on the goddamned wall.

In school I read about this writer who said he was like that, and if he could write down what was bothering him, what was pushing his skull from the inside, he could find relief, so I'm going to try that and hope for the best, because I've got to tell somebody, and I sure as hell can't tell Mommy-dear this, not that I can really tell her anything, but I've got to let this out of me and I only wish I could write faster, put it down as fast as I think.

This guy, Clyde Edson, he's really different and he's changed my life and I can feel it, I know it, it's down in my guts, squirming around like some kind of cancer, eating at me from the inside out, changing me into something new and fresh.

Being around Clyde is like being next to pure power, yeah, like that. Energy comes off of him in waves that nearly knock you down, and it's almost as if I'm absorbing that energy, and like maybe Clyde is sucking something out of me, something he can use, and the thought of that, of me giving Clyde something, whatever it is, makes me feel strong and whole. I mean, being around Clyde is like touching evil, or like that sappy Star Wars *shit about being seduced by the Dark Side of The Force, or some such fucking malarky. But you see, this seduction by the Dark Side, it's a damn good fuck, a real jism-spurter, kind that makes your eyes bug, your back pop and your asshole pucker.*

Maybe I don't understand this yet, but I think it's sort of like this guy I read about once, this philosopher whose name I can't remember, but who said something about becoming a Superman. Not the guy with the cape. I'm not talking comic book, do-gooder crap here, I'm talking the real palooka. Can't remember just what he said, but from memory of what I read, and from the way I feel now, I figure that Clyde and I are two of the chosen, the Supermen of now, this moment, mutants for the future. I see it sort of like this: man was once a wild animal type that made right by the size of his muscles and not by no bullshit government and laws. Time came when he had to become civilized to survive all the other hardnoses, but now that time has passed 'cause most of the hardnoses have died off and there isn't anything left but a bunch of fucking pussies who couldn't find their ass with a road map or figure how to wipe it without a blueprint. But you see, the mutations are happening again. New survivors are being born, and instead of that muck scientists say we crawled out of in the first place, we're crawling out of this mess the pussies have created with all their human rights shit and laws to protect the weak. Only this time, it isn't like before. Man might have crawled out of that slime to escape the sharks of the sea back then, but this time it's the goddamned sharks that are crawling out and we're mean sonofabitches with razor-sharp teeth and hides like fresh-dug gravel. And most different of all, there's a single-mindness about us that just won't let up.

I don't know if I'm saying this right, it's not all clear in my head and it's hard to put into words, but I can feel it, goddamnit, I can feel it. Time has come when we've become too civilized, overpopulated, so evolution has taken care of that, it's created a social mutation—Supermen like Clyde and me.

Clyde, he's the raw stuff, sewer sludge. He gets what he wants because he doesn't let anything stand in the way of what he wants, nothing. God, the conversations we had the last couple of days . . . See now, lost my train of thought . . . Oh yeah, the social mutations.

You see, I thought I was some kind of fucking freak all this time. But what it is, I'm just new, different. I mean, from as far back as I can remember, I've been different. I just don't react the way other people do, and I didn't understand why. Crying over dead puppies and shit like that. Big fucking deal. Dog's dead, he's dead. What the fuck do I care? It's the fucking dog that's dead, not me, so why should I be upset?

I mean, I remember this little girl next door that had this kitten when we were kids. She was always cooing and petting that little mangy bastard. And one day my Dad—that was before he got tired of the Old Lady's whining and ran off, and good riddance, I say—sent me out to mow the yard. He had this thing about the yard being mowed, and he had this thing about me doing it. Well, I'm out there mowing it, and there's that kitten, wandering around in our yard. Now, I was sick of that kitten, Mr. Journal, so I picked it up and petted it, went to the garage and got myself a trowel. I went out in the front yard and dug a nice deep hole and put that kitten in it, all except the head, I left that sticking up. I patted the dirt around its neck real tight, then I went back and got the lawn mower, started it and began pushing it toward that little fucking cat. I could see its head twisting and it started moving its mouth—meowing, but I couldn't hear it, though I wish I could have—and I pushed the mower slowlike toward it, watching the grass chute from time to time, making sure the grass was really coming out of there in thick green blasts, and then I'd look up and see that kitten. When I got a few feet from it, I noticed that I was on a hard. I mean, I had a pecker you could have used for a cold chisel.

When I was three feet away, I started to push that thing at a trot, and when I hit that cat, what a sound, and I had my eye peeled on that mower chute, and for a moment there was green and then there was red with green and hunks of ragged, grey fur spewing out, twisting onto the lawn.

Far as I knew, no one ever knew what I did. I just covered up the stump of the cat's neck real good and went on about my business. Later that evening when I was finishing up, the little shit next door came home and I could hear her calling out, "Kitty, kitty, kitty," it was all I could do not to fall down behind the mower laughing. But I kept a straight face, and when she came over and asked if I'd seen Morris—can you get that, Morris?—I said, "No, I'm sorry, I haven't," and she doesn't even get back to her house before she's crying and calling for that little fucking cat again.

Ah, but so much for amusing sidelights, Mr. Journal. I guess the point I'm trying to make is people get themselves tied up and concerned with the damndest things, dogs and cats, stuff like that. I've yet to come across a dog or cat with a good, solid idea.

God, it feels good to say what I want to say for a change, and to have someone like Clyde who not only understands, but agrees, sees things the same way. Feels good to realize why all the Boy Scout good deed shit never made me feel diddlyshit. Understand now why the good grades and being called smart never thrilled me either. Was all bullshit, that's why. We Supermen don't go for that petty stuff, doesn't mean dick to us. Got no conscience 'cause a conscience isn't anything but a bullshit tool to make you a goddamned pussy, a candy-ass coward. We do what we want, as we please, when we want. I got this feeling that there are more and more like Clyde and me, and in just a little more time, we new ones will rule. And those who are born like us won't feel so out of step, because they'll know by then that the way they feel is okay, and that this is a dog eat dog world full of fucking red, raw meat, and there won't be any bullshit, pussy talk from them, they'll just go out and find that meat and eat it.

These new ones aren't going to be like the rest of the turds who have a clock to tell them when to get up in the morning, a boss that tells them what to do all day and a wife to nag them into doing it to keep her happy lest she cut off the pussy supply. No, no more of that. That old dog ain't going to hunt no more. From then on it'll be every man for himself, take what you want, take the pussy you want, whatever. What a world that would be, a world where every sonofabitch on the block is as mean as a junkyard dog. Every day would be an adventure, a constant battle of muscle and wits.

Oh man, the doors that Clyde has opened for me. He's something else. Just a few days ago I felt like I was some kind of freak hiding out in this world, then along comes Clyde and I find out that the freaks are plentiful, but the purely sane, like Clyde and me, are far and few—least right now. Oh yeah, that Clyde . . . it's not because he's so smart, either. Least not in a book-learned sense. The thing that impresses me about him is the fact that he's so raw and ready to bite, to just take life in his teeth and shake that motherfucker until the shit comes out.

Me and Clyde are like two halves of a whole. I'm blond and fair, intelligent, and he's dark, short and muscular, just able to read. I'm his gears and he's my oil, the stuff that makes me run right. We give to each other . . . What we give is . . . Christ, this will sound screwy, Mr. Journal, but the closest I can come to describing it is psychic energy. We feed off each other.

Jesus Fucking H. Christ, starting to ramble. But feel better. That writer's idea must be working because I feel drained. Getting this out is like having been constipated for seventeen years of my life, and suddenly I've taken a laxative and I've just shit the biggest turd that can be shit by man, bear or elephant, and it feels so goddamned good, I want to yell to the skies.

Hell, I've had it. Feel like I been on an all-night fuck with a nympho on Spanish Fly. Little later Clyde's supposed to come by, and I'm going out the window, going with him to see The House. He's told me about it, and it sounds really fine. He says he's going to show me some things I've never seen before. Hope so.

Damn, it's like waiting to be blessed with some sort of crazy, magical power or something. Like being given the ability to strike people with leprosy or wish some starlet up all naked and squirming on the rack and you with a dick as long and hard and hot as a heated poker, and her looking up at you and yelling for you to stick it to her before she cums just looking at you. Something like that, anyway.

Well, won't be long now and Clyde will be here. Guess I need to go sit over by the window, Mr. Journal, so I won't miss him. If Mom finds me missing after a while, things could get a little sticky, but I doubt she'll report her only, loving son to the parole board. Would be tacky. I always just tell her I'll be moving out just as soon as I can

get me a job, and that shuts her up. Christ, she acts like
she's in love with me or something, isn't natural.

  Enough of this journal shit. Bring on the magic, Clyde.

5

Two midnight shadows seemed to blow across the yard of
the Blackwood home. Finally, those shadows broke out of
the overlapping darkness of the trees, hit the moonlight
and exploded into two teenagers. Clyde and Brian, running fast and hard. Their heels beat a quick, sharp rhythm
on the sidewalk, like the too-fast ticking of clocks; time-
pieces from the Dark Side, knocking on toward a grue-
some destiny.

After a moment the running stopped. Doors slammed.
A car growled angrily. Lights burst on, and the black '66
sailed away from the curb. It sliced down the quiet street
like a razor being sliced down a vein, cruised between
dark houses where only an occasional light burned behind
a window like a fearful gold eye gazing through a contact
lens.

A low-slung, yellow dog making its nightly trashcan
route crossed the street, fell into the Chevy's headlights.

The car whipped for the dog, but the animal was fast
and lucky and only got its tail brushed before making the
curb.

A car door flew open in a last attempt to bump the dog,
but the dog was too far off the street. The car bounced up
on the curb briefly, then lurched back onto the pavement.

The dog was gone now, blending into the darkness of a
tree-shadowed yard.

The door slammed and the motor roared loudly. The
car moved rapidly off into the night, and from its open
windows, carried by the wind, came the high wild sound
of youthful laughter.

6

The House, as Clyde called it, was just below Stoker
Street, just past where it intersected King, not quite book-

ended between the two streets, but nearby, on a more narrow one. And there it waited.

Almost reverently, like a hearse that has arrived to pick up the dead, the black '66 Chevy entered the drive, parked.

Clyde and Brian got out, stood looking up at the house for a moment, considering it as two monks would a shrine.

Brian felt a sensation of trembling excitement, and although he would not admit it, a tinge of fear.

The House was big, old, grey and ugly. It looked gothic, out of step with the rest of the block. Like something out of Poe or Hawthorne. It crouched like a falsely obedient dog. Upstairs two windows showed light, seemed like cold, rectangular eyes considering prey.

The moon was bright enough that Brian could see the dead grass in the yard, the dead grass in all the yards down the block. It was the time of year for dead grass, but to Brian's way of thinking, this grass looked browner, deader. It was hard to imagine it ever being alive, ever standing up tall and bright and green.

The odd thing about The House was the way it seemed to command the entire block. It was not as large as it first appeared—though it was large—and the homes about it were newer and more attractive. They had been built when people still cared about the things they lived in, before the era of glass and plastic and builders who pocketed the money that should have been used on foundation and structure. Some of the houses stood a story above the gothic nightmare, but somehow they had taken on a run-down, anemic look, as if the old grey house was in fact some sort of alien vampire that could impersonate a house by day, but late at night it would turn its head with a wood-grain creak, look out of its cold, rectangle eyes and suddenly stand to reveal thick peasant-girl legs and feet beneath its firm wooden skirt, and then it would start to stalk slowly and crazily down the street, the front door opening to reveal long, hollow, woodscrew teeth, and it would pick a house and latch onto it, fold back its rubbery front porch lips and burrow its many fangs into its brick or wood and suck out the architectural grace and all the love its builders had put into it. Then, as it turned to leave, bloated, satiated, the grass would die beneath its steps and it would creep and creak back down the street to find its place, and it would sigh deeply, contentedly, as it settled once more, and the energy and grace of the newer houses, the loved houses, would bubble inside its chest. Then it would sleep, digest, and wait.

"Let's go in," Clyde said.

The walk was made of thick white stones. They were cracked and weather swollen. Some of them had partially tumbled out of the ground dragging behind a wad of dirt and grass roots that made them look like abscessed teeth that had fallen from some giant's rotten gums.

Avoiding the precarious stepping-stones, they mounted the porch, squeaked the screen and groaned the door open. Darkness seemed to crawl in there. They stepped inside.

"Hold it," Clyde said. He reached and hit the wall switch.

Darkness went away, but the light wasn't much. The overhead fixture was coated with dust and it gave the room a speckled look, like sunshine through camouflage netting.

There was a high staircase to their left and it wound up to a dangerous-looking landing where the railing dangled out of line and looked ready to fall. Beneath the stairs, and to the far right of the room, were many doors. Above, behind the landing, were others, a half dozen in a soldier row. Light slithered from beneath the crack of one.

"Well?" Clyde said.

"I sort of expect Dracula to come down those stairs any moment."

Clyde smiled. "He's down here with you, buddy. Right here."

"What nice teeth you have."

"Uh-huh, real nice. How about a tour?"

"Lead on."

"The basement first?"

"Whatever."

"All right, the basement then. Come on."

Above them, from the lighted room, came the sound of a girl giggling, then silence.

"Girls?" Brian asked.

"More about that later."

They crossed the room and went to a narrow doorway with a recessed door. Clyde opened it. It was dark and foul-smelling down there, the odor held you like an embrace.

Brian could see the first three stair steps clearly, three more in shadow, the hint of one more, then nothing.

"Come on," Clyde said.

Clyde didn't bother with the light, if there was one. He stepped on the first step and started down.

Brian watched as Clyde was consumed by darkness. Cold air washed up and over him. He followed.

At the border of light and shadow, Brian turned to look behind him. There was only a rectangle of light to see, and that light seemed almost reluctant to enter the basement, as if it were too fearful.

Brian turned back, stepped into the veil of darkness, felt his way carefully with toe and heel along the wooden path. He half-expected the stairs to withdraw with a jerk and pull him into some creature's mouth, like a toad tongue that had speared a stupid fly. It certainly smelled bad enough down there to be a creature's mouth.

Brian was standing beside Clyde now. He stopped, heard Clyde fumble in his leather jacket for something. There was a short, sharp sound like a single cricket-click, and a match jumped to life, waved its yellow-red head around, cast the youngsters' shadows on the wall, made them look like monstrous Siamese twins, or some kind of two-headed, four-armed beast.

Water was right at their feet. Another step and they would have been in it. A bead of sweat trickled from Brian's hair, ran down his nose and fell off. He realized that Clyde was testing him.

"Basements aren't worth a shit around this part of the country," Clyde said, "except for a few things they're not intended for."

"Like what?"

"You'll find out in plenty of time. Besides, how do I know I can trust you?"

That hurt Brian, but he didn't say anything. The first rule of being a Superman was to be above that sort of thing. You had to be strong, cool. Clyde would respect that sort of thing.

Clyde nodded at the water. "That's from last month's storm."

"Nice place if you raise catfish."

"Yeah."

The match went out. And somehow, Brian could sense Clyde's hand behind him, in a position to shove, considering it. Brian swallowed quietly, said very coolly, "Now what?"

After a long moment, Brian sensed Clyde's hand slip away, heard it crinkle into the pocket of his leather jacket. Clyde said, "Let's go back, unless you want to swim a little. Want to do that?"

"Didn't bring my trunks. Wouldn't want you to see my wee-wee."

Clyde laughed. "What's the matter, embarrassed at only having an inch?"

"Naw, was afraid you'd think it was some kind of big water snake and you'd try to cut it."

"How'd you know I had a knife?"

"Just figures."

"Maybe I like you."

"Big shit." But it was a big shit to Brian, and he was glad for the compliment, though he wasn't about to let on.

Clyde's jacket crinkled. Another match flared.

"Easy turning," Clyde said, "these stairs are narrow, maybe rotten."

Brian turned briskly, started up ahead of Clyde.

"Easy, I said."

Brian stopped. He was just at the edge of the light. He turned, smiled down. He didn't know if Clyde could see his smile in the match light or not, but he hoped he could feel it. He decided to try a little ploy of his own.

"Easy, hell," he said. "Didn't you bring me down here just to see if I'd panic? To see if those creaky stairs and that water and you putting a hand behind me would scare me?''

Clyde's match went out. Brian could no longer see him clearly. That made him nervous.

''Guess that was the idea,'' Clyde said from the darkness.

Another match smacked to life.

''Thought so.''

Brian turned, started up, stepping firmly, but not hurriedly. The stairs rocked beneath his feet.

It felt good to step into the room's speckled light. Brian sighed softly, took a deep breath. It was a musty breath, but it beat the sour, rotten smell of the basement. He leaned against the wall, waited.

After what seemed like a long time, Clyde stepped out of the basement and closed the door. He turned to look at Brian, smiled.

(What nice teeth you have.)

''You'll do,'' Clyde said softly. ''You'll do.''

Now came the grand tour. Clyde led Brian through rooms stuffed with trash; full of the smell of piss, sweat, sex and dung; through empty rooms, cold and hollow as the inside of a petrified god's heart.

Rooms. So many rooms.

Finally the downstairs tour was finished and it was time to climb the stairs and find out what was waiting behind those doors, to look into the room filled with light.

They paused at the base of the stairs. Brian laid a hand on Clyde's shoulder.

''How in hell did you come by all this?'' he asked.

Clyde smiled.

''Is it yours?'' Brian asked.

''All mine,'' Clyde said. ''Got it easy. Everything I do comes easy. One day I decided to move in and I did.''

''How did you—''

''Hang on, listen: You see, this was once a fancy apartment house. Had a lot of old folks as customers, sort of an old fossil box. I needed a place to stay, was living on the streets then. I liked it here, but didn't have any money.

So I found the caretaker. Place had a full-time one then. Guy with a crippled leg.

"I say to this gimp, I'm moving into the basement—wasn't full of water then—and if he don't like it, I'll push his face in for him. Told him if he called the cops I'd get him on account of I'm a juvenile and I've been in and out of kiddie court so many times I got a lunch card. Told him I knew about his kids, how pretty that little daughter of his was, how pretty I thought she'd look on the end of my dick. Told him I'd put her there and spin her around on it like a top. I'd done my homework on the old fart, knew all about him, about his little girl and little boy.

"So, I scared him good. He didn't want any trouble and he let me and the cunt I was banging then move in."

A spark moved in Clyde's eyes. "About the cunt, just so you know I play hardball, she isn't around anymore. She and the brat she was going to have are taking an extended swimming lesson."

"You threw her in the bay?"

Clyde tossed his head at the basement.

"Ah," Brian said, and he felt an erection, a real blue-veiner. Something warm moved from the tips of his toes to the base of his skull, foamed inside his brain. It was as if his bladder had backed up and filled his body with urine. Old Clyde had actually killed somebody and had no remorse, was in fact proud. Brian liked that. It meant Clyde was as much of a Superman as he expected. And since Clyde admitted the murder to him, he knew he trusted him, considered him a comrade, a fellow Superman.

"What happened next?" Brian asked. It was all he could do not to lick his lips.

"Me and the cunt moved in. Couple guys I knew wanted to come too, bring their cunts along. I let them. Before long there's about a half dozen of us living in the god-damned basement. We got the caretaker to see we got fed, and he did it too on account of he was a weenie, and we kept reminding him how much we like little-girl pussy. I got to where I could describe what we wanted to do to her real good."

"Anyway, that went on for a while, then one day he

doesn't show up with the grub. Found out later that he'd packed up the dumpling wife, the two ankle-biters and split. So I say to the guys—by the way, don't ask no cunt nothing, they got opinions on everything and not a bit of it's worth stringy dogshit, unless you want to know the best way to put a tampon in or what color goes well with blue . . . so, I say to the guys, this ain't no way to live, and we start a little storm trooper campaign. Scared piss out of some of the old folks, roughed up an old lady, nailed her dog to the door by its ears.''

''Didn't the cops come around?''

''Yeah. They came and got us on complaints, told us to stay out. But what could they do? No one had seen us do a damn thing except those complaining, and it was just our word against theirs. They made us move out though.''

''So we went and had a little talk with the manager, made a few threats, got a room out of the deal and started paying rent. By this time we had the cunts hustling for us, bouncing tail on the streets and bringing in a few bucks. Once we start paying rent, what can they say? But we keep up the storm trooper campaign, just enough to keep it scary around here. Before long the manager quit and all the old folks hiked.''

''What about the owner?''

''He came around. We paid the rent and he let us stay. He's a slumlord anyway. It was the old folks kept the place up. After they left, it got pretty trashy, and this guy wasn't going to put out a cent on the place. He was glad to take our money and run. We were paying him more than all the old codgers together. The pussy business was really raking in the coins. And besides, he don't want to make us mad, know what I mean?''

''Some setup.''

''It's sweet all right. Like being a juvenile. The courts are all fucked up on that one. They don't know what to do with us, so they usually just say the hell with us. It's easier to let us go than to hassle with us. After you're eighteen life isn't worth living. That's when the rules start to apply to us too. Right now we're just misguided kids who'll straighten out in time.''

"I hear that."

"Good. Let's go upstairs. Got some people I want you to meet."

"Yeah?"

"A girl I want you to fuck."

"Yeah?"

"Yeah. Got this one cunt that's something else. Thirteen years old, a runaway or something. Picked her up off the street about a month ago. Totally wiped out in the brain department, not that a cunt's got that much brain to begin with, but this one is a clean slate. But, man, does she have tits. They're big as footballs. She's as good a fuck as a grown woman."

"This going to cost me?"

"You kidding? You get what you want, no charge—money anyway."

"What's that mean?"

"I want your soul, not your money."

Brian grinned. "So what are you, the devil? Thought you were Dracula."

"I'm both of them."

"Do I have to sign something in blood?"

Clyde laughed hysterically. "Sure, that's a good one. Blood. Write something in fucking blood. I like you, Brian, I really do."

So Brian saw the dark rooms upstairs, and finally the one with the light and the people.

The room stank. There was a mattress on the floor and there was a nude girl on the mattress and there was a nude boy on the girl and the girl was not moving but the boy was moving a lot.

On the other side of the mattress a naked blond girl squatted next to a naked boy. The girl had enormous breasts and dark brown eyes. The boy was stocky and square-jawed. They lifted their heads as Clyde and Brian came in, and Brian could see they were stoned to the max. The two smiled at them in unison, as if they had but one set of facial muscles between them.

The boy riding the girl grunted, once, real loud. After

a moment he rolled off her smiling, his penis half-hard, dripping.

The girl on the mattress still did not move. She lay with her eyes closed and her arms by her sides.

"This is Loony Tunes," Clyde said, pointing to the boy who had just rolled off the girl. "This is Stone," he said, pointing to the stocky boy. "If he talks, I've never heard it." He did not introduce either girl. "This is all we got around here right now, cream of the crop."

The girl on the mattress still had not moved.

The one called Loony Tunes laughed once in a while, for no apparent reason.

Clyde said, "Go ahead and tend to your rat killing, me and Brian got plans." Then he snapped his fingers and pointed to the nude girl with the big breasts and the silly smile.

She stood up, wavering a bit. With ten pounds and something to truly smile about, she might have been pretty. She looked like she needed a bath.

Clyde held out his hand. She came around the mattress and took it. He put an arm around her waist.

The one called Stone crawled on top of the girl on the mattress.

She still did not move.

Brian could see now that her eyes were actually only half-closed and her eyeballs were partly visible. They looked as cool and expressionless as marbles.

Stone took hold of his sudden erection and put it in her.

She still did not move.

Stone began to grunt.

Loony Tunes laughed.

She still did not move.

"Come on," Clyde said to Brian, "the next room."

So they went out of there, the big-eyed girl sandwiched between them.

There was a small mattress in the closet in the next room, and Clyde, feeling his way around in the dark with experienced ease, pulled it out. He said, "Keeping in practice for when I quit paying the light bill, learning to be a bat.''

"I see," Brian said. The girl leaned against him. She muttered something once, but it made no sense. She was so high on nose candy and cheap wine she didn't know where she was or who she was. She smelled like mildewed laundry.

After Clyde had tossed the mattress on the floor, he took his clothes off, called them over. The girl leaned on Brian all the way across the room.

When they were standing in front of Clyde, he said, "This is the big-titted, thirteen-year-old I told you about. Looks older, don't she?" But he didn't wait for Brian to answer. He said loudly to the girl, "Come here."

She crawled on the mattress. Brian took his clothes off. They all lay down together. The mattress smelled of dirt, wine and sweat.

And that night Brian and Clyde had the thirteen-year-old, and later, when Brian tried to think back on the moment, he would not be able to remember her face, only that she was blond, had massive breasts and dark eyes like pools of fresh-perked coffee, pools that went down and down into her head like wet tunnels to eternity.

She was so high they could have poked her with knives and she would not have felt it. She was just responding in automaton fashion. Clyde had it in her ass and Brian had it in her mouth, and they were pumping in unison, the smell of their exertion mingling with hers, filling the room.

The girl was slobbering and choking on Brian's penis and he was ramming it harder and harder into her mouth, and he could feel her teeth scraping his flesh, making his cock bleed, and it seemed to him that he was extending all the way down her throat, all the way through her, and that the head of his penis was touching Clyde's and Clyde's penis was like the finger of God giving life to the clay form of Adam, and that he was Adam, and he was receiving that spark from the Holy On High, and for the power and the glory he was grateful; made him think of the Frankenstein monster and how it must have felt when its creator threw the switch and drove the power of the storm through its body and above the roll of the thunder and the crackling flash of lightning Dr. Frankenstein yelled at the top of his lungs, *"It's alive!"*

Then he and Clyde came in white-hot-atomic-blast unison and in Brian's mind it was the explosive ending of the old world and the Big Bang creation of the new . . .

Only the sound of panting now, the pleasant sensation of his organ draining into the blond's mouth.

Clyde reached out and touched Brian's hand, squeezed his fingers, and Clyde's touch was as cold and clammy as the hand of death.

Clyde drove Brian home. Brian stole silently into the house and climbed the stairs. Once in his room he went to the window to look out. He could hear Clyde's '66 Chevy in the distance, and though it was a bright night and he could see real far, he could not see as far as Clyde had gone.

And later:

back at The House the girl Clyde and Brian had shared would start to wail and fight invisible harpies in her head, and Clyde would take her to the basement for a little swim. The body of the girl on the mattress would follow suit. Neither managed much swimming;

and there would be a series of unprecedented robberies that night all over the city;

and in a little quiet house near Galveston Bay, an Eagle Scout and honor student would kill his father and rape his mother;

and an on-duty policeman with a fine family and plenty of promotion to look forward to would pull over to the curb on a dark street and put his service revolver in his mouth and pull the trigger, coating the back windshield with brains, blood and clinging skull shrapnel;

and a nice meek housewife in a comfortable house by Sea Arama would take a carving knife to her husband's neck while he slept; would tell police later that it was because he said he didn't like the way she'd made the roast that night, which was ridiculous since he'd liked it fixed exactly that same way the week before.

All in all, it was a strange night in Galveston, Texas. A lot of dogs howled.

THE FAT MAN
AND THE ELEPHANT

For Pat LoBrutto

The signs were set in relay and went on for miles. The closer you got to the place the bigger they became. They were so enthusiastic in size and brightness of paint it might be thought you were driving to heaven and God had posted a sure route so you wouldn't miss it. They read:

WORLD'S LARGEST GOPHER!
ODDITIES!
SEE THE SNAKES! SEE THE ELEPHANT!
SOUVENIRS!
BUTCH'S HIGHWAY MUSEUM AND EMPORIUM!

But Sonny knew he wasn't driving to heaven. Butch's was far from heaven and he didn't want to see anything but the elephant. He had been to the Museum and Emporium many times, and the first time was enough for the sights—because there weren't any.

The World's Largest Gopher was six feet tall and inside a fenced-in enclosure. It cost you two dollars on top of the dollar admission fee to get in there and have a peek at it and feel like a jackass. The gopher was a statue, and it wasn't even a good statue. It looked more like a dog standing on its haunches than a gopher. It had a strained, constipated look on its homely face, and one of its two front teeth had been chipped off by a disappointed visitor with a rock.

The snake show wasn't any better. Couple of dead, stuffed rattlers with the rib bones sticking through their

98

taxidermied hides, and one live, but about to go, cotton mouth who didn't have any fangs and looked a lot like a deflated bicycle tire when it was coiled and asleep. Which was most of the time. You couldn't wake the sonofabitch if you beat on the glass with a rubber hose and yelled FIRE!

There were two main souvenirs. One was the armadillo purses, and the other was a miniature statue of the gopher with a little plaque on it that read: I SAW THE WORLD'S LARGEST GOPHER AT BUTCH'S HIGHWAY MUSEUM AND EM-PORIUM OFF HIGHWAY 59. And the letters were so crowded on there you had to draw mental slashes between the words. They sold for a dollar fifty apiece and they moved right smart. In fact, Butch made more money on those (75¢ profit per statue) than he did on anything else, except the cold drinks which he marked up a quarter. When you were hot from a long drive and irritated about actually seeing the World's Largest Gopher, you tended to spend money foolishly on soda waters and gopher statues.

Or armadillo purses. The armadillos came from Hank's Armadillo Farm and Hank was the one that killed them and scooped their guts out and made purses from them. He lacquered the bodies and painted them gold and tossed glitter in the paint before it dried. The 'dillos were quite bright and had little zippers fixed into their bellies and a rope handle attached to their necks and tails so you could carry them upside down with their sad, little feet pointing skyward.

Butch's wife had owned several of the purses. One Fourth of July she and the week's receipts had turned up missing along with one of her 'dillo bags. She and the purse and the receipts were never seen again. Elrod down at the Gulf station disappeared too. Astute observers said there was a connection.

But Sonny came to see the elephant, not buy souvenirs or look at dead snakes and statues. The elephant was dif-ferent from the rest of Butch's stuff. It was special.

It wasn't that it was beautiful, because it wasn't. It was in bad shape. It could hardly even stand up. But the first time Sonny had seen it, he had fallen in love with it. Not in the romantic sense, but in the sense of two great souls encountering one another. Sonny came back time after time to see it when he needed inspiration, which of late, with the money dwindling and his preaching services not bringing in the kind of offerings he thought they should, was quite often.

Sonny wheeled his red Chevy pickup with the GOD LOVES EVEN FOOLS LIKE ME sticker on the back windshield through the gate of Butch's and paid his dollar for admission, plus two dollars to see the elephant.

Butch was sitting at the window of the little ticket house as usual. He was toothless and also wore a greasy, black work cap, though Sonny couldn't figure where the grease came from. He had never known Butch to do any kind of work, let alone something greasy—unless you counted the serious eating of fried chicken. Butch just sat there in the window of the little house in his zip-up coveralls (summer or winter) and let Levis Garrett snuff drip down his chin while he played with a pencil or watched a fly dive bomb a jelly doughnut. He seldom talked, unless it was to argue about money. He didn't even like to tell you how much admission was. It was like it was some secret you were supposed to know, and when he did finally reveal it, it was as if he had given up part of his heart.

Sonny drove his pickup over to the big barn where the elephant stayed, got out and went inside.

Candy, the ancient clean-up nigger, was shoving some dirt around with a push broom, stirring up dust mostly. When Candy saw Sonny wobble in, his eyes lit up.

"Hello there, Mr. Sonny. You done come to see your elephant, ain't you?"

"Yeah, I have," Sonny said.

"That's good, that's good." Candy looked over Sonny's shoulder at the entrance, then glanced at the back of the barn. "That's good, and you right on time too, like you always is."

Candy held out his hand.

Sonny slipped a five into it and Candy folded it carefully and put it in the front pocket of his faded khakis, gave it a pat like a good dog, then swept up the length of the barn. When he got to the open door, he stood there watching, waiting for Mr. Butch to go to lunch, like he did every day at eleven-thirty sharp.

And sure enough, there he went in his black Ford pickup out the gate of Butch's Museum and Emporium. Then came the sound of the truck stopping and the gate being locked. Butch closed the whole thing down every day for lunch rather than leave it open for the nigger to tend. Anyone inside the Emporium at that time was just shit out of luck. They were trapped there until Butch came back from lunch thirty minutes later, unless they wanted to go over the top or ram the gate with their vehicle.

It wasn't a real problem however. Customers seldom showed up mid-day, dead of summer. They didn't seem to want to see the World's Largest Gopher at lunch time.

Which was why Sonny liked to come when he did. He and Candy had an arrangement.

When Candy heard Butch's truck clattering up the highway, he dropped the broom, came back and led Sonny over to the elephant stall.

"He in this one today, Mr. Sonny."

Candy took out a key and unlocked the chainlink gate that led inside the stall and Sonny stepped inside and Candy said what he always said. "I ain't supposed to do this now. You supposed to do all your looking through this gate." Then, without waiting for a reply he closed the gate behind Sonny and leaned on it.

The elephant was lying on its knees and it stirred slightly. Its skin creaked like tight shoes and its breathing was heavy.

"You wants the usual, Mr. Sonny?"

"Does it have to be so hot this time? Ain't it hot enough in here already?"

"It can be anyway you wants it, Mr. Sonny, but if you wants to do it right, it's got to be hot. You know I'm telling the truth now, don't you?"

"Yeah . . . but it's so hot."

"Don't do no good if it ain't, Mr. Sonny. Now we got to get these things done before Mr. Butch comes back. He ain't one for spir'tual things. That Mr. Butch ain't like you and me. He just wants that dollar. You get that stool and sit yourself down, and I'll be back dreckly, Mr. Sonny.''

Sonny sat the stool upright and perched his ample butt on it, smelled the elephant shit and studied the old pachyderm. The critter didn't look as if it had a lot of time left, and Sonny wanted to get all the wisdom from it he could.

The elephant's skin was mottled grey and more wrinkled than a bloodhound's. Its tusks had been cut off short years before and they had turned a ripe lemon yellow, except for the jagged tips and they were the color of dung. Its eyes were skummy and it seldom stood anymore, not even to shit. Therefore, its flanks were caked with it. Flies had collected in the mess like raisins spread thickly on rank chocolate icing. When the old boy made a feeble attempt to slap at them with his tail, they rose up en masse like bad omens.

Candy changed the hay the elephant lay on now and then, but not often enough to rid the stall of the stink. With the heat like it was, and the barn being made of tin and old oak, it clung to the structure and the elephant even when the bedding was fresh and the beast had been hosed down. But that was all right with Sonny. He had come to associate the stench with God.

The elephant was God's special animal—shit smell and all. God had created the creature in the same way he had created everything else—with a wave of his majestic hand (Sonny always imagined the hand bejeweled with rings). But God had given the elephant something special—which seemed fair to Sonny, since he had put the poor creature in the land of crocodiles and niggers—and that special something was wisdom.

Sonny had learned of this from Candy. He figured since Candy was born of niggers who came from Africa, he knew about elephants. Sonny reasoned that elephant love was just the sort of information niggers would pass down to one another over the years. They probably passed along other stuff that wasn't of importance too, like the best bones for your nose and how to make wooden dishes you could put inside your lips so you could flap them like Donald Duck. But the stuff on the elephants would be the good stuff.

He was even more certain of this when Candy told him on his first visit to see the elephant that the critter was most likely his totem. Candy had taken one look at him and said that. It surprised Sonny a bit that Candy would even consider such things. He seemed like a plain old clean-up nigger to him. In fact, he had hired Candy to work for him before. The sort of work you wanted a nigger to do, hot and dirty. He'd found Candy to be slow and lazy and at the end of the day he had almost denied him the two dollars he'd promised. He could hardly see that he'd earned it. In fact, he'd gotten the distinct impression that Candy was getting uppity in his old age and thought he deserved a white man's wages.

But, lazy or not, Candy did have wisdom—least when it came to elephants. When Candy told him he thought the elephant was his totem, Sonny asked how he had come by that, and Candy said, "You big and the elephant is big, and you both tough-hided and just wise as Old Methus'la. And you can attract them gals just like an ole bull elephant can attract them elephant females, now can't you? Don't lie to Candy now, you know you can."

This was true. All of it. And the only way Candy could have known about it was to know he was like the elephant and the elephant was his totem. And the last thing about attracting the women, well, that was the thing above all that convinced him that the nigger knew his business.

Course, even though he had this ability to attract the women, he had never put it to bad use. That wouldn't be God's way. Some preachers, men of God or not, would have taken advantage of such a gift, but not him. That wouldn't be right.

It did make him wonder about Louise though. Since the Lord had seen fit to give him this gift, why in the world had he ended up with her? What was God's master plan there? She was a right nice Christian woman on the inside, but the outside looked like a four car pileup. She could use some work.

He couldn't remember what it was that had attracted

him to her in the first place. He had even gone so far as to look at old pictures of them together to see if she had gotten ugly slowly. But no, she'd always been that way. He finally had to blame his choice on being a drinking man in them days and a sinner. But now, having lost his liquor store business, and having sobered to God's will and gotten a little money (though that was dwindling), he could see her for what she was.

Fat and ugly.

There, he'd thought it clearly. But he did like her. He knew that. There was something so wonderfully Christian about her. She could recite from heart dozens of Bible verses, and he'd heard her give good argument against them that thought white man came from monkey, and a better argument that the nigger did. But he wished God had packaged her a little better. Like in the body of his next door neighbor's wife for instance. Now there was a Godly piece of work.

It seemed to him, a man like himself, destined for great things in God's arena, ought to at least have a wife who could turn heads toward her instead of away from her. A woman like that could help a man go far.

There wasn't any denying that Louise had been a big help. When he married her she had all that insurance money, most of which they'd used to buy their place and build a church on it. But the settlement was almost run through now, and thinking on it, he couldn't help but think Louise had gotten cheated.

Seemed to him that if your first husband got kicked to death by a wild lunatic that the nut house let out that very afternoon calling him cured, they ought to have to fork up enough money to take care of the man's widow for the rest of her life. And anyone she might remarry, especially if that person had some medical problems, like a trick back, and couldn't get regular work anymore.

Still, they had managed what she had well; had gotten some real mileage out of the four hundred thousand. There was the land and the house and the church and the four hundred red-jacketed, leatherette Bibles that read in gold, gilt letters on the front: THE MASTER'S OWN BAPTIST MIN-

ISTRIES INC., SONNY GUY OFFICIATING. And there were some little odds and ends here and there he couldn't quite recall. But he felt certain not a penny had been wasted. Well, maybe those seven thousand bumper stickers they bought that said GO JESUS on them was a mistake. They should have made certain that the people who made them were going to put glue on the backs so they'd stick to something. Most folks just wouldn't go to the trouble to tape them on the bumpers and back glasses of their automobiles, and therefore weren't willing to put out four-fifty per sticker.

But that was all right. Mistakes were to be expected in a big enterprise. Even if it was for God, The Holy Ghost, and The Lord Jesus Crucified.

Yet, things weren't going right, least not until he started visiting the elephant. Now he had him some guidance and there was this feeling he had that told him it was all going to pay off. That through this creature of the Lord he was about to learn God's *grand-doise plan* for his future. And when he did learn it, he was going to start seeing those offering plates (a bunch of used hubcaps bought cheap from the wrecking yard) fill up with some serious jack.

Candy came back with the electric heater, extension cord and tarp. He had a paper bag in one back pocket, his harmonica in the other. He looked toward the entrance, just in case Butch should decide for the first time in his life to come back early.

But no Butch.

Candy smiled and opened the stall's gate.

"Here we go, Mr. Sonny, you ready to get right with God and the elephant?"

Sonny took hold of the tarp and pulled it over his head and Candy came in and found places to attach all four corners to the fence near the ground and draped it over the old elephant who squeaked its skin and turned its head ever so slightly and rolled its goo-filled eyes.

"Now you just keep you seat, Mr. Bull Elephant," Candy said, "and we all gonna be happy and ain't none of us gonna get trampled."

Candy stooped back past Sonny on his stool and crawled

out from under the tarp and let it fall down Sonny's back to the ground. He got the electric heater and pushed it under the tarp next to Sonny's stool, then he took the extension cord and went around and plugged it into one of the barn's deadly-looking wall sockets. He went back to the tarp and lifted it up and said to Sonny, "You can turn it on now, Mr. Sonny. It's all set up."

Sonny sighed and turned the heater on. The grillwork went pink, then red, and the fan in the machine began to whirl, blowing the heat at him.

Candy, who still had his face under the tarp, said, "You got to lean over it now to get the full effects, Mr. Sonny. Get that heat on you good. Get just as hot as a nigger field hand."

"I know," Sonny said. "I remember how to do it."

"I knows you do, Mr. Sonny. You great for remembering, like an elephant. It heating up in there good?"

"Yeah."

"Real hot?"

"Yeah."

"That's good. Make you wonder how anyone wouldn't want to do good and stay out of hell, don't it, Mr. Sonny? I mean it's hotter under here than when I used to work out in that hot sun for folks like you, and I bet when I drop this here tarp it just gonna get hotter, and then that heat and that stink gonna build up in there and things gonna get right for you . . . Here's you paper bag."

Candy took the bag out of his back pocket and gave it to Sonny. "Remember now," Candy said, "when you get good and full of that shit-smell and that heat, you put this bag over you face and you start blowing like you trying to push a grapefruit through a straw. That gonna get you right for the ole elephant spirit to get inside you and do some talking at you 'cause it's gonna be hot as Africa and you gonna be out of breath just like niggers dancing to drums, and that's how it's got to be."

"Ain't I done this enough to know, Candy?"

"Yes suh, you have. Just like to earns my five dollars and see a good man get right with God."

Candy's head disappeared from beneath the tarp and

when the tarp hit the ground it went dark in there except
for the little red lines of the heater grate, and for a moment
all Sonny could see was the lumpy shape of the elephant
and the smaller lumps of his own knees. He could hear the
elephant's labored breathing and his own labored breathing. Outside, Candy began to play nigger music on the
harmonica. It filtered into the hot tent and the notes were
fire ants crawling over his skin and under his overalls.
The sweat rolled down him like goat berries.

After a moment, Candy began to punctuate the harmonica notes with singing. "Sho gonna hate it when the elephant dies. Hot in here, worse than outside, and I'm sho
gonna hate it when the elephant dies." A few notes on the
harmonica. "Yes suh, gonna be bad when the pachyderm's
dead, ain't gonna have five dollars to buy Coalie's bed."
More notes. "Come on brother can you feel the heat. I'm
calling to you Jesus, cross my street."

Sonny put the bag over his face and began to blow viciously. He was blowing so hard he thought he would
knock the bottom out of the bag, but that didn't happen.
He grew dizzy, very dizzy, felt stranger than the times
before. The harmonica notes and singing were far away
and he felt like a huge hunk of ice cream melting on a hot
stone. Then he didn't feel the heat anymore. He was flying. Below him the ribs of the heater were little rivers of
molten lava and he was falling toward them from a great
height. Then the rivers were gone. There was only darkness and the smell of elephant shit, and finally that went
away and he sat on his stool on a sunny landscape covered
in tall grass. But he and his stool were taller than the
grass, tall as an elephant itself. He could see scrubby trees
in the distance and mountains and to the left of him was
a blue-green line of jungle from which came the constant
and numerous sounds of animals. Birds soared overhead
in a sky bluer than a jay's feathers. The air was as fresh
as a baby's first breath.

There was a dot in the direction of the mountains and
the dot grew and became silver-grey and there was a wink
of white on either side of it. The dot became an elephant
and the closer it came the more magnificent it looked, its

skin tight and grey and its tusks huge and long and porcelain-white. A fire sprang up before the elephant and the grass blazed in a long, hot line from the beast to the stool where Sonny sat. The elephant didn't slow. It kept coming. The fire didn't bother it. The blaze wrapped around its massive legs and licked at its belly like a lover's tongue. Then the elephant stood before him and they were eye to eye; the tusks extended over Sonny's shoulders. The trunk reached out and touched his cheek; it was as soft as a woman's lips.

The smell of elephant shit filled the air and the light went dark and another smell intruded, the smell of burning flesh. Sonny felt pain. He let out a whoop. He had fallen off the stool on top of the heater and the heater had burned his chest above the bib of his overalls.

There was light again. Candy had ripped off the tarp and was pulling him up and sitting him on the stool and righting the electric heater. "Now there, Mr. Sonny, you ain't on fire no more. You get home you get you some shaving cream and put on them burns, that'll make you feel right smart again. Did you have a good trip?"

"Africa again, Candy," Sonny said, the hot day air feeling cool to him after the rancid heat beneath the tarp. "And this time I saw the whole thing. It was all clearer than before and the elephant came all the way up to me."

"Say he did?" Candy said looking toward the barn door.

"Yeah, and I had a revelation."

"That's good you did, Mr. Sonny. I was afraid you wasn't gonna have it before Mr. Butch come back. You gonna have to get out of here now. You know how Mr. Butch is, 'specially since his wife done run off with that ole 'diller purse and the money that time. Ain't been a fit man to take a shit next to since."

Candy helped Sonny to his feet and guided him out of the stall and leaned him against it.

"A firewalking elephant," Sonny said. "Soon as I seen it, it come to me what it all meant."

"I'm sho glad of that, Mr. Sonny."

Candy looked toward the open door to watch for Butch. He then stepped quickly into the stall, jammed the paper bag in his back pocket and folded up the tarp and put it under his arm and picked the heater up by the handle and carried it out, the cord dragging behind it. He sat the tarp and the heater down and closed the gate and locked it. He looked at the elephant. Except for a slight nodding of its head it looked dead.

Candy got hold of the tarp and the heater again and put them in their place. He had no more than finished when he heard Butch's truck pulling up to the gate. He went over to Sonny and took him by the arm and smiled at him and said, "It sho been a pleasure having you, and the elephant done went and gave you one of them rav'lations too. And the best one yet, you say?"

"It was a sign from God," Sonny said.

"God's big on them signs. He's always sending someone a sign or a bush on fire or a flood or some such thing, ain't he, Mr. Sonny?"

"He's given me a dream to figure on, and in that dream he's done told me some other things he ain't never told any them other preachers."

"That's nice of him, Mr. Sonny. He don't talk to just everyone. It's the elephant connection does it."

Butch drove through the open gate and parked his truck in the usual spot and started for the ticket booth. He had the same forward trudge he always had, like he was pushing against a great wind and not thinking it was worth it.

"The Lord has told me to expand the minds of Baptists," Sonny said.

"That's a job he's given you, Mr. Sonny."

"There is another path from the one we've been taking. Oh, some of the Baptist talk is all right, but God has shown me that firewalking is the correct way to get right with the holy spirit."

"Like walking on coals and stuff?"

"That's what I mean."

"You gonna walk on coals, Mr. Sonny?"

"I am."

"I'd sho like to see that, Mr. Sonny, I really would."

Candy led Sonny out to the pickup and Sonny opened

the door and climbed in, visions of firewalking Baptists trucking through his head.

"You gonna do this with no shoes on?" Candy asked, closing the pickup door for Sonny.

"It wouldn't be right to wear shoes. That would be cheating. It wouldn't have a purpose."

"Do you feet a mite better."

Sonny wasn't listening. He found the keys in his overalls and touched the red furrows on his chest that the heater had made. He was proud of them. They were a sign from God. They were like the trenches of fire he would build for his Baptists. He would teach them to walk the trenches and open their hearts and souls and trust their feet to Jesus. And not mind putting a little something extra in the offering plate. People would get so excited he could move those red leatherette Bibles.

"Lord be praised," Sonny said.

"Ain't that the truth," Candy said.

Sonny backed the truck around and drove out of the gate onto the highway. He felt like Moses must have felt when he was chosen to lead the Jews out of the wilderness. But he had been chosen instead to to lead the Baptists into a new way of Salvation by forming a firewalking branch of the Baptist church. He smiled and leaned over the steering wheel letting it touch the hot wounds on his chest. Rows of rich converts somewhere beyond the horizon of his mind stepped briskly through trenches of hot coals, smiling.

HELL THROUGH A WINDSHIELD

For T.E.D. Klein

"We are drive-in mutants.
We are not like other people.
We are sick.
We are disgusting.
We believe in blood.
In breasts,
And in beasts.
We believe in Kung Fu City.
If life had a vomit meter,
We'd be off the scale.
As long as one single drive-in remains
On the planet Earth,
We will party like jungle animals.
We will boogie till we puke.
Heads will roll.
The drive-in will never die.
Amen."

("The Drive-In Oath," by Joe Bob Briggs)

The drive-in theater may have been born in New Jersey, but it had the good sense to come to Texas to live. Throughout the 'fifties and 'sixties it thrived here like a fungus on teenage lusts and families enticed by the legendary Dollar Night or Two Dollars a Carload.

And even now—though some say the drive-in has seen its heyday in the more populated areas, you can drive on in there any night of the week—particularly Special Nights

111

and Saturday—and witness a sight that sometimes makes the one on the screen boring in comparison.

You'll see lawn chairs planted in the backs of pickups, or next to speakers, with cowboys and cowgirls planted in the chairs, beer cans growing out of their fists, and there'll be the sputterings of barbeque pits and the aromas of cooking meats rising up in billows of smoke that slowly melts into the clear Texas sky.

Sometimes there'll be folks with tape decks whining away, even as the movie flickers across the three story screen and their neighbors struggle to hear the crackling speaker dialogue over ZZ Top doing "The Tube Snake Boogie." There'll be lovers sprawled out on blankets spread between two speaker posts, going at it so hot and heavy they ought to just go on and charge admission. And there's plenty of action in the cars too. En route to the concession stand a discerning eye can spot the white moons of un-Levied butts rising and falling to a steady, rocking rhythm just barely contained by well-greased shocks and 4-ply tires.

What you're witnessing is a bizarre subculture in action. One that may in fact be riding the crest of a new wave.

Or to put it another way: Drive-ins are crazy, but they sure are fun.

The drive-in theater is over fifty years old, having been spawned in Camden, New Jersey June 6th, 1933 by a true visionary—Richard Milton Hollingshead.

Camden, as you may know, was the last home of Walt Whitman, and when one considers it was the death place of so prestigious an American poet, it is only fitting that it be the birthplace of such a poetic and All-American institution as the drive-in theater. Or as my dad used to call them, "the outdoor picture show."

Once there were over 4,000 drive-ins in the United States, now there are about 3,000, and according to some experts, they are dropping off fast. However, in Texas there is a re-emergence and new interest in the passion pits of old. They have become nearly as sacred as the armadillo. The Lone Star State alone has some 209 outdoor theaters in operation, and many of these are multi-screen jobs with different movies running concurrently alongside one another. Not long ago, Gordon McLendon, "The Drive-in Business King," erected the I-45 in Houston, a drive-in capable of holding up to three thousand automobiles. In fact, it claims to be the biggest drive-in in existence.

Why does the drive-in thrive in Texas when it's falling off elsewhere? Three reasons.

(1) *Climate.* Generally speaking, Texas has a pretty comfortable climate year round. (2) *A car culture.* Texas is the champion state for automobile registration, and Texans have this thing about their cars. The automobile has replaced the horse not only as a mode of transportation, but as a source of mythology. If the Texan of old was supposedly half human and half horse, the modern Texan is half human and half automobile. Try and separate a Texan from his car, or mass transit that sucker against his will, and you're likely to end up kissing grillwork at sixty-five miles an hour. (3) *Joe Bob Briggs.*

Okay, start the background music. Softly please, a humming version of "The Eyes of Texas." And will all true Texans please remove your hats while we have a short discussion of Joe Bob Briggs, The Patron Saint Of Texas Drive-ins, He Who Drives Behind The Speaker Rows, and columnist for *The Dallas Times Herald.* In fact, his column, *Joe Bob Goes to the Drive-in,* is the most popular feature in the paper. As it should be, because Joe Bob—who may be the pseudonym for the *Herald*'s regular film critic John Bloom—don't talk no bullcorn, and he don't bother with "hardtop" movie reviews. He's purely a drive-in kind of guy, and boy does he have style.

Here's an example, part of a review for *The Evil Dead:* "Five teenagers become Spam-in-a-cabin when they head for the woods and start turning into flesh-eating zombies. Asks a lot of moral questions, like, 'If your girlfriend turns zombie on you, what do you do? Carve her into itty-bitty pieces or look the other way?' One girl gets raped by the woods. Not in the woods. *By* the woods. The only way to kill zombies: total dismemberment. This one could make "Saw" eligible for the Disney Channel."

Single-handedly, with that wild column of his—which not only reports on movies, but on the good times and bad times of Joe Bob himself—he has given the drive-in a new mystique. Or to be more exact, made the non-drive-in goers aware of it, and reminded the rest of us just how much fun the outdoor picture show can be.

Joe Bob's popularity has even birthed a yearly Drive-in Movie Festival—somewhat sacrilegiously held indoors this year—that has been attended in the past by such guests as Roger Corman, King Of The B's, and this year by "Big Steve," known to some as Stephen King. (If you movie watchers don't recognize the name, he's a writer-feller.) "Big Steve" was given the solemn honor of leading off the 1984 ceremonies with Joe Bob's "drive-in oath" and arrived wearing his JOE BOB BRIGGS IS A PERSONAL FRIEND OF MINE tee-shirt.

The festival has also sported such features as The Custom Car Rally, Ralph The Diving Pig (sure hate I missed the boy's act), the stars of *The Texas Chainsaw Massacre*, Miss Custom Body of 1983, "unofficial custom bodies" and Joe Bob his own self. And last, but certainly not least, along with this chic gathering, a number of new movies like *Bloodsuckers From Outer Space* and *Future-Kill* made their world premieres.

What more could you ask from Joe Bob?

Kill the music. Hats on.

The drive-ins I grew up with went by a number of names: The Apache, The Twin Pines, The River-road being a few examples. And though they varied somewhat in appearance, basically they were large lots filled with speaker posts—many of which were minus their speakers, due to absent-minded patrons driving off while they were still hooked to their windows, or vandals—a concession stand, a screen at least three stories high (sometimes six), a swing, see-saw and merry-go-round up front for the kiddies, all this surrounded by an ugly six foot, moon-shimmering tin fence.

They all had the same bad food at the concessions. Hot dogs that tasted like rubber hoses covered in watery mustard, popcorn indistinguishable from the cardboard containers that held it, drinks that were mostly water and ice, and candy so old the worms inside were dead either of old age or sugar diabetes.

And they all came with the *same* restroom. It was as if The Apache, Riverroad, and Twin Pines were equipped with warping devices that activated the moment you stepped behind the wooden "modesty fence." Suddenly, at the speed of thought, you were whisked away to a concrete bunker with floors either so tacky your shoes stuck to it like cat hairs to honey, or so flooded in water you needed skis to make it to the urinals or the john, the latter of which was forever doorless, the hinges hanging like frayed tendons. And both of these public conveniences were invariably stuffed full of floating cigarette butts, candy wrappers and used prophylactics.

Rather than take my life into my own hands in these rather seedy enclosures, I often took my chances battling constipation or urinating into a Coke cup and pouring the prize out the window. The idea of standing over one of those odoriferous urinals—and there was always this item of crayoned wisdom above them: "Remember, crabs can pole vault"—and having something ugly, fuzzy, multilegged and ravenous leap out on me was forever foremost in my mind. Nor did I find those initialed and graffiti carved seats—when there were seats at all—the more inviting. I figured that no matter how precariously I might perch myself, some nameless horror from the pits of sewerdom would find access to that part of my anatomy I most prized.

In spite of these unpleasantries, come Saturday night, a bunch of us guys—the ones who couldn't get dates—would cruise over there, stopping a quarter mile outside the place to stuff one member of our party in the trunk, this always the fellow who had the least money to pool toward entrance fees, having blown it on beer, Playboy magazines and prophylactics that would certainly rot in his wallet.

Then we would drive up to the pay booth and promptly be asked, "Got anybody in the trunk?"

Obviously we were a suspicious-looking lot, but we never admitted to a body in the trunk, and for some reason we were never forced to open up. After we had emphatically denied that we would even consider it, and the ticket seller had eyed us over for a while, trying to break our resolve, he would take our money and we would drive inside.

My Plymouth Savoy was rigged so that the man in the trunk could push the back seat from the inside, and it would fold down, allowing our unthrifty, and generally greasy, contortionist to join our party.

That Savoy, what a car, what a drive-in machine. What a death trap. It took a two man crew to drive it. The gas pedal always stuck to the floor, and when you came whizzing up to a red light you had to jerk your foot off the gas, go for the brake and yell "Pedal." Then your co-pilot would dive for the floorboards, grab the pedal and yank it up just in time to keep us from plowing broadside into an unsuspecting motorist. However, that folding back seat made the sticking pedal seem like a minor liability, and the Savoy was a popular auto with the drive-in set.

The drive-in gave me many firsts. The first sexual action I ever witnessed was there, and I don't mean on the screen. At the Apache the front row was somewhat on an incline, and if the car in front of you was parked just right, and you were lying on the roof of your car, any activity going on in the back seat of the front row car was quite visible to you, providing it was a moonlit night and the movie playing was a particularly bright one.

The first sexual activity that included me, also occurred at a drive-in, but that is a personal matter, and enough said.

The first truly vicious fight I ever saw was at The Riverroad. A fellow wearing a cowboy hat got into some kind of a shindig with a hatless fellow in front of my Savoy. I've no idea what started the fight, but it was a good one, matched only by a live Championship Wrestling match at the Cottonbowl.

Whatever the beef, the fellow with the hat was the sharper of the two, as he had him a three foot length of two-by-four, and all the other fellow had was a bag of popcorn. Even as the zombies of *Night of the Living Dead* shuffled across the screen, The Hat laid a lick on Hatless's noggin that sounded like a beaver's tail slapping water. Popcorn flew and the fight was on.

The Hat got Hatless by the lapel and proceeded to knock knots on his head faster than you could count them, and though Hatless was game as all-get-out, he couldn't fight worth a damn. His arms flew over The Hat's shoulders and slapped his back like useless whips of spaghetti, and all the while he just kept making The Hat madder by calling him names and making rude accusations about the man's family tree and what members of it did to one another when the lights were out.

For a while there, The Hat was as busy as the lead in a samurai movie, but finally the rhythm of his blows—originally akin to a Ginger Baker drum solo—died down, and this indicated to me that he was getting tired, and had I been Hatless, this would have been my cue to scream sharply once, then flop at The Hat's feet like a dying fish, and finally pretend to go belly up right there in the lot. But this boy either had the I.Q. of a can of green beans, or was in such a near-comatose state from the beating, he didn't have the good sense to shut up. In fact his language became so vivid, The Hat found renewed strength and delivered his blows in such close proximity that the sound of wood to skull resembled the angry rattling of a diamond-back snake.

Finally, Hatless tried to wrestle The Hat to the ground and then went tumbling over my hood, shamelessly knocking loose my prized hood ornament, a large, in-flight swan that lit up when the lights were on, and ripping off half of The Hat's cowboy shirt in the process.

A bunch of drive-in personnel showed up then and tried to separate the boys. That's when the chili really hit the fan. There were bodies flying all over that lot as relatives and friends of the original brawlers suddenly dealt themselves in. One guy got crazy and ripped a speaker and

wire smooth off a post and went at anyone and everybody
with it. And he was good too. Way he whipped that baby
about made Bruce Lee and his nunchukas look like a third
grade carnival act.

While this went on, a fellow in the car to the right of
us, oblivious to the action on the lot, wrapped up in *Night
of the Living Dead,* and probably polluted on Thunderbird
wine, was yelling in favor of the zombies, "Eat 'em, eat
'em!''

Finally the fight moved on down the lot and eventually
dissipated. About half an hour later I looked down the row
and saw Hatless crawling out from under a white Cadillac
festooned with enough curb feelers to make it look like a
centipede. He sort of went on his hands and knees for a
few yards, rose to a squatting run, and disappeared into
a winding maze of automobiles.

Them drive-in folks, what kidders.

The drive-in is also the source for my darkest fantasy—
I refrain from calling it a nightmare, because after all these
years it has become quite familiar, a sort of grim friend.
For years now I've been waiting for this particular dream
to continue, take up a new installment, but it always ends
on the same enigmatic note.

Picture this: a crisp summer night in Texas. A line of
cars winding from the pay booth of a drive-in out to the
highway, then alongside it for a quarter mile or better.
Horns are honking, children are shouting, mosquitoes are
buzzing. I'm in a pickup with two friends who we'll call
Dave and Bob. Bob is driving. On the rack behind us is a
twelve gauge shotgun and a baseball bat, "a bad-ass per-
suader." A camper is attached to the truck bed, and in
the camper we've got lawn chairs, coolers of soft drinks
and beer, enough junk food to send a hypoglycemic to the
stars.

What a night this is. Dusk to Dawn features, two dollars
a carload. Great movies like *The Tool Box Murders, Night
of the Living Dead, Day of the Dead, Zombies* and *I Dis-
member Mama.*

We finally inch our way past the pay booth and dart

inside. It's a magnificent drive-in, like the I-45, big enough for 3,000 cars or better. Empty paper cups, popcorn boxes, chili and mustard stained hot dog wrappers blow gently across the lot like paper tumbleweeds. And there, standing stark-white against a jet-black sky is a portal into another dimension; the six story screen.

We settle on a place near the front, about five rows back. Out come the lawn chairs, the coolers and the eats. Before the first flick sputters on and Cameron Mitchell opens that ominous box of tools, we're through an economy size bag of "tater" chips, a quart of Coke and half a sack of chocolate cookies.

The movie starts, time is lost as we become absorbed in the horrifyingly campy delights of *Tool Box*. We get to the part where Mitchell is about to use the industrial nailer on a young lady he's been watching shower, and suddenly—

there is a light, so red and bright the images on the screen fade. Looking up, we see a great, crimson comet hurtling towards us. Collision with the drive-in is imminent. Or so it seems, then, abruptly the *comet smiles.* Just splits down the middle to show a mouth full of grinning, jagged teeth not too unlike a power saw blade. It seems that instead of going out of life with a bang, we may go out with a crunch. The mouth gets wider, and the comet surprises us by whipping up, dragging behind it a fiery tail that momentarily blinds us.

When the crimson washes from our eyeballs and we look around, all is as before. At first glance anyway. Because closer observation reveals that everything outside the drive-in, the highway, the trees, the tops of houses and buildings that had been visible above the surrounding tin fence, are gone. There is only blackness, and we're talking BLACKNESS here, the kind of dark that makes fudge pudding look pale. It's as if the drive-in has been ripped up by the roots and miraculously stashed in limbo somewhere. But if so, we are not injured in any way, and the electricity still works. There are lights from the concession stand, and the projector continues to throw the images of *Tool Box* on the screen.

About this time a guy in a station wagon, fat wife beside him, three kids in the back, panics, guns the car to life and darts for the exit. His lights do not penetrate the blackness, and as the car hits it, inch by inch it is consumed by the void. A moment later nothing.

A cowboy with a hatfull of toothpicks and feathers, gets out of his pickup and goes over there. He stands on the tire-buster spears, extends his arm . . . And never in the history of motion pictures or real life have I heard such a scream. He flops back, his arm gone from the hand to elbow. He rolls on the ground. By the time we get over there the rest of his arm is collapsing, as if bone and tissue have gone to mush. His hat settles down on a floppy mess that a moment before was his head. His whole body folds in and oozes out of his clothes in what looks like sloppy vomit. I carefully reach out and take hold of one of his boots, upend it, a loathsome mess pours out and strikes the ground with a plopping sound.

We are trapped in the drive-in.

Time goes by, no one knows how much. It's like the Edgar Rice Burroughs stories about Pellucidar. Without the sun or moon to judge by, time does not exist. Watches don't help either. They've all stopped. We sleep when sleepy, eat when hungry. And the movies flicker on. No one even suggests cutting them off. Their light and those of the concession stand are the only lights, and should we extinguish them, we might be lost forever in a void to match the one outside of the drive-in fence.

At first people are great. The concession folks bring out food. Those of us who have brought food, share it. Everyone is fed.

But as time passes, people are not so great. The concession stand people lock up and post guards. My friends and I are down to our last kernels of popcorn and we're drinking the ice and water slush left in the coolers. The place smells of human waste, as the restrooms have ceased to function altogether. Gangs are forming, even cults based on the movies. There is a Zombie Cult that stumbles and staggers in religious mockery of the ''dead'' on the screen. And with the lack of food an acute problem, they have taken to human sacrifice and cannibalism. Bob takes down the shotgun. I take down the baseball bat. Dave has taken to wearing a hunting knife he got out of the glove box.

Rape and murder are wholesale, and even if you've a mind to, there's not much you can do about it. You've got to protect your little stretch of ground, your automobile, your universe. But against our will we are forced into the role of saviours when a young girl runs against our truck while fleeing her mother, father and older brother. Bob jerks her inside the truck, holds the family—who are a part of the Zombie Cult and run as if they are cursed with a case of the rickets—at bay with the shotgun. They start to explain that as the youngest member of the family, it's only right that she give herself up to them to provide sustenance. A chill runs up my back. Not so much because it is a horrible thing they suggest, but because I too am hungry, and for a moment they seem to make good sense.

Hunger devours the family's common sense, and the father leaps forward. The shotgun rocks against Bob's shoulder and the man goes down, hit in the head, the way you have to kill zombies. Then the mother is on me, teeth and nails. I swing the bat and down she goes, thrashing at my feet like a headless chicken.

Trembling, I hold the bat before me. It is caked with blood and brains. I fall back against the truck and throw up. On the screen the zombies are feasting on bodies from an exploded pickup.

Rough for the home team. Time creeps by. We are weak. No food. No water. We find ourselves looking at the rotting corpses outside our pickup far too long. We catch the young girl eating their remains, but we do nothing. Somehow, it doesn't seem so bad. In fact, it looks inviting. Food right outside the truck, on the ground, ready for the taking.

But when it seems we are going to join her, there is a red light in the sky. The comet is back, and once again it swoops down, collision looks unavoidable, it smiles with its jagged teeth, peels up and whips its bright tail. And when the glow burns away from our eyes, it is daylight and there is a world outside the drive-in.

A sort of normalcy returns. Engines are tried. Batteries have been unaffected by the wait. Automobiles start up and begin moving toward the exit in single file, as if nothing has ever happened.

Outside, the highway we come to is the same, except the yellow line has faded and the concrete has buckled in spots. But nothing else is the same. On either side of the highway is a great, dank jungle. It looks like something out of a lost world movie.

As we drive along—we're about the fifth automobile in line—we see something move up ahead, to the right. A massive shape steps out of the foliage and onto the highway. It is a Tyrannosaurus Rex covered in bat-like parasites, their wings opening and closing slowly, like contented butterflies sipping nectar from a flower.

The dinosaur does nothing. It gives our line of metal bugs the once over, crosses the highway and is enveloped by the jungle again.

The caravan starts up once more. We drive onward into this prehistoric world split by a highway out of our memories.

I'm riding shotgun and I glance in the wing-mirror on my side. In it I can see the drive-in screen, and though the last movie should still be running, I can't make out any movement there. It looks like nothing more than an oversized slice of Wonder Bread.

Fade out.

That's the dream. And even now when I go to a drive-in, be it the beat up Lumberjack here with its cheap, tin screen, or anywhere else, I find myself occasionally glancing at the night sky, momentarily fearing that out of the depths of space there will come a great, red comet that will smile at me with a mouthful of sawblade teeth and whip its flaming tail.

DOWN BY THE SEA
NEAR THE GREAT BIG ROCK

For John Maclay

Down by the sea near the great big rock, they made their camp and toasted marshmallows over a small, fine fire. The night was pleasantly chill and the sea spray cold. Laughing, talking, eating the gooey marshmallows, they had one swell time; just them, the sand, the sea and the sky, and the great big rock.

The night before they had driven down to the beach, to the camping area; and on their way, perhaps a mile from their destination, they had seen a meteor shower, or something of that nature. Bright lights in the heavens, glowing momentarily, seeming to burn red blisters across the ebony sky.

Then it was dark again, no meteoric light, just the natural glow of the heavens—the stars, the dime-size moon.

They drove on and found an area of beach on which to camp, a stretch dominated by pale sands and big waves, and the great big rock.

Toni and Murray watched the children eat their marshmallows and play their games, jumping and falling over the great big rock, rolling in the cool sand. About midnight, when the kids were crashed out, they walked along the beach like fresh-found lovers, arm in arm, shoulder to shoulder, listening to the sea, watching the sky, speaking words of tenderness.

"I love you so much," Murray told Toni, and she repeated the words and added, "and our family too."

They walked in silence now, the feelings between them words enough. Sometimes Murray worried that they did not talk as all the marriage manuals suggested, that so much of what he had to say on the world and his work fell on the ears of others, and that she had so little to truly say to him. Then he would think: What the hell? I know how I feel. Different messages, unseen, unheard, pass between us all the time, and they communicate in a fashion words cannot.

He said some catch phrase, some pet thing between them, and Toni laughed and pulled him down on the sand. Out there beneath that shiny-dime moon, they stripped and loved on the beach like young sweethearts, experiencing their first night together after long expectation.

It was nearly two a.m. when they returned to the camper, checked the children and found them sleeping comfortably as kittens full of milk.

They went back outside for awhile, sat on the rock and smoked and said hardly a word. Perhaps a coo or a purr passed between them, but little more.

Finally they climbed inside the camper, zipped themselves into their sleeping bags and nuzzled together on the camper floor.

Outside the wind picked up, the sea waved in and out, and a slight rain began to fall.

Not along after, Murray awoke and looked at his wife in the crook of his arm. She lay there with her face a grimace, her mouth opening and closing like a guppie, making an ''uhhh, uhh,'' sound.

A nightmare perhaps. He stroked the hair from her face, ran his fingers lightly down her cheek and touched the hollow of her throat and thought: What a nice place to carve out some fine, white meat . . .

What in the hell is wrong with me? Murray thought, and he rolled away from her, out of the bag. He dressed, went outside and sat on the rock. With shaking hands on his knees, buttocks resting on the warmth of the stone, he brooded. Finally he dismissed the possibility that such a thought had actually crossed his mind, smoked a cigarette and went back to bed.

He did not know that an hour later Toni awoke and bent

over him and looked at his face as if it were something to squash. But finally she shook it off and slept.

The children tossed and turned. Little Roy squeezed his hands open, closed, open, closed. His eyelids fluttered rapidly.

Robyn dreamed of striking matches.

Morning came and Murray found that all he could say was, "I had the oddest dream."

Toni looked at him, said, "Me, too," and that was all.

Placing lawn chairs on the beach, they put their feet on the rock and watched the kids splash and play in the waves; watched as Roy mocked the sound of the *Jaws* music and made fins with his hands and chased Robyn through the water as she scuttled backwards and screamed with false fear.

Finally they called the children from the water, ate a light lunch, and, leaving the kids to their own devices, went in for a swim.

The ocean stroked them like a mink-gloved hand. Tossed them, caught them, massaged them gently. They washed together, laughing, kissing—

Then tore their lips from one another as up on the beach they heard a scream.

Roy had his fingers gripped about Robyn's throat, held her bent back over the rock and was putting a knee in her chest. There seemed no play about it. Robyn was turning blue.

Toni and Murray waded for shore, and the ocean no longer felt kind. It grappled with them, held them, tripped them with wet, foamy fingers. It seemed an eternity before they reached the shore, yelling at Roy.

Roy didn't stop. Robyn flopped like a dying fish.

Murray grabbed the boy by the hair and pulled him back, and for a moment, as the child turned, he looked at his father with odd eyes that did not seem his, but looked instead as cold and firm as the great big rock.

Murray slapped him, slapped him so hard Roy spun and went down, stayed there on hands and knees, panting.

Murray went to Robyn, who was already in Toni's arms, and on the child's throat were blue-black bands like thin, ugly snakes.

"Baby, baby, are you okay?" Toni asked over and over. Murray wheeled, strode back to the boy, and Toni was now yelling at him, crying, "Murray, Murray, easy now. They were just playing and it got out of hand."

Roy was on his feet, and Murray, gritting his teeth, so angry he could not believe it, slapped the child down.

"MURRAY," Toni yelled, and she let go of the sobbing Robyn and went to stay his arm, for he was already raising it for another strike. "That's no way to teach him not to hit, not to fight."

Murray turned to her, almost snarling, but then his face relaxed and he lowered his hand. Turning to the boy, feeling very criminal, Murray reached down to lift Roy by the shoulder. But Roy pulled away, darted for the camper.

"Roy," he yelled, and started after him. Toni grabbed his arm.

"Let him be," she said. "He got carried away and he knows it. Let him mope it over. He'll be all right." Then softly: "I've never known you to get that mad."

"I've never been so mad before," he said honestly.

They walked back to Robyn, who was smiling now. They all sat on the rock, and about fifteen minutes later Robyn got up to see about Roy. "I'm going to tell him it's okay," she said. "He didn't mean it." She went inside the camper.

"She's sweet," Toni said.

"Yeah," Murray said, looking at the back of Toni's neck as she watched Robyn move away. He was thinking that he was supposed to cook lunch today, make hamburgers, slice onions; big onions cut thin with a freshly sharpened knife. He decided to go get it.

"I'll start lunch," he said flatly, and stalked away.

As he went, Toni noticed how soft the back of his skull looked, so much like an over-ripe melon.

She followed him inside the camper.

Next morning, after the authorities had carried off the bodies, taken the four of them out of the blood-stained, fire-gutted camper, one detective said to another:

"Why does it happen? Why would someone kill a nice

family like this? And in such horrible ways . . . set fire to it afterwards?''

The other detective sat on the huge rock and looked at his partner, said tonelessly, ''Kicks maybe.''

That night, when the moon was high and bright, gleaming down like a big spotlight, the big rock, satiated, slowly spread its flippers out, scuttled across the sand, into the waves, and began to swim toward the open sea. The fish that swam near it began to fight.

TRAINS NOT TAKEN

For Lee Schultz

Dappled sunlight danced on the Eastern side of the train. The boughs of the great cherry trees reached out along the tracks and almost touched the cars, but not quite; they had purposely been trimmed to fall short of that.

James Butler Hickok wondered how far the rows of cherry trees went. He leaned against the window of the Pullman car and tried to look down the track. The speed of the train, the shadows of the trees and the illness of his eyesight did not make the attempt very successful. But the dark line that filled his vision went on and on and on.

Leaning back, he felt more than just a bit awed. He was actually seeing the famous Japanese cherry trees of the Western Plains; one of the Great Cherry Roads that stretched along the tracks from mid-continent to the Black Hills of the Dakotas.

Turning, he glanced at his wife. She was sleeping, her attractive, sharp-boned face marred by the pout of her mouth and the tight lines around her eyes. That look was a perpetual item she had cultivated in the last few years, and it stayed in place both awake or asleep. Once her face held nothing but laughter, vision and hope, but now it hurt him to look at her.

For a while he turned his attention back to the trees, allowing the rhythmic beat of the tracks, the overhead hiss of the fire line and the shadows of the limbs to pleasantly massage his mind into white oblivion.

After a while, he opened his eyes, noted that his wife had left her seat. Gone back to the sleeping car, most likely. He did not hasten to join her. He took out his pocket watch and looked at it. He had been asleep just under an hour. Both he and Mary Jane had had their breakfast early, and had decided to sit in the parlor car and watch the people pass. But they had proved disinterested in their fellow passengers and in each other, and had both fallen asleep.

Well, he did not blame her for going back to bed, though she spent a lot of time there these days. He was, and had been all morning, sorry company.

A big man with a blond goatee and mustache came down the aisle, spotted the empty seat next to Hickok and sat down. He produced a pipe and a leather pouch of tobacco, held it hopefully. "Could I trouble you for a light, sir?"

Hickok found a lucifer and lit the pipe while the man puffed.

"Thank you," the man said. "Name's Cody. Bill Cody."

"Jim Hickok."

They shook hands.

"Your first trip to the Dakotas?" Cody asked.

Hickok nodded.

"Beautiful country, Jim, beautiful. The Japanese may have been a pain in the neck in their time, but they sure know how to make a garden spot of the world. White men couldn't have grown sagebrush or tree moss in the places they've beautified."

"Quite true," Hickok said. He got out the makings and rolled himself a smoke. He did this slowly, with precision, as if the anticipation and preparation were greater than the final event. When he had rolled the cigarette to his satisfaction, he put a lucifer to it and glanced out the window. A small, attractive stone shrine, nestled among the cherry trees, whizzed past his vision.

Glancing back at Cody, Hickok said, "I take it this is not your first trip?"

"Oh no, no. I'm in politics. Something of an ambassador, guess you'd say. Necessary that I make a lot of trips this way. Cementing relationships with the Japanese, you know. To pat myself on the back a bit, friend, I'm respon-

sible for the cherry road being expanded into the area of
the U.S. Sort of a diplomatic gesture I arranged with the
Japanese.''

"Do you believe there will be more war?''

"Uncertain. But with the Sioux and the Cheyenne forming up again, I figure the yellows and the whites are going
to be pretty busy with the reds. Especially after last
week.''

"Last week?''

"You haven't heard?''

Hickok shook his head.

"The Sioux and some Cheyenne under Crazy Horse and
Sitting Bull wiped out General Custer and the Japanese
General Miyamoto Yoshii.''

"The whole command?''

"To the man. U.S. Cavalry and Samurai alike.''

"My God!''

"Terrible. But I think it's the last rise for the red man,
and not to sound ghoulish, but I believe this will further
cement Japanese and American relationships. A good
thing, considering a number of miners in Cherrywood,
both white and yellow, have found gold. In a case like
that, it's good to have a common enemy.''

"I didn't know that either.''

"Soon the whole continent will know, and there will be
a scrambling to Cherrywood the likes you've never seen.''

Hickok rubbed his eyes. Blast the things. His sight was
good in the dark or in shadowed areas, but direct sunlight
stabbed them like needles.

At the moment Hickok uncovered his eyes and glanced
toward the shadowed comfort of the aisle, a slightly over-
weight woman came down it tugging on the ear of a little
boy in short pants. "John Luther Jones,'' she said, "I've
told you time and time again to leave the Engineer alone.
Not to ask so many questions.'' She pulled the boy on.

Cody looked at Hickok, said softly: "I've never seen a
little boy that loves trains as much as that one. He's always
trying to go up front and his mother is on him all the time.
She must have whipped his little butt three times yesterday. Actually, I don't think the Engineer minds the boy.''

Hickok started to smile, but his attention was drawn to an attractive young woman who was following not far behind mother and son. In Dime Novels she would have been classified as "a vision." Health lived on her heart-shaped face as surely as ill-content lived on that of his wife. Her hair was wheat-ripe yellow and her eyes were as green as the leaves of a spring-fresh tree. She was sleek in blue and white calico with a thick, black Japanese cloth belt gathered about her slim waist. All the joy of the world was in her motion, and Hickok did not want to look at her and compare her to his wife, but he did not want to lose sight of her either, and it was with near embarrassment that he turned his head and watched her pass until the joyful swing of her hips waved him goodbye, passing out of sight into the next car of the train.

When Hickok settled back into his seat, feeling somewhat warm under the collar, he noticed that Cody was smiling at him.

"Kind of catches the eye, does she not?" Cody said. "My wife, Louisa, noticed me noticing the young thing yesterday, and she has since developed the irritating habit of waving her new Japanese fan in front of my face 'accidentally,' when she passes."

"You've seen her a lot?"

"Believe she has a sleeping car above the next parlor car. I think about that sleeping car a bunch. Every man on this train that's seen her, probably thinks about that sleeping car a bunch."

"Probably so."

"You single?"

"No."

"Ah, something of a pain sometimes, is it not? Well, friend, must get back to the wife, least she think I'm chasing the sweet, young thing. And if the Old Woman were not on this trip, I just might be."

Cody got up, and with a handshake and a politician wave, strode up the aisle and was gone.

Hickok turned to look out the window again, squinting somewhat to comfort his eyes. He actually saw little. His vision was turned inward. He thought about the girl. He had been more than a bit infatuated with her looks. For the first time in his life, infidelity crossed his mind.

Not since he had married Mary Jane and become a clerk, had he actually thought of trespassing on their marriage agreement. But as of late the mere sight of her was like a wound with salt in it.

After rolling and smoking another cigarette, Hickok rose and walked back toward his sleeping car, imagining that it was not his pinch-faced wife he was returning to, but the blond woman and her sexual heaven. He imagined that she was on her first solo outing. Going out West to meet the man of her dreams. Probably had a father who worked as a military officer at the fort outside of Cherrywood, and now that Japanese and American relations had solidified considerably, she had been called to join him. Perhaps the woman with the child was her mother and the boy her brother.

He carried on this pretty fantasy until he reached the sleeping car and found his cabin. When he went inside, he found that Mary Jane was still sleeping.

She lay tossed out on the bunk with her arm thrown across her eyes. Her sour, puckering lips had not lost their bitterness. They projected upwards like the mouth of an active volcano about to spew. She had taken off her clothes and laid them neatly over the back of a chair, and her somewhat angular body was visible because the sheet she had pulled over herself had fallen half off and lay draped only over her right leg and the edge of the bunk. Hickok noted that the glass decanter of whiskey on the little table was less than half full. As of this morning only a drink or two had been missing. She had taken more than enough to fall comfortably back to sleep again, another habit of recent vintage.

He let his eyes roam over her, looking for something that would stir old feelings—not sexual but loving. Her dark hair curled around her neck. Her shoulders, sharp as Army sabres, were her next most obvious feature. The light through the windows made the little freckles on her alabaster skin look like some sort of pox. The waist and hips that used to excite him still looked wasp-thin, but the sensuality and lividness of her flesh had disappeared. She was just thin from not eating enough. Whiskey was now often her breakfast, lunch and supper.

A tinge of sadness crept into Hickok as he looked at this angry, alcoholic lady with a life and a husband that had not lived up to her romantic and wealthy dreams. In the last two years she had lost her hope and her heart, and the bottle had become her lifeblood. Her faith in him had died, along with the little girl look in her once-bright eyes.

Well, he had had his dreams too. Some of them a bit wild perhaps, but they had dreamed him through the dullness of a Kansas clerkery that had paid the dues of the flesh but not of the mind.

Pouring himself a shot from the decanter, he sat on the wall bench and looked at his wife some more. When he got tired of that, he put his hand on the bench, but found a book instead of wood. He picked it up and looked at it. It was titled: *Down the Whiskey River Blue,* by Edward Zane Carroll Judson.

Hickok placed his drink beside him and thumbed through the book. It did not do much for him. As were all of Judson's novels, it was a sensitive and overly-poetic portrayal of life in our times. It was in a word, boring. Or perhaps he did not like it because his wife liked it so much. Or because she made certain that he knew the Dime Novels he read by Sam Clemens and the verse by Walt Whitman were trash and doggerel. She was the sensitive one, she said. She stuck to Judson and poets like John Wallace Crawford and Cincinnatus Hiner.

Well, she could have them.

Hickok put the book down and glanced at his wife. This trip had not worked out. They had designed it to remold what had been lost, but no effort had been expended on her part that he could see. He tried to feel guilty, conclude that he too had not pushed the matter, but that simply was not true. She had turned him into bad company with her sourness. When they had started out he had mined for their old love like a frantic prospector looking for color in a vein he knew was long worked out.

Finishing his drink, he stretched out on the long bench,

used the Judson book for a pillow, folded an arm across his eyes. He found the weight of his discontent was more able than Morpheus to bring sleep.

When he awoke, it was because his wife was running a finger along the edge of his cheek, tracing his jawbone with it. He looked into her smiling face, and for a moment he thought he had dreamed all the bad times and that things were fine and as they should be; imagined that time had not put a weight on their marriage and that it was shortly after their wedding when they were very much on fire with each other. But the rumble of the train assured him that this was not the case, and that time had indeed passed. The moment of their marriage was far behind.

Mary Jane smiled at him, and for a moment the smile held all of her lost hopes and dreams. He smiled back at her. At that moment he wished deeply that they had had children. But it had never worked. One of them had a flaw and no children came from their couplings.

She bent to kiss him and it was a warm kiss that tingled him all over. In that moment he wanted nothing but their marriage and for it to be good. He even forgot the young girl he had seen while talking to Cody.

They did not make love, though he hoped they would. But she kissed him deeply several times and said that after bath and dinner they would go to bed. It would be like old times. When they often performed the ceremony of pleasure.

After the Cherokee porter had filled their tub with water and after she had bathed and he had bathed in the dregs of her bath and they had toweled themselves dry, they laughed while they dressed. He kissed her and she kissed him back, their bodies pushed together in familiar ritual, but the ritual was not consummated. Mary Jane would have nothing of that. "After dinner," she said. "Like old times."

"Like old times," he said.

Arm in arm they went to the dining car, dressed to the hilt and smiling. They paid their dollar and were conducted to their table where they were offered a drink to begin the meal. As if to suggest hope for later, he denied one, but Mary Jane did not follow his lead. She had one, then another.

When she was on her third drink and dinner was in the process of being served, the blond woman with the sunshine smile came in and sat not three tables down from them. She sat with the matronly woman and the little boy who loved trains. He found that he could not take his eyes off the young lady.

"Are you thinking about something?" Mary Jane asked.

"No, not really. Mind was wandering," he said. He smiled at her and saw that her eyes were a trifle shiny with drunkenness.

They ate in near silence and Mary Jane drank two more whiskeys.

When they went back to the cabin, she was leaning on him and his heart had fallen. He knew the signs.

They went into their cabin and he hoped she was not as far along in drunkenness as he thought. She kissed him and made movements against his body with hers. He felt desire.

She went to the bed and undressed, and he undressed by the bench seat and placed his clothes there. He turned down the lamp and climbed into bed with her.

She had fallen asleep. Her breath came out in alcoholic snores. There would be no love making tonight.

He lay there for a while and thought of nothing. Then he got up, dressed, went into the cars to look for some diversion, a poker game perhaps.

No poker game was to be found and no face offered any friendly summons to him. He found a place to sit in the parlor car where the overhead lamp was turned down and there was no one sitting nearby. He got out the makings, rolled himself a smoke, and was putting a lucifer to it when Cody fell into the seat across from him. Cody had his pipe like before. "You'd think I'd have found some lucifers of my own by now, wouldn't you?"

Hickok thought just that, but he offered his still burning light to Cody. Cody bent forward and puffed the flame into his packed pipe. When it was lit he sat back and said, "I thought you had turned in early. I saw you leave the dining car."

"I didn't see you."

"You were not looking in my direction. I was nearby."

Hickok understood what Cody was implying, but he did not acknowledge. He smoked his cigarette furiously.

"She is quite lovely," Cody said.

"I guess I made a fool out of myself looking at her. She is half my age."

"I meant your wife, but yes, the girl is a beauty. And she has a way with her eyes, don't you think?"

Hickok grunted agreement. He felt like a schoolboy who had been caught looking up the teacher's dress.

"I was looking too," Cody said. "You see, I don't care for my wife much. You?"

"I want to, but she is not making it easy. We're like two trains on different tracks. We pass close enough to wave, but never close enough to touch."

"My God, friend, but you are a poet."

"I didn't mean to be."

"Well, mean to. I could use a bit of color and poetry in my life."

"An ambassador is more colorful than a clerk."

"An ambassador is little more than a clerk who travels. Maybe it's not so bad, but I just don't feel tailored to it."

"Then we are both cut from the wrong cloth, Cody."

Hickok finished his cigarette and looked out into the night. The shapes of the cherry trees flew by, looked like multi-armed men waving gentle goodbyes.

"It seems I have done nothing with my life," Hickok said after a while, and he did not look at Cody when he said it. He continued to watch the night and the trees. "Today when you told me about Custer and Yoshii, I did not feel sadness. Surprise, but not sadness. Now I know why. I envy them. Not their death, but their glory. A hundred years from now, probably more, they will be remembered. I will be forgotten a month after my passing—if it takes that long.''

Cody reached over and opened a window. The wind felt cool and comfortable. He tapped his pipe on the outside of the train. Sparks flew from it and blew down the length of the cars like fireflies in a blizzard. Cody left the window open, returned his pipe to his pocket.

''You know,'' Cody said, ''I wanted to go out West during the Japanese Wars: the time the Japanese were trying to push down into Colorado on account of the gold we'd found there, and on account of we'd taken the place away from them back when it was a part of New Japan. I was young then and I should have gone. I wanted to be a soldier. I might have been a great scout, or a buffalo hunter had my life gone different then.''

''Do you sometimes wonder that your dreams are your real life, Cody? That if you hope for them enough they become solid? Maybe our dreams are our trains not taken.''

''Come again.''

''Our possible futures. The things we might have done had we just edged our lives another way.''

''I hadn't thought much about it actually, but I like the sound of it.''

''Will you laugh if I tell you my dream?''

''How could I? I've just told you mine.''

''I dream that I'm a gunman—and with these light-sensitive eyes that's a joke. But that's what I am. One of those long haired shootists like in the Dime Novels, or that real life fellow Wild Jack McCall. I even dream of lying face down on a card table, my pistol career ended by some skulking knave who didn't have the guts to face me and so shot me from behind. It's a good dream, even with the death, because I am remembered, like those soldiers who died at The Little Big Horn. It's such a strong dream I like to believe that it is actually happening somewhere, and that I am that man that I would rather be.''

''I think I understand you, friend. I even envy Morse and these damn trains; him and his telegraph and *'pulsating energy.'* Those discoveries will make him live forever.

Every time a message is flashed across the country or a train bullets along on the crackling power of its fire line, it's like thousands of people crying his name.''

"Sometimes—a lot of the time—I just wish that for once I could live a dream.''

They sat in silence. The night and the shadowed limbs of the cherry trees fled by, occasionally mixed with the staggered light of the moon and the stars.

Finally Cody said, "To bed. Cherrywood is an early stop." He opened his pocket watch and looked at it. "Less than four hours. The wife will awake and call out the Cavalry if I'm not there.''

As Cody stood, Hickok said, "I have something for you." He handed Cody a handful of lucifers.

Cody smiled. "Next time we meet, friend, perhaps I will have my own." As he stepped into the aisle he said, "I've enjoyed our little talk.''

"So have I," Hickok said. "I don't feel any happier, but I feel less lonesome.''

"Maybe that's the best we can do.''

Hickok went back to his cabin and did not try to be overly quiet. There was no need. Mary Jane, when drunk, slept like an anvil.

He slipped out of his clothes and crawled into bed. Lay there feeling the warmth of his wife's shoulder and hip; smelling the alcoholic aroma of her breath. He could remember a time when they could not crawl into bed together without touching and expressing their love. Now he did not want to touch her and he did not want to be touched by her. He could not remember the last time she had bothered to tell him she loved him, and he could not remember the last time he had said it and it was not partly a lie.

Earlier, before dinner, the old good times had been recalled and for a few moments he adored her. Now he lay beside her feeling anger. Anger because she would not try. Or could not try. Anger because he was always the one to try, the one to apologize, even when he felt he was not wrong. Trains on a different track going opposite directions, passing fast in the night, going nowhere really. That was them.

Closing his eyes, he fell asleep instantly and dreamed of the blond lovely in blue and white calico with a thick, black Japanese belt. He dreamed of her without the calico, lying there beside him white-skinned and soft and passionate and all the things his wife was not.

And when the dream ended, so did his sleep. He got up and dressed and went out to the parlor car. It was empty and dark. He sat and smoked a cigarette. When that was through he opened a window, felt and smelled the wind. It was a fine night. A lover's night.

Then he sensed the train was slowing.

Cherrywood already?

No, it was still too early for that. What gave here?

In the car down from the one in which he sat, a lamp was suddenly lit, and there appeared beside it the chiseled face of the Cherokee porter. Behind him, bags against their legs, were three people: the matronly lady, the boy who loved trains and the beautiful blond woman.

The train continued to slow. Stopped.

By God, he thought, they are getting off.

Hickok got out his little, crumpled train schedule and pressed it out on his knee. He struck a lucifer and held it down behind the seat so that he could read. After that he got out his pocket watch and held it next to the flame. Two-fifteen. The time on his watch and that on the schedule matched. This was a scheduled stop—the little town and fort outside of Cherrywood. He had been right in his daydreaming. The girl was going here.

Hickok pushed the schedule into his pocket and dropped the dead match on the floor. Even from where he sat, he could see the blond woman. As always, she was smiling. The porter was enjoying the smile and he was giving her one back.

The train began to stop.

For a moment, Hickok imagined that he too were getting off here and that the blond woman was his sweetheart. Or better yet, would be. They would meet in the railway station and strike up some talk and she would be one of those new modern women who did not mind a man buying her a drink in public. But she would not be like his wife. She would drink for taste and not effect.

They would fall instantly in love, and on occasion they would walk in the moonlight down by these tracks, stand beneath the cherry trees and watch the trains run by. And afterwards they would lie down beneath the trees and make love with shadows and starlight as their canopy. When it was over, and they were tired of satisfaction, they would walk arm in arm back towards the town, or the fort, all depending.

The dream floated away as the blond woman moved down the steps and out of the train. Hickok watched as the porter handed down their bags. He wished he could still see the young woman, but to do that he would have to put his head out the window, and he was old enough that he did not want to appear foolish.

Goodbye, Little Pretty, he thought. I will think and dream of you often.

Suddenly he realized that his cheeks were wet with tears. God, but he was unhappy and lonely. He wondered if behind her smiles the young woman might be lonely too.

He stood and walked toward the light even as the porter reached to turn it out.

"Excuse me," Hickok said to the man. "I'd like to get off here."

The porter blinked. "Yes sir, but the schedule only calls for three."

"I have a ticket for Cherrywood, but I've changed my mind, I'd like to get off here."

"As you wish, sir." The porter turned up the lamp. "Best hurry, the train's starting. Watch your step. Uh, any luggage?"

"None."

Briskly, Hickok stepped down the steps and into the night. The three he had followed were gone. He strained his eyes and saw between a path of cherry trees that they were walking toward the lights of the rail station.

He turned back to the train. The porter had turned out the light and was no longer visible. The train sang its song. On the roof he saw a ripple of blue-white fulmination jump along the metal fire line. Then the train made a sound like a boiling teapot and began to move.

For a moment he thought of his wife lying there in their cabin. He thought of her waking in Cherrywood and not finding him there. He did not know what she would do, nor did he know what he would do.

Perhaps the blond woman would have nothing to do with him. Or maybe, he thought suddenly, she is married or has a sweetheart already.

No matter. It was the ambition of her that had lifted him out of the old funeral pyre, and like a phoenix fresh from the flames, he intended to stretch his wings and soar.

The train gained momentum, lashed shadows by him. He turned his back on it and looked through the cherry-wood path. The three had reached the rail station and had gone inside.

Straightening his collar and buttoning his jacket, he walked toward the station and the pretty blond woman with a face like a hopeful heart.

TIGHT LITTLE STITCHES
IN A DEAD MAN'S BACK

For Ardath Mayhar

From the journal of Paul Marder
(Boom!)

That's a little scientist joke, and the proper way to begin this. As for the purpose of this notebook, I'm uncertain. Perhaps to organize my thoughts and not go insane.

No. Probably so I can read it and feel as if I'm being spoken to. Maybe neither of those reasons. It doesn't matter. I just want to do it, and that is enough.

What's new?

Well, Mr. Journal, after all these years I've taken up martial arts again—or at least the forms and calisthenics of Tae Kwon Do. There is no one to spar with here in the lighthouse, so the forms have to do.

There is Mary, of course, but she keeps all her sparring verbal. And as of late, there is not even that. I long for her to call me a sonofabitch. Anything. Her hatred of me has cured to 100% perfection and she no longer finds it necessary to speak. The tight lines around her eyes and mouth, the emotional heat that radiates from her body like a dreadful cold sore looking for a place to lie down, is voice enough for her. She lives only for the moment when she (the cold sore) can attach herself to me with her needles, ink and thread. She lives only for the design on my back.

That's all I live for as well. Mary adds to it nightly and I enjoy the pain. The tattoo is of a great, blue mushroom cloud, and in the cloud, etched ghost-like, is the face of

142

our daughter, Rae. Her lips are drawn tight, eyes are closed and there are stitches deeply pulled to simulate the lashes. When I move fast and hard they rip slightly and Rae cries bloody tears.

That's one reason for the martial arts. The hard practice of them helps me to tear the stitches so my daughter can cry. Tears are the only thing I can give her.

Each night I bare my back eagerly to Mary and her needles. She pokes deep and I moan in pain as she moans in ecstasy and hatred. She adds more color to the design, works with brutal precision to bring Rae's face out in sharper relief. After ten minutes she tires and will work no more. She puts the tools away and I go to the full-length mirror on the wall. The lantern on the shelf flickers like a jack-o-lantern in a high wind, but there is enough light for me to look over my shoulder and examine the tattoo. And it is beautiful. Better each night as Rae's face becomes more and more defined.

Rae.

Rae. God, can you forgive me, sweetheart?

But the pain of the needles, wonderful and cleansing as they are, is not enough. So I go sliding, kicking and punching along the walkway around the lighthouse, feeling Rae's red tears running down my spine, gathering in the waistband of my much-stained canvas pants.

Winded, unable to punch and kick any more, I walk over to the railing and call down into the dark, "Hungry?"

In response to my voice a chorus of moans rises up to greet me.

Later, I lie on my pallet, hands behind my head, examine the ceiling and try to think of something worthy to write to you, Mr. Journal. So seldom is there anything. Nothing seems truly worthwhile.

Bored of this, I roll on my side and look at the great light that once shone out to the ships, but is now forever snuffed. Then I turn the other direction and look at my wife sleeping on her bunk, her naked ass turned toward me. I try to remember what it was like to make love to her, but it is difficult. I only remember that I miss it. For a long moment I stare at my wife's ass as if it is a mean mouth about to open and reveal teeth. Then I roll on my back again, stare at the ceiling, and continue this routine until daybreak.

Mornings I greet the flowers, their bright red and yellow blooms bursting from the heads of long-dead bodies that will not rot. The flowers open wide to reveal their little black brains and their feathery feelers, and they lift their blooms upward and moan. I get a wild pleasure out of this. For one crazed moment I feel like a rock singer appearing before his starry-eyed audience.

When I tire of the game I get the binoculars, Mr. Journal, and examine the eastern plains with them, as if I expect a city to materialize there. The most interesting thing I have seen on those plains is a herd of large lizards thundering north. For a moment, I considered calling Mary to see them, but I didn't. The sound of my voice, the sight of my face, upsets her. She loves only the tattoo and is interested in nothing more.

When I finish looking at the plains, I walk to the other side. To the west, where the ocean was, there is now nothing but miles and miles of cracked, black sea bottom. Its only resemblances to a great body of water are the occasional dust storms that blow out of the west like dark tidal waves and wash the windows black at mid-day. And the creatures. Mostly mutated whales. Monstrously large, sluggish things. Abundant now where once they were near extinction. (Perhaps the whales should form some sort of GREENPEACE organization for humans now. What do you think, Mr. Journal? No need to answer. Just another one of those little scientist jokes.)

These whales crawl across the sea bottom near the lighthouse from time to time, and if the mood strikes them, they rise on their tails and push their heads near the tower and examine it. I keep expecting one to flop down on us, crushing us like bugs. But no such luck. For some unknown reason the whales never leave the cracked sea bed to venture onto what we formerly called the shore. It's as if they live in invisible water and are bound by it. A racial memory perhaps. Or maybe there's something in that cracked black soil they need. I don't know.

Besides the whales I suppose I should mention I saw a shark once. It was slithering along at a great distance and the tip of its fin was winking in the sunlight. I've also seen some strange, legged fish and some things I could not put a name to. I'll just call them whale food since I saw one of the whales dragging his bottom jaw along the ground one day, scooping up the creatures as they tried to beat a hasty retreat.

Exciting, huh? Well, that's how I spend my day, Mr. Journal. Roaming about the tower with my glasses, coming in to write in you, waiting anxiously for Mary to take hold of that kit and give me the signal. The mere thought of it excites me to erection. I suppose you could call that our sex act together.

And what was I doing the day they dropped The Big One?

Glad you asked that Mr. Journal, really I am.

I was doing the usual. Up at six, did the shit, shower and shave routine. Had breakfast. Got dressed. Tied my tie. I remember doing the latter, and not very well, in front of the bedroom mirror, and noticing that I had shaved poorly. A hunk of dark beard decorated my chin like a bruise.

Rushing to the bathroom to remedy that, I opened the door as Rae, naked as the day of her birth, was stepping from the tub.

Surprised, she turned to look at me. An arm went over her breasts, and a hand, like a dove settling into a fiery bush, covered her pubic area.

Embarrassed, I closed the door with an "excuse me" and went about my business—unshaved. It was an innocent thing. An accident. Nothing sexual. But when I think of her now, more often than not, that is the first image that comes to mind. I guess it was the moment I realized my baby had grown into a beautiful woman.

That was also the day she went off to her first day of college and got to see, ever so briefly, the end of the world.

And it was the day the triangle—Mary, Rae and myself—shattered.

If my first memory of Rae alone is that day, naked in the bathroom, my foremost memory of us as a family is when Rae was six. We used to go to the park and she would ride the merry-go-round, swing, teeter-totter, and finally my back. ("I want to piggy Daddy.") We would gallop about until my legs were rubber, then we would stop at the bench where Mary sat waiting. I would turn my back to the bench so Mary could take Rae down, but always before she did, she would reach around from behind, caressing Rae, pushing her tight against my back, and Mary's hands would touch my chest.

God, but if I could describe those hands. She still has hands like that, after all these years. They are long and sleek and artistic. Naturally soft, like the belly of a baby rabbit. And when she held Rae and me that way, I felt that no matter what happened in the world, we three could stand against it and conquer.

But now the triangle is broken and the geometry gone away.

So the day Rae went off to college and was fucked into oblivion by the dark, pelvic thrust of the bomb, Mary drove me to work. Me, Paul Marder, big shot with The Crew. One of the finest, brightest young minds in the industry. Always teaching, inventing and improving on our nuclear threat, because, as we often joked, "We cared enough to send only the very best."

When we arrived at the guard booth, I had out my pass, but there was no one to take it. Beyond the chain-link gate there was a wild mêlée of people running, screaming, falling down.

I got out of the car and ran to the gate. I called out to a man I knew as he ran by. When he turned his eyes were wild and his lips were flecked with foam. "The missiles are flying," he said, then he was gone, running madly.

I jumped in the car, pushed Mary aside and stomped on the gas. The Buick leaped into the fence, knocking it asunder. The car spun, slammed into the edge of a building and went dead. I grabbed Mary's hand, pulled her from the car and we ran toward the great elevators. We made one just in time. There were others running for it as the door closed, and the elevator went down. I still remember the echo of their fists on the metal as it began to drop. It was like the rapid heartbeat of something dying.

And so the elevator took us to the world of Down Under and we locked it off. There we were in a five-mile layered city designed not only as a massive office and laboratory, but as a impenetrable shelter. It was our special reward for creating the poisons of war. There was food, shelter, medical supplies, films, books, you name it. Enough to last two thousand people for a hundred years. Of the two thousand it was designed for, perhaps eleven hundred made it. The others didn't run fast enough from the parking lot or the other buildings, or they were late for work, or maybe they had called in sick.

Perhaps they were the lucky ones. They might have died in their sleep. Or while they were having a morning quickie with the spouse. Or perhaps as they lingered over that last cup of coffee.

Because you see, Mr. Journal, Down Under was no paradise. Before long suicides were epidemic. I considered it myself from time to time. People slashed their throats, drank acid, took pills. It was not unusual to come out of your cubicle in the morning and find people dangling from pipes and rafters like ripe fruit.

There were also the murders. Most of them performed by a crazed group who lived in the deeper recesses of the unit and called themselves the Shit Faces. From time to time they smeared dung on themselves and ran amok, clubbing men, women, and children born Down Under, to death. It was rumored they ate human flesh.

We had a police force of sorts, but it didn't do much. It didn't have a sense of authority. Worse, we all viewed ourselves as deserving victims. Except for Mary, we had all helped to blow up the world.

Mary came to hate me. She came to the conclusion I had killed Rae. It was a realization that grew in her like a drip growing and growing until it became a gushing flood of hate. She seldom talked to me. She tacked up a picture of Rae and looked at it most of the time.

Topside she had been an artist, and she took that up again. She rigged a kit of tools and inks and became a tattooist. Everyone came to her for a mark. And though each was different, they all seemed to indicate one thing: I fucked up. I blew up the world. Brand me.

Day in and day out she did her tattoos, having less and less to do with me, pushing herself more and more into this work until she was as skilled with skin and needles as she had been Topside with brush and canvas. And one night, as we lay on our separate pallets, feigning sleep, she said to me, "I just want you to know how much I hate you."

"I know," I said.

"You killed Rae."

"I know."

"Say you killed her, you bastard. Say it."

"I killed her," I said, and meant it.

Next day I asked for my tattoo. I told her of this dream that came to me nightly. There would be darkness, and out of this darkness would come a swirl of glowing clouds, and the clouds would meld into a mushroom shape, and out of that—torpedo-shaped, nose pointing skyward, striding on ridiculous cartoon legs—would step The Bomb.

There was a face painted on The Bomb, and it was my face. And suddenly the dream's point of view would change, and I would be looking out of the eyes of that painted face. Before me was my daughter. Naked. Lying on the ground. Her legs wide apart. Her sex glazed like a wet canyon.

And I/The Bomb, would dive into her, pulling those silly feet after me, and she would scream. I could hear it echo as I plunged through her belly, finally driving myself out of the top of her head, then blowing to terminal orgasm. And the dream would end where it began. A mushroom cloud. Darkness.

When I told Mary the dream and asked her to interpret it in her art, she said, "Bare your back," and that's how the design began. An inch of work at a time—a painful inch. She made sure of that.

Never once did I complain. She'd send the needles home as hard and deep as she could, and though I might moan or cry out, I never asked her to stop. I could feel those fine hands touching my back and I loved it. The needles. The hands. The needles. The hands.

And if that was so much fun, you ask, why did I come Topside?

You ask such probing questions, Mr. Journal. Really you do, and I'm glad you asked that. My telling you will be like a laxative, I hope. Maybe if I just let the shit flow I'll wake up tomorrow and feel a lot better about myself.

Sure. And it will be the dawning of a new Pepsi generation as well. It will have all been a bad dream. The alarm clock will ring, I'll get up, have my bowl of Rice Krispies and tie my tie.

Okay, Mr. Journal. The answer. Twenty years or so after we went Down Under, a fistful of us decided it couldn't be any worse Topside than it was below. We made plans to go see. Simple as that. Mary and I even talked a little. We both entertained the crazed belief Rae might have survived. She would be thirty-eight. We might have been hiding below like vermin for no reason. It could be a brave new world up there.

I remember thinking these things, Mr. Journal, and half-believing them.

We outfitted two sixty-foot crafts that were used as part of our transportation system Down Under, plugged in the half-remembered codes that opened the elevators, and drove the vehicles inside. The elevator lasers cut through the debris above them and before long we were Topside. The doors opened to sunlight muted by grey-green clouds and a desert-like landscape. Immediately I knew there was no brave new world over the horizon. It had all gone to hell in a fiery handbasket, and all that was left of man's millions of years of development were a few pathetic humans living Down Under like worms, and a few others crawling Topside like the same.

We cruised about a week and finally came to what had once been the Pacific Ocean. Only there wasn't any water now, just that cracked blackness.

We drove along the shore for another week and finally saw life. A whale. Jacobs immediately got the idea to shoot one and taste its meat.

Using a high-powered rifle he killed it, and he and seven others cut slabs off it, brought the meat back to cook. They invited all of us to eat, but the meat looked greenish and there wasn't much blood and we warned him against it. But Jacobs and the others ate it anyway. As Jacobs said, "It's something to do."

A little later on Jacobs threw up blood and his intestines boiled out of his mouth, and not long after those who had shared the meat had the same thing happen to them. They died crawling on their bellies like gutted dogs. There wasn't a thing we could do for them. We couldn't even bury them. The ground was too hard. We stacked them like cordwood along the shoreline and moved camp down a way, tried to remember how remorse felt.

And that night, while we slept as best we could, the roses came.

Now, let me admit, Mr. Journal, I do not actually know how the roses survive, but I have an idea. And since you've agreed to hear my story—and even if you haven't, you're going to anyway—I'm going to put logic and fantasy together and hope to arrive at the truth.

These roses lived in the ocean bed, underground, and at night they came out. Up until then they had survived as parasites of reptiles and animals, but a new food had arrived from Down Under. Humans. Their creators actually. Looking at it that way, you might say we were the gods who conceived them, and their partaking of our flesh and blood was but a new version of wine and wafer.

I can imagine the pulsating brains pushing up through the sea bottom on thick stalks, extending feathery feelers, and tasting the air out there beneath the light of the moon—which through those odd clouds gave the impression of a pus-filled boil—and I can imagine them uprooting and dragging their vines across the ground toward the shore where the corpses lay.

Thick vines sprouted little, thorny vines, and these moved up the bank and touched the corpses. Then, with a lashing motion, the thorns tore into the flesh, and the vines, like snakes, slithered through the wounds and inside. Secreting a dissolving fluid that turned the innards to the consistency of watery oatmeal, they slurped up the mess, and the vines grew and grew at amazing speed, moved and coiled through the bodies, replacing nerves and shaping into the symmetry of the muscles they had devoured, and lastly they pushed up through the necks, into the skulls, ate tongues and eyeballs and sucked up the mouse-grey brains like soggy gruel. With an explosion of skull shrapnel, the roses bloomed, their tooth-hard petals expanding into beautiful red and yellow flowers, hunks of human heads dangling from them like shattered watermelon rinds.

In the center of these blooms a fresh, black brain pulsed and feathery feelers once again tasted air for food and breeding grounds. Energy waves from the floral brains shot through the miles and miles of vines that were knotted inside the bodies, and as they had replaced nerves, muscles and vital organs, they made the bodies stand. Then those corpses turned their flowered heads toward the tents where we slept, and the blooming corpses (another little scientist joke there if you're into English idiom, Mr. Journal) walked, eager to add the rest of us to their animated bouquet.

I saw my first rose-head while I was taking a leak.

I had left the tent and gone down to the shore line to relieve myself, when I caught sight of it out of the corner of my eye. Because of the bloom I first thought it was Susan Myers. She wore a thick, wooly Afro that surrounded her head like a lion's mane, and the shape of the thing struck me as her silhouette. But when I zipped and turned, it wasn't an Afro. It was a flower blooming out of Jacobs. I recognized him by his clothes and the hunk of his face that hung off one of the petals like a worn-out hat on a peg.

In the center of the blood-red flower was a pulsating sack, and all around it little wormy things squirmed. Directly below the brain was a thin proboscis. It extended toward me like an erect penis. At its tips, just inside the opening, were a number of large thorns.

A sound like a moan came out of that proboscis, and I stumbled back. Jacob's body quivered briefly, as if he had been besieged by a sudden chill, and ripping through his flesh and clothes, from neck to foot, was a mass of thorny, wagging vines that shot out to five feet in length.

With an almost invisible motion, they waved from west to east, slashed my clothes, tore my hide, knocked my feet out from beneath me. It was like being hit by a cat-o-nine-tails.

Dazed, I rolled onto my hands and knees, bear-walked away from it. The vines whipped against my back and butt, cut deep.

Every time I got to my feet, they tripped me. The thorns not only cut, they burned like hot ice picks. I finally twisted away from a net of vines, slammed through one last shoot, and made a break for it.

Without realizing it, I was running back to the tent. My body felt as if I had been lying on a bed of nails and razor blades. My forearm hurt something terrible where I had used it to lash the thorns away from me. I glanced down at it as I ran. It was covered in blood. A strand of vine about two feet in length was coiled around it like a garter snake. A thorn had torn a deep wound in my arm, and the vine was sliding into the wound.

Screaming, I held my forearm in front of me like I had just discovered it. The flesh, where the vine had entered, rippled and made a bulge that looked like a junkie's favorite vein. The pain was nauseating. I snatched at the vine, ripped it free. The thorns turned against me like fishhooks.

The pain was so much I fell to my knees, but I had the vine out of me. It squirmed in my hand, and I felt a thorn gouge my palm. I threw the vine into the dark. Then I was up and running for the tent again.

The roses must have been at work for quite some time

before I saw Jacobs, because when I broke back into camp yelling, I saw Susan, Ralph, Casey and some others, and already their heads were blooming, skulls cracking away like broken model kits.

Jane Calloway was facing a rose-possessed corpse, and the dead body had its hands on her shoulders, and the vines were jetting out of the corpse, weaving around her like a web, tearing, sliding inside her, breaking off. The proboscis poked into her mouth and extended down her throat, forced her head back. The scream she started came out a gurgle.

I tried to help her, but when I got close, the vines whipped at me and I had to jump back. I looked for something to grab, to hit the damn thing with, but there was nothing. When next I looked at Jane, vines were stabbing out of her eyes, and her tongue, now nothing more than lava-thick blood, was dripping out of her mouth onto her breasts, which like the rest of her body, were riddled with stabbing vines.

I ran away then. There was nothing I could do for Jane. I saw others embraced by corpse hands and tangles of vines, but now my only thought was Mary. Our tent was to the rear of the campsite, and I ran there as fast as I could.

She was lumbering out of our tent when I arrived. The sound of screams had awakened her. When she saw me running she froze. By the time I got to her, two vine-riddled corpses were coming up on the tent from the left side. Grabbing her hand I half pulled, half dragged her away from there. I got to one of the vehicles and pushed her inside.

I locked the doors just as Jacobs, Susan, Jane, and others appeared at the windshield, leaning over the rocket-nosed hood, the feelers around their brain sacs vibrating like streamers in a high wind. Hands slid greasily down the windshield. Vines flopped and scratched and cracked against it like thin bicycle chains.

I got the vehicle started, stomped the accelerator, and the rose-heads went flying. One of them, Jacobs, bounced over the hood and splattered into a spray of flesh, ichor, and petals.

I had never driven the vehicle, so my maneuvering was rusty. But it didn't matter. There wasn't exactly a traffic rush to worry about.

After an hour or so, I turned to look at Mary. She was staring at me, her eyes like the twin holes of a double-barreled shotgun. They seemed to say, "More of your doing," and in a way she was right. I drove on.

Daybreak we came to the lighthouse. I don't know how it survived. One of those quirks. Even the glass was un-broken. It looked like a great stone finger shooting us the bird.

The vehicle's tank was near empty, so I assumed here was as good a place to stop as any. At least there was shelter, something we could fortify. Going on until the vehicle was empty of fuel didn't make much sense. There wouldn't be any more fill-ups, and there might not be any more shelter like this.

Mary and I (in our usual silence) unloaded the supplies from the vehicle and put them in the lighthouse. There was enough food, water, chemicals for the chemical toi-let, odds and ends, extra clothes, to last us a year. There were also some guns. A Colt .45 revolver, two twelve-gauge shotguns and a .38, and enough shells to fight a small war.

When everything was unloaded, I found some old fur-niture downstairs, and using tools from the vehicle, tried to barricade the bottom door and the one at the top of the stairs. When I finished, I thought of a line from a story I had once read, a line that always disturbed me. It went something like, "Now we're shut in for the night."

Days. Nights. All the same. Shut in with one another, our memories and the fine tattoo.

A few days later I spotted the roses. It was as if they had smelled us out. And maybe they had. From a distance, through the binoculars, they reminded me of old women in bright sun hats.

It took them the rest of the day to reach the lighthouse,

and they immediately surrounded it, and when I appeared at the railing they would lift their heads and moan.

And that, Mr. Journal, brings us up to now.

I thought I had written myself out, Mr. Journal. Told the only part of my life story I would ever tell, but now I'm back. You can't keep a good world destroyer down.

I saw my daughter last night and she's been dead for years. But I saw her, I did, naked, smiling at me, calling to ride piggyback.

Here's what happened.

It was cold last night. Must be getting along winter. I had rolled off my pallet onto the cold floor. Maybe that's what brought me awake. The cold. Or maybe it was just gut instinct.

It had been a particularly wonderful night with the tattoo. The face had been made so clear it seemed to stand out from my back. It had finally become more defined than the mushroom cloud. The needles went in hard and deep, but I've had them in me so much now I barely feel the pain. After looking in the mirror at the beauty of the design, I went to bed happy, or as happy as I can get.

During the night the eyes ripped open. The stitches came out and I didn't know it until I tried to rise from the cold, stone floor and my back puckered against it where the blood had dried.

I pulled myself free and got up. It was dark, but we had a good moonspill that night and I went to the mirror to look. It was bright enough that I could see Rae's reflection clearly, the color of her face, the color of the cloud. The stitches had fallen away and now the wounds were spread wide, and inside the wounds were eyes. Oh, God, Rae's blue eyes. Her mouth smiled at me and her teeth were very white.

Oh, I hear you, Mr. Journal. I hear what you're saying. And I thought of that. My first impression was that I was about six bricks shy of a load, gone 'round the old bend. But I know better now. You see, I lit a candle and held it over my shoulder, and with the candle and the moonlight,

I could see even more clearly. It was Rae all right, not just a tattoo.

I looked over at my wife on the bunk, her back to me, as always. She had not moved.

I turned back to the reflection. I could hardly see the outline of myself, just Rae's face smiling out of that cloud.

"Rae," I whispered, "is that you?"

"Come on, Daddy," said the mouth in the mirror, "that's a stupid question. Of course, it's me."

"But . . . You're . . . you're . . ."

"Dead?"

"Yes . . . Did . . . did it hurt much?"

She cackled so loudly the mirror shook. I could feel the hairs on my neck rising. I thought for sure Mary would wake up, but she slept on.

"It was instantaneous, Daddy, and even then, it was the greatest pain imaginable. Let me show you how it hurt."

The candle blew out and I dropped it. I didn't need it anyway. The mirror grew bright and Rae's smile went from ear to ear—literally—and the flesh on her bones seemed like crêpe paper before a powerful fan, and that fan blew the hair off her head, the skin off her skull and melted those beautiful blue eyes and those shiny white teeth of hers to a putrescent goo the color and consistency of fresh bird shit. Then there was only the skull, and it heaved in half and flew backwards into the dark world of the mirror and there was no reflection now, only the hurtling fragments of a life that once was and was now nothing more than swirling cosmic dust.

I closed my eyes and looked away.

"Daddy?"

I opened them, looked over my shoulder into the mirror. There was Rae again, smiling out of my back.

"Darling," I said, "I'm so sorry."

"So are we," she said, and there were faces floating past her in the mirror. Teenagers, children, men and women, babies, little embryos swirling around her head like planets around the sun. I closed my eyes again, but I could not keep them closed. When I opened them the multitudes of swirling dead, and those who had never had a chance to live, were gone. Only Rae was there.

"Come close to the mirror, Daddy."

I backed up to it. I backed until the hot wounds that were Rae's eyes touched the cold glass and the wounds became hotter and hotter and Rae called out, "Ride me piggy, Daddy," and then I felt her weight on my back, not the weight of a six-year-old child or a teenage girl, but a great weight, like the world was on my shoulders and bearing down.

Leaping away from the mirror I went hopping and whooping about the room, same as I used to in the park. Around and around I went, and as I did, I glanced in the mirror. Astride me was Rae, lithe and naked, red hair fanning around her as I spun. And when I whirled by the mirror again, I saw that she was six years old. Another spin and there was a skeleton with red hair, one hand held high, the jaws open and yelling, "Ride 'em cowboy."

"How?" I managed, still bucking and leaping, giving Rae the ride of her life. She bent to my ear and I could feel her warm breath. "You want to know how I'm here, Daddy-dear? I'm here because you created me. Once you laid between Mother's legs and thrust me into existence, the two of you, with all the love there was in you. This time you thrust me into existence with your guilt and Mother's hate. Her thrusting needles, your arching back. And now I've come back for one last ride, Daddy-o. Ride, you bastard, ride."

All that while I had been spinning, and now as I glimpsed the mirror, I saw wall to wall faces, weaving in, weaving out, like smiling stars, and all those smiles opened wide and words came out in chorus, "Where were you when they dropped The Big One?"

Each time I spun and saw the mirror again, it was a new scene. Great flaming winds scorching across the world, babies turning to fleshy jello, heaps of charred bones, brains boiling out of the heads of men and women like backed up toilets overflowing, The Almighty, Glory Hallelujah, Ours Is Bigger Than Yours Bomb hurtling forward, the mirror going mushroom white, then clear, and me, spinning, Rae pressed tight against my back, melting like butter on a griddle, evaporating into the eye wounds on my back, and finally me alone, collapsing to the floor beneath the weight of the world.

Mary never awoke.
The vines outsmarted me.

A single strand found a crack downstairs somewhere and wound up the steps and slipped beneath the door that led into the tower. Mary's bunk was not far from the door, and in the night, while I slept and later while I spun in front of the mirror and lay on the floor before it, it made its way to Mary's bunk, up between her legs, and entered her sex effortlessly.

I suppose I should give the vine credit for doing what I had not been able to do in years, Mr. Journal, and that's enter Mary. Oh God, that's a funny one, Mr. Journal. Real funny. Another little scientist joke. Let's make that a mad scientist joke, what say? Who but a madman would play with the lives of human beings by constantly trying to build the bigger and better boom machine?

So what of Rae, you ask?

I'll tell you. She is inside me. My back feels the weight. She twists in my guts like a corkscrew. I went to the mirror a moment ago, and the tattoo no longer looks like it did. The eyes have turned to crusty sores and the entire face looks like a scab. It's as if the bile that made up my soul, the unthinking, nearsightedness, the guilt that I am, has festered from inside and spoiled the picture with pustule bumps, knots and scabs.

To put it in layman's terms, Mr. Journal, my back is infected. Infected with what I am. A blind, senseless fool.

The wife?

Ah, the wife. God, how I loved that woman. I have not really touched her in years, merely felt those wonderful hands on my back as she jabbed the needles home, but I never stopped loving her. It was not a love that glowed any more, but it was there, though hers for me was long gone and wasted.

This morning when I got up from the floor, the weight

of Rae and the world on my back, I saw the vine coming up from beneath the door and stretching over to her. I yelled her name. She did not move. I ran to her and saw it was too late. Before I could put a hand on her, I saw her flesh ripple and bump up, like a den of mice were nesting under a quilt. The vines were at work. (Out goes the old guts, in goes the new vines.)

There was nothing I could do for her.

I made a torch out of a chair leg and an old quilt, set fire to it, burned the vine from between her legs, watched it retreat, smoking, under the door. Then I got a board, nailed it along the bottom, hoping it would keep others out for at least a little while. I got one of the twelve-gauges and loaded it. It's on the desk beside me, Mr. Journal, but even I know I'll never use it. It was just something to do, as Jacobs said when he killed and ate the whale. Something to do.

I can hardly write any more. My back and shoulders hurt so bad. It's the weight of Rae and the world.

I've just come back from the mirror and there's very little left of the tattoo. Some blue and black ink, a touch of red that was Rae's hair. It looks like an abstract painting now. Collapsed design, running colors. It's real swollen. I look like the hunchback of Notre Dame.

What am I going to do, Mr. Journal?

Well, as always, I'm glad you asked me that. You see, I've thought this out.

I could throw Mary's body over the railing before it blooms. I could do that. Then I could doctor my back. It might even heal, though I doubt it. Rae wouldn't let that happen, I can tell you now. And I don't blame her. I'm on her side. I'm just a walking dead man and have been for years.

I could put the shotgun under my chin and work the trigger with my toe, or maybe push it with the very pen I'm using to create you, Mr. Journal. Wouldn't that be neat? Blow my brains to the ceiling and sprinkle you with my blood.

But as I said, I loaded the gun because it was something to do. I'd never use it on myself or Mary.

You see, I want Mary. I want her to hold Rae and me one last time like she used to in the park. And she can. There's a way.

I've drawn all the curtains and made curtains out of blankets for those spots where there aren't any. It'll be sunup soon and I don't want that kind of light in here. I'm writing this by candlelight and it gives the entire room a warm glow. I wish I had wine. I want the atmosphere to be just right.

Over on Mary's bunk she's starting to twitch. Her neck is swollen where the vines have congested and are writhing toward their favorite morsel, the brain. Pretty soon the rose will bloom (I hope she's one of the bright yellow ones, yellow was her favorite color and she wore it well) and Mary will come for me.

When she does, I'll stand with my naked back to her. The vines will whip out and cut me before she reaches me, but I can stand it. I'm used to pain. I'll pretend the thorns are Mary's needles. I'll stand that way until she folds her dead arms around me and her body pushes up against the wound she made in my back, the wound that is our daughter Rae. She'll hold me so the vines and the proboscis can do their work. And while she holds me, I'll grab her fine hands and push them against my chest, and it will be we three again, standing against the world, and I'll close my eyes and delight in her soft, soft hands one last time.

THE WINDSTORM PASSES

For Ardath Mayhar

The winter I come to believe in signs and omens was the baddest old winter we'd ever seen. The winter I turned fifteen.

It had come a rare snow that year, and even rarer for East Texas, it had actually stuck to the ground and got thick. Along came the wind, colder than ever, and it turned the snow to ice. It was beautiful, like sugar and egg-white icing on a cake, but it wasn't nothing to enjoy after the excitement of first seeing it come down. I had to get out in it and do chores, and that made me wish for a lot of sunshine and a time to go fishing.

Third day after it snowed and things had gotten real icy, I was out cutting some firewood from the woodlot and I found a madman in a ditch.

I'd already chopped down a tree and was trimming the limbs off of it, waiting for Papa who was coming across the way with a cross cut so we could saw it up into firewood sizes. While I was trimming I heard a voice.

"I got a message. Get out of this ditch, I got a message."

Clutching the axe tight, I went over and looked in the ditch, and there was a man. His face was as blue as my Mama's eyes; Papa says they're so blue the sky looks white beside them, even on the sky's best day. His long, oily hair had stuck to the ground and frozen there so that the clumped strands looked like snakes or fat worms trying to find holes to crawl into. There were icicles hanging off his eyelids and he was barefoot.

I screamed for Papa. He tossed down the saw and came running as fast as he could go on that ice. We got down in the ditch, hauled the feller up, pulling out some of his frozen hair in the doing. He was wearing a baggy old pair of faded black suit pants with the rear busted out, and his butt was hanging free and bare. It was darker than his face, looked a bit like a split, overripe watermelon gone dark in the sun. His feet and hands were somewhere between the blue of his face and the blue-black of his butt. The shirt he had on was three sizes too big, and when Papa and I had him standing, the wind came a-whistling along and flapped the feller's shirt around him till he looked like a scarecrow we was trying to poke in the ground.

We got him up to the house, laid him out on the kitchen table. He looked like he'd had it. Didn't move, just laid there, eyes closed, breathing slow. Then, all of a sudden, his eyes snapped open and he shot out a bony hand and grabbed Papa by the coat collar. He pulled himself to a sitting position until his face was right even with Papa's and said, ''I got a message from the Lord. You are doomed, brother, doomed to the wind 'cause it's going to blow you away.'' Then he closed his eyes, laid back down and let go of Papa's coat.

''Easy there,'' Papa said. But about that time the feller gave a shake, like he was going to have a rigor, then he went still as a turnip. Papa felt for a pulse and put his ear to the feller's chest looking for a heartbeat. From the expression on Papa's face, I could tell he hadn't found neither.

''He dead, Papa?''

''Couldn't get no deader, son,'' Papa said, lifting his head from the feller's chest.

Mama, who'd sort of been standing off to the side watching, came over now. ''You know him, Harold?'' she asked.

''Think this is Hazel Onin's boy,'' Papa said.

''The crazy boy?''

''I just seen him the once, but I think it's him. They had him on a leash out in the yard one summer, had this colored feller leading him around, and the boy was running on all fours, howling and trying to lift his leg to pee on things. His pants were all wet.''

"How pitiful," Mama said.

I knew of Hazel Onin's crazy boy, but if he had a name I'd never heard it. He'd always been crazy, but not so crazy at first that they couldn't let him run free. He was just considered peculiar. When he was eighteen he got religion real bad, took to preaching. Then right after he turned twenty he tried to rape this little high yeller gal he was teaching some Bible verses to, and that's when the Onins throwed him in the attic room, locked and barred the windows. If he'd been out of that room since that time, I'd never heard of it till now.

I'm ashamed of it now, but when I was twelve or thirteen, me and some of the other boys used to have to walk by there on our way to and from school, and the madman would holler out from his barred windows at us, "Repent, 'cause you're all going to have a bad fall," then he'd go to singing some old gospel song, and it gave me the jitters 'cause there was an echo up there in that attic, and it made it seem there was someone else inside singing along with him. Someone with a voice as deep and trembly as Old Man Death ought to have.

Johnny Clarence used to pull his pants down, bend over and show his naked butt to the madman, and we'd follow his lead on account of we didn't want to be considered no chickens. Then we'd all take off out of there running, hoopin' and a hollerin', pulling our pants and suspenders up as we ran.

But we'd quit going there long time back, as had almost everyone in town. They moved Main Street when the railroad came through on the other side, and from then on the town built up over there. They even tore down and rebuilt the school house on that side, and there wasn't no need for us to come that way no more. We could cut shorter by going another way. And after that, I mostly forgot about the madman prophet.

"It's such a shame," Mama said. "Poor boy."

"It's a blessing, is what it is," Papa said. "He don't

look like he's been eating so good to me, and I bet that's because the Onins ain't feeding him like they ought to. They figure him a shame and a curse from God, and they've treated him like it was his fault his head ain't no good ever since he was born.''

"He was dangerous, Harold," Mama said. "Remember that little high yeller girl?"

"Ain't saying he ought to have been invited to a church social. But they didn't have to treat him like an animal."

"Guess it's not ours to judge," Mama said.

"Damn sure don't matter now," Papa said.

"What do you think he meant about that thing he said, Papa?" I asked. "About the wind and all?"

"Didn't mean nothing, son. Just crazy talk. Go on out and hitch up the wagon and I'll get him wound up in a sheet. We'll take him back to the Onins. Maybe they'll want to stuff him and put him in the attic window so folks can see him as they walk or ride by. Or they could charge two bits for folks to come inside and look at him. Kind of pull his arm with a string so it looks like he's waving at them.''

"That's quite enough, Harold," Mama said. "Don't talk like that in front of the boy."

Papa grumbled something, went out of the room for a sheet, and I went out to the barn and hitched the mules up. I drove the wagon up to the front door, went in to help Papa carry the body out. Not that it really took both of us. He was as light as a big, empty corn husk. But somehow, the two of us carrying him seemed a lot more respectable than just tossing him over a shoulder and slamming him down in the wagon bed.

We took the body over to the Onins, and if they was broke up about it, I missed the signs. They looked like they'd just finally gotten some stomach tonic to work, and had made that long put off and desired trip to the outhouse.

Papa didn't say nothing stern to them, though I expected him to, since he wasn't short on honest words. But I figure he didn't see no need in it now.

Mrs. Onin stood in the doorway all the time, didn't

come out to the wagon bed while the body was there. After Mr. Onin unwound the sheet and took a look at the madman's face, said what a sad day it was and all, he asked us if we'd mind putting the body in the toolshed.

We did, and when we got back to the wagon Mrs. Onin was waiting by it. Mr. Onin offered us a dollar for bringing the body home, but of course, Papa wouldn't take it.

Before we climbed up on the wagon, Mrs. Onin said, "He'd been yelling all morning from upstairs, saying how an angel from God wearing a suit coat and a top hat, had brought him a message he was supposed to pass on. Kept sayin' the angel was giving him a test, see if he deserved heaven after what he done to that little girl."

Papa went ahead and climbed on the wagon, took hold of the lines. With his head, he motioned me up.

"Then we didn't hear nothing no more," Mr. Onin said. "I went up there to check on him and he'd pulled the bars out of one of the windows and got out. I don't reckon how he did that, as he'd never been able to do it before, and them bars was as sturdy as the day I put them in, no rotten wood around the sills or nothing."

Papa had taken out his pocket knife and tobacco bar, and he was cutting him a chaw off it. "Reckon you went right then to the sheriff to tell him your boy run off," Papa said, and there was that edge to his voice, like when he finds me peeing out back too close to the house.

"Naw," Mr. Onin said looking at the ground. "I didn't. Figured cold as he was, he'd come on back."

"Don't matter none now, does it?" Papa said.

"No," Mr. Onin said. "He's out of his misery now."

"Thems as true a words as you've spoke," Papa said.

"I'll be getting your sheet back to you," Mr. Onin said.

"Don't want it," Papa said. He clucked up the mules and we started off.

When we were out of earshot of the house, I said, "Papa, you really think they thought that crazy feller would go back because it was cold?"

"Why in hell would he want to go back to that attic? I don't reckon it was all that warm. I figure they thought he'd freeze and they'd be rid of him."

We didn't say anything else until we got home, then wasn't none of the talking about the madman or the Onins. Mama didn't even mention it after she saw Papa's face.

Just before supper, Papa went out on the porch to smoke his pipe, and I went out to the barn to toss the mules and milk cow some hay. I was out there tossing and smelling that animal smell, thinking how it reminded me of my whole life, that smell. Reminded me of Mama and Papa, warm nights with very little breeze, cold nights with the fire stoked up big and warm, late suppers, tall tales in front of the fireplace, standing on the porch or looking out the windows at the morning, noon or night, spring, summer, winter or fall. And that smell, always there, like a friend who had on some peculiar, if not bad smelling, toilet water. It was in the floorboards of the house, in the yard, thick in the barn. A smell that even now moves me backwards and forwards in time.

So there I was, throwing hay, thinking this fine life would go on forever, and all of a sudden I felt it before it happened.

I quit tossing hay, turned to look out the barn door. It was like I was looking at a painting, things had gone so still. The sky had turned yellow. The late birds quit singing and the mules and the milk cow turned their heads to look out of doors too.

Way off I heard it, a sound like a locomotive making the grade, burning that timber. Only there wasn't a track within ten miles of us. Outside the sky went from yellow to black, from still to windy. Pine straw, dust, and all manner of things began whipping by. I knew what was happening: twister.

I dropped the pitchfork, dove for the inside of an old shovel scoop mule sled, and no sooner had I hit face down and put my hands over my head, then it hit.

I caught a glimpse of a cow flying by, legs splayed like she thought she could stop the tug of the wind easy as she could stop the tug of a rope. Then the cow was gone and the sled started to move.

After that, everything started happening so quickly I'm not certain what I saw. Lots of things flying by, and I could hardly breathe. The sled might have gone as high as thirty feet, 'cause when I came down it was hard. Hadn't been for the ice, I'd probably have been driven into the ground like a cork in a bottle. But the sled hit the ice and started sliding, throwing up dirty, hard snow on either side of me. Ice pieces hit me in the face, then the sled fetched up against something solid, a stump probably, and I went flying out of it, hit the ice, whirled around and around, came to rest in that ditch where I'd found the madman.

I passed out for a while, and I dreamed. Dreamed I was in the sled again, flying through the air, and there was our house, lifting up from the ground, floor and all. It flew right past me, rising fast. In the brief instant it moved in front of me, I saw Mama. She was standing at the window. All the glass was blown out, and she was clinging to the sill with both hands. Her eyes were as big and blue as her china saucers, and her red hair had come undone and was blowing and whipping around her like a brush fire.

The house shot on up, and when I looked up to see, there wasn't nothing but whirling blackness with little chunks of wood and junk disappearing into it.

"Mama," I said, and I must have said it a lot of times, 'cause that's what woke me up. The sound of my voice calling Mama.

I tried to stand, but my ankle wasn't having it. It hurt like hell, and when I looked down, I saw my boot and sock had been ripped off by the blow, and the ankle was as big as a coiled cottonmouth snake.

I put a hand on the edge of the ditch, dug my fingers through the ice and pulled myself up, taking some of the skin off my naked foot as I did. It was so cold the flesh had frozen to the ground and it had peeled off when I moved, like sweetgum bark.

Once I was out of the ditch, I started crawling across the ice, dragging my useless foot behind me. Little chunks of skin came off my palms, so I had to get down and pull myself forward on my coat-sleeved forearms.

I hadn't gone far before I found Papa. He was sitting in his rocking chair, and in one hand he held his pipe and it was still smoking. The porch the chair had been sitting on was gone, but Papa was rocking gently in what remained of the wind. And the pitchfork I'd tossed before diving into the sled was sticking out of his chest like it had growed there. I didn't see a drop of blood. His eyes were open and staring, and every time that chair rocked forward, he seemed to look and nod at me.

Behind Papa, where the house ought to have been, wasn't nothing. It was like it hadn't never been built. I quit crawling and started crying. Did that till there wasn't nothing in me to cry, and the cold started making me so numb I just wanted to lay there and freeze at Papa's feet like an old dog. I felt like if I wasn't his killer, I was at least a helper, having tossed down the very pitchfork that had murdered him.

It started to rain little ice pellets, and somehow the pain of those things pounding on me, gave me the will to crawl toward a heap of hay that had been tossed there by the wind. By the time I got to the pile and looked back, Papa wasn't rocking no more. Those runners had froze to the ground and his black hair had turned white from the ice that had stuck to him.

I worked my way into the hay and tried to pull as much of it over me as I could. Doing that wore me out, and I fell asleep wondering about Mama, wondering what had happened to her, hoping she was alive.

The wind picked up again, took most of my hay away, but by then I didn't care. I awoke remembering that I'd had that dream about Mama and the house again. Even though I didn't have much hay on me, it didn't seem so cold anymore. I figured it was either warming up, or I was getting used to it. Course, wasn't neither of them things. I was freezing to death, and would have too, if not for Mr. Parks and his boys.

Mr. Parks was our nearest neighbor, about three miles east. It turned out he had been chopping wood when the sky turned yellow. Later he told me about it, and he said it was as strange as a blue-eyed hound dog, and unlike any twister he'd ever seen. Said the yellow sky went black, then this dark cloud grew a tail and came a-wagging out of the sky like a happy pup, the tail getting thicker as it dipped. When it touched down he figured the place it hit was right close to our farm, so he hitched up a wagon and came on out.

It was slow go for him and his two boys, on account of the ice and them having to stop now and then to clear the road of blown over trees. But they made it to our place about dark, and Mr. Parks said first thing he saw was Papa in that rocker. He said it was like the stem of Papa's pipe was pointing to where I lay, half in, half out of some hay.

They figured me for dead at first, I looked so bad. But when they saw I was alive, they loaded me in the wagon, covered me in some old feed sacks and a couple half-wet blankets and started out of there.

Turned out that foot of mine was broke bad. The doctor came out to the Parks place, set it, and didn't charge me a cent. He said he owed Papa from last fall for a bushel of taters, but I knew that was just a friendly lie. Doc Ryan hadn't never owed nobody nothing.

Mr. and Mrs. Parks offered me a place to stay after the funeral, but I told them I'd go back to our place and try to make a go of it there.

Johnny Parks, who used to whip the hell out of me twice a week on them weeks when we both managed to go a full week to school, made me a pair of solid crutches out of hickory, and I went to Papa's funeral on them. Mama, as if there was something to my dream, wasn't never found, and for that matter, they couldn't hardly find no pieces of the house. There was plenty of barn siding around, but of the house there was only a few floorboards, some wood shingles and some broken glass. Maybe it's silly, but I like to think that old storm just come and got her and hauled her off to a better place, like that little old gal in that book *The Wizard of Oz*.

Mr. Parks made Papa a tombstone out of a piece of river slate, chiseled some nice words on it:

HERE LIES HAROLD FOGG,
KILT BY A TORNADER,
AND HERE LIES THE MEMRY OF GLENDA FOGG
WHO WAS CARRIED OFF BY

THE SAME TORNADER
AND WASN'T NEVER FOUND.
NOT EVEN THE PIECES.

Beneath that was some dates on when they was born and died, and a line about them being survived by one son, Buster Fogg, meaning me, of course.

Over the protest of Mr. and Mrs. Parks, I had them take me out to the place and I set me up a tent there. They left me a lot of food and some hand-me-down clothes from their boys, then they went off saying they'd be back to check on me right regular. Mr. Parks even offered me some money and the loan of his mule, but I said I had to think on it.

This tent Mr. Parks had given me was a good one, and I managed to get around well enough on my crutches to gather barn siding and use what tools I could find to build a floor in it. I could have got Mr. Parks and his boys to do that for me, but I couldn't bring myself to ask them to, not after all they'd done. And besides, I had my pride. Matter of fact, that was about all I had right then. That and the place.

Well, it took me a couple of days what should have taken a few hours, but I got the tent fixed up real good and cozy finally. But it wasn't no replacement for the house and Mama and Papa. I'd have even liked to have heard them fussing over how much firewood Papa should have laid in, which was one of them things he was always a little lazy on, and was finally glad to pass most of the job along to me. I could just imagine Mama telling him as she looked at the last few sticks of stove wood, "I told you so."

On the morning after I'd spent my first night on my finished floor, I got out to take a real good look at things, and see what I could manage on crutches.

There were dead chickens lying all about, like feather dusters, pieces of wood and one mule lying on his back, legs sticking up in the air like a table blowed over.

Well, wasn't none of this something I hadn't already seen, but now with the flooring in, and my immediate comfort attended to, I found I just couldn't face picking up dead chickens and burning a mule carcass.

I went back inside the tent and felt sorry for myself, as that's all there was to do in there, besides eat, and I'd done that till I was about to pop. I didn't even have a book to reread, as all them had got blowed away with the house.

About a week went by, and I'd maybe got half the chickens picked up and tossed off in the ditch by the woodlot, and gotten the mule burned to nothing besides bones, when this slick-looking feller in a buckboard showed up.

"Howdy, young feller," he said, climbing down from his rig. "You must be Buster Fogg."

I admitted I was, and up close I saw that snazzy black suit and narrow brim hat he had on were even snappier than they'd looked from a distance. The hat and suit were as black as fresh charcoal and the pants had creases in them sharp enough to cut your throat. And the feller was all smiles. He looked to have more teeth than Main Street had bricks.

"Glad I caught you home," he said, and he took off his hat and held it over his chest as if contemplating a prayer.

"Whatsit I can do for you?" I asked. "Maybe you'd like to come in the tent, get out of this cold."

"No, no. What I have to say won't take but a moment. My name is Purdue. Jack Purdue. I'm the banker from town."

Well, right off I knew what it was and I didn't want to hear it, but I knew I was going to anyway.

"Your father's bill has come due, son, and I hate it something awful, and I know it's a bad time and all, but I'm going to need that money by about . . . ," he stopped for a moment to look generous, ". . . say noon tomorrow. Least half."

"I ain't got a penny, Mr. Purdue," I said. "Papa had the money, but everything got blowed away in the storm. If you could just give some time—"

He put his hat on and looked real sad about things, almost like it was his farm he was losing.

"I'm afraid not, son. It's an awful duty I got, but it's my duty."

I told him again about the money blowing away, how Papa had saved it up from selling stuff during the farm season, doing odd jobs around and all, and that I could do the same, providing he gave my leg time to heal so I could get a job. Just to work on his sympathy some, I then went on to tell him the whole horrible truth about how Papa was killed and Mama blowed away like so much outhouse paper, and when I got through I figured I'd told it real good, 'cause his eyes looked a little moist.

"That," he said, not hardly able to speak, "is without a doubt, the saddest story I've ever heard. And of course I knew all about it, son, but somehow, hearing it from you, the last survivor of the Fogg family, makes it all the more dreadful."

He kind of choked up there on the end of his words, and I figured I had him pretty good, so I throwed in how us Foggs had pride and all, and that I'd never let a due bill go unpaid, if he'd just give me the time to raise the money.

Well, he told me he was tore all to hell up about it, but business was business, sad story or not. And as he wiped some of the water out of his eyes with the back of his hand, he told me he would give me until tomorrow evening instead of noon, because he reckoned someone who'd been through what I had deserved a little more time.

"But that ain't enough," I said.

"I'm sorry, son, that's the best I can do, and that goes against the judgement of the bank. I'm sticking my neck out to do that."

"You are the bank, Purdue," I said. "Who you fooling? It ain't me. We all know you're the bank."

"I understand your grief, your torment," he said, just like one of the characters from some of them Dime Novels Papa bought from time to time, "but business is business."

"You said that."

"Yes I did." With that, Mr. Purdue turned and walked back to his buckboard. He called out to me as I stood there leaning defeated on my crutches. "I tell you, son, that is the saddest story I've ever heard, and I've heard some. Tragic. This will hang over my head from here on out, right over my head," he showed me exactly where it would be hanging with his hand, "until my dying day."

He stood there with one foot up on the buckboard step a moment, looking as downcast as a young rooster without any hens, then he climbed up and cracked the whip gently over the heads of his horses. There must have been some pretty heavy tears in his eyes as he left, 'cause when he turned the buckboard around, the left wheels rolled right over Papa's grave.

My farming days were over before they even got started. And I'll tell you, right then and there, I decided I wasn't going to pick up another dead chicken to make the place look nicer. In fact, I went over to the ditch, got the ones I throwed down there out and chunked them around sorta like they had been. Then I went back to my tent and wished I hadn't burned that old dead mule up.

The smartest thing to do would have been to go on over to Mr. and Mrs. Parks, even if it did take me all damned day on them crutches, but I just couldn't. Us Foggs have our pride. I decided to set out for town, get me a job there, make my own way. Surely there was something I could do till my leg healed up and I got me a solid job.

I figured if I started early, like tomorrow morning, I could maybe make town by nightfall, crutches or not. I'd probably fall down and bust it a few times, but that didn't matter none.

Well, as I said, us Foggs are proud, and maybe just a little bit stupid, so next morning I set out as planned, leaving the tent behind, carrying with me some hard bread, jerked meat, and dried fruit in a sack.

I must have fell down a half a dozen times before I got to the road, but then I could crutch along better, 'cause there was a lot less ice there.

By noon my underarms were so sore from the rubbing of them crutches that they were bleeding and making blisters that kept popping as I went.

Stopping about then, I sat down on a rock and my coattails, ate me some bread and jerky, and fretted things over. While I was fretting, I heard this sound and looked up.

It was bells on a harness I had heard, and the harness was attached to eight big mules pulling a bright red wagon driven by a big black man wearing a long, dark coat and a top hat. When the sun hit his teeth they flashed like a pearl-handled revolver.

As the wagon made a little curve in the road, I got a glimpse at the side, and I could see there was a cage fixed there, balancing out the barrels of water and supplies on the other side.

At first I thought what was in the cage was a deformed colored feller, but when it got closer, I seen it was some kind of animal covered in hair. It was about the ugliest, scariest damned thing I'd ever seen.

Right then I was feeling a might less proud than I had been that morning, so I got them crutches under me and hobbled out into the road and waved one hand at the man on the wagon.

The wagon slowed and pulled alongside of me. The driver yelled, "Whoa, you old ugly mules," and the harness bells ceased to shake.

I could see the animal in the cage real good now, but I still couldn't figure on what it was. There was some yellow words painted above the cage that said THE MAGIC WAGON, and to the right of the cage was a little sign with some fancy writing on it that read:

Magic Tricks, Trick Shooting, Fortune Telling,
Wrestling Ape, Side Amusements,
Medicine For What Ails You,
And All At Reasonable Prices.

Sounded pretty good to me.

"You look like you could use a ride, white boy," the big colored man said.

"Yes sir, I could at that," I said.

"You don't say yes sir to a nigger." I turned to see who had said that, and there was this feller standing in faded, red long johns and moccasins with blond hair down to his shoulders and a skimpy little blond mustache over his lip. He had his arms crossed, holding his elbows against the cold. He'd obviously come out of the back of the wagon, but he'd walked out so quiet I hadn't even known he was there till he spoke.

When I didn't say nothing, he added, "This here's my wagon. He just works for me. I say who rides and who don't, and I say you don't."

"I got some jerky, canned taters and beans I can trade for a ride, and I'll sit up there on the seat."

"If you was riding, you sure would," the blond man said. "But you ain't riding." He turned back to the wagon and I noticed the flap on his long johns was down. I snickered just a little, and he turned around to stare at me. He had eyes like a couple of gun barrels, cold and ugly grey.

"I don't need no beans or sweet taters," he said suddenly, then he started back to the wagon.

"He can ride up here with me if he's got a mind to," said the colored man.

The white feller spun around and came stomping back. "What did you say?"

"I said he could ride up here with me if he's got a mind to," the colored man said, moving his lips real slow like, as if he was talking to an idiot. "It's too cold for a boy to be out here, especially one on crutches."

"You're getting mighty uppity for a nigger," the white feller said. "Mighty uppity for a nigger who works for me."

"Maybe I is," the colored feller said. "And it worries me something awful, Mister Billy Bob. I get so worried abouts it I can't get me no good sleep at night. I wake up wondering if Mister Billy Bob is put out with me, and if I truly is getting uppity."

Mister Billy Bob pointed his finger at the colored feller and shook it. "Keep it up, nigger. Just keep it up and you're going to wake up with a crowd of buzzards around you. Hear?"

"I hear," the colored feller said. It was almost a yawn.

Billy Bob started back for the wagon again, gave me a glimpse of his exposed butt, turned and came back. He shook his finger at the colored feller again. "Albert," he said, "you and me, we going to have to have us a serious

Come To Jesus meeting, get some things straight. Like who's the nigger and who ain't."

"I do need some pointers on that, Mister Billy Bob. I get a trifle confused sometime."

Billy Bob stood there for a moment like he was going to stare Albert down off the wagon seat, but he finally gave it up. "All right, you," he said to me. "You can ride, but it's going to cost you them beans and taters, hear?"

I nodded.

This time Billy Bob turned and went into the wagon, the moon of his butt my last sight of him, the slamming of the door my last sound.

I turned and looked up at Albert. He was leaning down with a big hand extended. Just before I took it, I got me another look at the critter in the cage, and when he looked at me he peeled back his lips to show his teeth, like maybe he was smiling.

When I was on the seat beside Albert, he said, "That Mister Billy Bob's going to need to get them buttons fixed on the seat of his drawers, ain't he?"

We laughed at that.

After we got moving good, Albert said, "You keep them beans and taters, boy. Taters upset my stomach, and beans they make Mister Billy Bob fart something awful. Just ain't no being around him."

"That's good of you to let me keep them," I said, " 'cause I ain't got no beans or taters. All I got is some hard bread and some jerked meat."

Albert let out a roar, like that was the funniest thing he'd ever heard. I could tell right then and there he didn't have no real respect for Billy Bob.

"That critter in the cage?" I asked, taking a long shot. "Is that some kind of bear what caught on fire or something?"

Albert laughed again. "Naw, it ain't no bear. That there is a jungle ape, comes from the same place as all us colored. They calls him a chimpanzee. Name's RotToe on account of he got him some kind of disease once and one of the toes on his right foot rotted off. Least that's what the feller who sold him to Billy Bob said."

I remembered the sign I'd read on the side of the wagon. "Wrestling Ape," I said.

"There you got it," Albert said.

I found a place for the crutches and the food bag, then I leaned back with my hands in my lap.

"You look a might bushed, little peckerwood. You wants to lay your head against my shoulder to rest, you go right ahead."

"No thanks," I said. But we hadn't gone too far down the road when I just couldn't keep my eyes open no more and I realized just how tired I really was. I lolled my head on Albert's big shoulder. I could smell the clean wool of his coat. And wasn't no time until I was asleep.

NIGHT THEY MISSED
THE HORROR SHOW

For Lew Shiner, a story that doesn't flinch

If they'd gone to the drive-in like they'd planned, none of this would have happened. But Leonard didn't like drive-ins when he didn't have a date, and he'd heard about *Night Of The Living Dead*, and he knew a nigger starred in it. He didn't want to see no movie with a nigger star. Niggers chopped cotton, fixed flats, and pimped nigger girls, but he'd never heard of one that killed zombies. And he'd heard too that there was a white girl in the movie that let the nigger touch her, and that peeved him. Any white gal that would let a nigger touch her must be the lowest trash in the world. Probably from Hollywood, New York, or Waco, some god-forsaken place like that.

Now Steve McQueen would have been all right for zombie killing and girl handling. He would have been the ticket. But a nigger? No sir.

Boy, that Steve McQueen was one cool head. Way he said stuff in them pictures was so good you couldn't help but think someone had written it down for him. He could sure think fast on his feet to come up with the things he said, and he had that real cool, mean look.

Leonard wished he could be Steve McQueen, or Paul Newman even. Someone like that always knew what to say, and he figured they got plenty of bush too. Certainly they didn't get as bored as he did. He was so bored he felt as if he were going to die from it before the night was out. Bored, bored, bored. Just wasn't nothing exciting about being in the Dairy Queen parking lot leaning on the front of his '64 Impala looking out at the highway. He figured maybe old crazy Harry who janitored at the high school might be right about them flying saucers. Harry was always seeing something. Bigfoot, six-legged weasels, all manner of things. But maybe he was right about the saucers. He'd said he'd seen one a couple nights back hovering over Mud Creek and it was shooting down these rays that looked like wet peppermint sticks. Leonard figured if Harry really had seen the saucers and the rays, then those rays were boredom rays. It would be a way for space critters to get at earth folks, boring them to death. Getting melted down by heat rays would have been better. That was at least quick, but being bored to death was sort of like being nibbled to death by ducks.

Leonard continued looking at the highway, trying to imagine flying saucers and boredom rays, but he couldn't keep his mind on it. He finally focused on something in the highway. A dead dog.

Not just a dead dog. But a DEAD DOG. The mutt had been hit by a semi at least, maybe several. It looked as if it had rained dog. There were pieces of that pooch all over the concrete and one leg was lying on the curbing on the opposite side, stuck up in such a way that it seemed to be waving hello. Doctor Frankenstein with a grant from Johns Hopkins and assistance from NASA couldn't have put that sucker together again.

Leonard leaned over to his faithful, drunk companion, Billy—known among the gang as Farto, because he was fart lighting champion of Mud Creek—and said, "See that dog there?"

Farto looked where Leonard was pointing. He hadn't noticed the dog before, and he wasn't nearly as casual about it as Leonard. The puzzle-piece hound brought back memories. It reminded him of a dog he'd had when he was thirteen. A big, fine German Shepherd that loved him better than his Mama.

Sonofabitch dog tangled its chain through and over a barbed wire fence somehow and hung itself. When Farto found the dog its tongue looked like a stuffed, black sock and he could see where its claws had just been able to scrape the ground, but not quite enough to get a toe hold.

It looked as if the dog had been scratching out some sort of a coded message in the dirt. When Farto told his old man about it later, crying as he did, his old man laughed and said, "Probably a goddamn suicide note."

Now, as he looked out at the highway, and his whiskey-laced Coke collected warmly in his gut, he felt a tear form in his eyes. Last time he'd felt that sappy was when he'd won the fart-lighting championship with a four-inch burner that singed the hairs of his ass and the gang awarded him with a pair of colored boxing shorts. Brown and yellow ones so he could wear them without having to change them too often.

So there they were, Leonard and Farto, parked outside the DQ, leaning on the hood of Leonard's Impala, sipping Coke and whiskey, feeling bored and blue and horny, looking at a dead dog and having nothing to do but go to a show with a nigger starring in it. Which, to be up front, wouldn't have been so bad if they'd had dates. Dates could make up for a lot of sins, or help make a few good ones, depending on one's outlook.

But the night was criminal. Dates they didn't have. Worse yet, wasn't a girl in the entire high school would date them. Not even Marylou Flowers, and she had some kind of disease.

All this nagged Leonard something awful. He could see what the problem was with Farto. He was ugly. Had the kind of face that attracted flies. And though being fart-lighting champion of Mud Creek had a certain prestige among the gang, it lacked a certain something when it came to charming the gals.

But for the life of him, Leonard couldn't figure his own problem. He was handsome, had some good clothes, and his car ran good when he didn't buy that old cheap gas. He even had a few bucks in his jeans from breaking into washaterias. Yet his right arm had damn near grown to the size of his thigh from all the whacking off he did. Last time he'd been out with a girl had been a month ago, and as he'd been out with her along with nine other guys, he wasn't rightly sure he could call that a date. He wondered about it so much, he'd asked Farto if he thought it qualified as a date. Farto, who had been fifth in line, said he didn't think so, but if Leonard wanted to call it one, wasn't no skin off his back.

But Leonard didn't want to call it a date. It just didn't have the feel of one, lacked that something special. There was no romance to it.

True, Big Red had called him Honey when he put the mule in the barn, but she called everyone Honey—except Stoney. Stoney was Possum Sweets, and he was the one who talked her into wearing the grocery bag with the mouth and eye holes. Stoney was like that. He could sweet talk the camel out from under a sand nigger. When he got through chatting Big Red down, she was plumb proud to wear that bag.

When finally it came his turn to do Big Red, Leonard had let her take the bag off as a gesture of good will. That was a mistake. He just hadn't known a good thing when he had it. Stoney had had the right idea. The bag coming off spoiled everything. With it on, it was sort of like balling the Lone Hippo or some such thing, but with the bag off, you were absolutely certain what you were getting, and it wasn't pretty.

Even closing his eyes hadn't helped. He found that the ugliness of that face had branded itself on the back of his eyeballs. He couldn't even imagine the sack back over her head. All he could think about was that puffy, too-painted face with the sort of bad complexion that began at the bone.

He'd gotten so disappointed, he'd had to fake an orgasm and get off before his hooter shriveled up and his Trojan fell off and was lost in the vacuum.

Thinking back on it, Leonard sighed. It would certainly be nice for a change to go with a girl that didn't pull the train or had a hole between her legs that looked like a manhole cover ought to be on it. Sometimes he wished he could be like Farto, who was as happy as if he had good sense. Anything thrilled him. Give him a can of Wolf Brand Chili, a big moon pie, Coke and whiskey and he could spend the rest of his life fucking Big Red and lighting the gas out of his asshole.

God, but this was no way to live. No women and no fun. Bored, bored, bored. Leonard found himself looking overhead for spaceships and peppermint-colored boredom rays, but he saw only a few moths fluttering drunkenly through the beams of the DQ's lights.

Lowering his eyes back to the highway and the dog, Leonard had a sudden flash. "Why don't we get the chain out of the back and hook it up to Rex there? Take him for a ride?"

"You mean drag his dead ass around?" Farto asked.

Leonard nodded.

"Beats stepping on a tack," Farto said.

They drove the Impala into the middle of the highway at a safe moment and got out for a look. Up close the mutt was a lot worse. Its innards had been mashed out of its mouth and asshole and it stunk something awful. The dog was wearing a thick, metal-studded collar and they fastened one end of their fifteen-foot chain to that and the other to the rear bumper.

Bob, the Dairy Queen manager, noticed them through the window, came outside and yelled, "What are you fucking morons doing?"

"Taking this doggie to the vet," Leonard said. "We think this sumbitch looks a might peeked. He may have been hit by a car."

"That's so fucking funny I'm about to piss myself," Bob said.

"Old folks have that problem," Leonard said.

Leonard got behind the wheel and Farto climbed in on the passenger side. They maneuvered the car and dog around and out of the path of a tractor-trailer truck just in time. As they drove off, Bob screamed after them, "I hope you two no-dicks wrap that Chevy piece of shit around a goddamn pole."

As they roared along, parts of the dog, like crumbs from a flaky loaf of bread, came off. A tooth here. Some hair there. A string of guts. A dew claw. And some unidentifiable pink stuff. The metal-studded collar and chain threw up sparks now and then like fiery crickets. Finally they hit seventy-five and the dog was swinging wider and wider on the chain, like it was looking for an opportunity to pass.

Farto poured him and Leonard up Cokes and whiskey as they drove along. He handed Leonard his paper cup and Leonard knocked it back, a lot happier now than he had been a moment ago. Maybe this night wasn't going to turn out so bad after all.

They drove by a crowd at the side of the road, a tan station wagon and a wreck of a Ford up on a jack. At a glance they could see that there was a nigger in the middle of the crowd and he wasn't witnessing to the white boys. He was hopping around like a pig with a hotshot up his ass, trying to find a break in the white boys so he could make a run for it. But there wasn't any break to be found and there were too many to fight. Nine white boys were knocking him around like he was a pinball and they were a malicious machine.

"Ain't that one of our niggers?" Farto asked. "And ain't that some of the White Tree football players that's trying to kill him?"

"Scott," Leonard said, and the name was dogshit in his mouth. It had been Scott who had outdone him for the position of quarterback on the team. That damn jig could put together a play more tangled than a can of fishing worms, but it damn near always worked. And he could run like a spotted-ass ape.

As they passed, Farto said, "We'll read about him to-morrow in the papers."

But Leonard drove only a short way before slamming on the brakes and whipping the Impala around. Rex swung way out and clipped off some tall, dried sunflowers at the edge of the road like a scythe.

"We gonna go back and watch?" Farto asked. "I don't think them White Tree boys would bother us none if that's all we was gonna do, watch."

"He may be a nigger," Leonard said not liking himself, "but he's our nigger and we can't let them do that. They kill him, they'll beat us in football."

Farto saw the truth of this immediately. "Damn right. They can't do that to our nigger."

Leonard crossed the road again and went straight for the White Tree boys, hit down hard on the horn. The White Tree boys abandoned beating their prey and jumped in all directions. Bullfrogs couldn't have done any better.

Scott stood startled and weak where he was, his knees bent in and touching one another, his eyes as big as pizza pans. He had never noticed how big grillwork was. It looked like teeth there in the night and the headlights looked like eyes. He felt like a stupid fish about to be eaten by a shark.

Leonard braked hard, but off the highway in the dirt it wasn't enough to keep from bumping Scott, sending him flying over the hood and against the glass where his face mashed to it then rolled away, his shirt snagging one of the windshield wipers and pulling it off.

Leonard opened the car door and called to Scott who lay on the ground, "It's now or never."

A White Tree boy made for the car, and Leonard pulled the taped hammer handle out from beneath the seat and stepped out of the car and hit him with it. The White Tree boy went down to his knees and said something that sounded like French but wasn't. Leonard grabbed Scott by the back of the shirt and pulled him up and guided him around and threw him into the open door. Scott scrambled over the front seat and into the back. Leonard threw the hammer handle at one of the White Tree boys and stepped back, whirled into the car behind the wheel. He put the car in gear again and stepped on the gas. The Impala lurched forward, and with one hand on the door Leonard flipped it wider and clipped a White Tree boy with it as if he were flexing a wing. The car bumped back on the highway and the chain swung out and Rex cut the feet out from under two White Tree boys as neatly as he had taken down the dried sunflowers.

Leonard looked in his rear view mirror and saw two White Tree boys carrying the one he had clubbed with the hammer handle to the station wagon. The others he and the dog had knocked down were getting up. One had kicked the jack out from under Scott's car and was using it to smash the headlights and windshield.

"Hope you got insurance on that thing," Leonard said.

"I borrowed it," Scott said, peeling the windshield wiper out of his T-shirt. "Here, you might want this." He dropped the wiper over the seat and between Leonard and Farto.

"That's a borrowed car?" Farto said. "That's worse."

"Nah," Scott said. "Owner don't know I borrowed it. I'd have had that flat changed if that sucker had had him a spare tire, but I got back there and wasn't nothing but the rim, man. Say, thanks for not letting me get killed, else we couldn't have run that ole pig together no more. Course, you almost run over me. My chest hurts."

Leonard checked the rear view again. The White Tree boys were coming fast. "You complaining?" Leonard said.

"Nah," Scott said, and turned to look through the back glass. He could see the dog swinging in short arcs and pieces of it going wide and far. "Hope you didn't go off and forget your dog tied to the bumper."

"Goddamn," said Farto, "and him registered too."

"This ain't so funny," Leonard said, "them White Tree boys are gaining."

"Well speed it up," Scott said.

Leonard gnashed his teeth. "I could always get rid of some excess baggage, you know."

"Throwing that windshield wiper out ain't gonna help," Scott said.

Leonard looked in his mirror and saw the grinning nigger in the back seat. Nothing worse than a comic coon. He didn't even look grateful. Leonard had a sudden horrid vision of being overtaken by the White Tree boys. What if he were killed with the nigger? Getting killed was bad enough, but what if tomorrow they found him in a ditch with Farto and the nigger? Or maybe them White Tree boys would make him do something awful with the nigger before they killed them. Like making him suck the nigger's dick or some such thing. Leonard held his foot all the way to the floor; as they passed the Dairy Queen he took a hard left and the car just made it and Rex swung

out and slammed a light pole then popped back in line
behind them.

The White Tree boys couldn't make the corner in the
station wagon and they didn't even try. They screeched
into a car lot down a piece, turned around and came back.
By that time the tail lights of the Impala were moving
away from them rapidly, looking like two inflamed hem-
orrhoids in a dark asshole.

"Take the next right coming up," Scott said, "then
you'll see a little road off to the left. Kill your lights and
take that."

Leonard hated taking orders from Scott on the field, but
this was worse. Insulting. Still, Scott called good plays on
the field, and the habit of following instructions from the
quarterback died hard. Leonard made the right and Rex
made it with them after taking a dip in a water-filled bar
ditch.

Leonard saw the little road and killed his lights and took
it. It carried them down between several rows of large tin
storage buildings, and Leonard pulled between two of them
and drove down a little alley lined with more. He stopped
the car and they waited and listened. After about five minutes, Farto said, "I think we skunked those father rap-
ers."

"Ain't we a team?" Scott said.

In spite of himself, Leonard felt good. It was like when
the nigger called a play that worked and they were all
patting each other on the ass and not minding what color
the other was because they were just creatures in football
suits.

"Let's have a drink," Leonard said.

Farto got a paper cup off the floorboard for Scott and
poured him up some warm Coke and whiskey. Last time
they had gone to Longview, he had peed in that paper cup
so they wouldn't have to stop, but that had long since been
poured out, and besides, it was for a nigger. He poured
Leonard and himself drinks in their same cups.

Scott took a sip and said, "Shit, man, that tastes kind
of rank."

"Like piss," Farto said.

Leonard held up his cup. ''To the Mud Creek Wildcats and fuck them White Tree boys.''

''You fuck 'em,'' Scott said. They touched their cups, and at that moment the car filled with light.

Cups upraised, the Three Musketeers turned blinking toward it. The light was coming from an open storage building door and there was a fat man standing in the center of the glow like a bloated fly on a lemon wedge. Behind him was a big screen made of a sheet and there was some kind of movie playing on it. And though the light was bright and fading out the movie, Leonard, who was in the best position to see, got a look at it. What he could make out looked like a gal down on her knees sucking this fat guy's dick (the man was visible only from the belly down) and the guy had a short, black revolver pressed to her forehead. She pulled her mouth off of him for an instant and the man came in her face then fired the revolver. The woman's head snapped out of frame and the sheet seemed to drip blood, like dark condensation on a window pane. Then Leonard couldn't see anymore because another man had appeared in the doorway, and like the first he was fat. Both looked like huge bowling balls that had been set on top of shoes. More men appeared behind these two, but one of the fat men turned and held up his hand and the others moved out of sight. The two fat guys stepped outside and one pulled the door almost shut, except for a thin band of light that fell across the front seat of the Impala.

Fat Man Number One went over to the car and opened Farto's door and said, ''You fucks and the nigger get out.'' It was the voice of doom. They had only thought the White Tree boys were dangerous. They realized now they had been kidding themselves. This was the real article. This guy would have eaten the hammer handle and shit a two-by-four.

They got out of the car and the fat man waved them around and lined them up on Farto's side and looked at them. The boys still had their drinks in their hands, and sparing that, they looked like cons in a lineup.

Fat Man Number Two came over and looked at the trio

and smiled. It was obvious the fatties were twins. They had the same bad features in the same fat faces. They wore Hawaiian shirts that varied only in profiles and color of parrots and had on white socks and too-short black slacks and black, shiny, Italian shoes with toes sharp enough to thread needles.

Fat Man Number One took the cup away from Scott and sniffed it. "A nigger with liquor," he said. "That's like a cunt with brains. It don't go together. Guess you was getting tanked up so you could put the old black snake to some chocolate pudding after a while. Or maybe you was wantin' some vanilla and these boys were gonna set it up."

"I'm not wanting anything but to go home," Scott said.

Fat Man Number Two looked at Fat Man Number One and said, "So he can fuck his mother."

The fatties looked at Scott to see what he'd say but he didn't say anything. They could say he screwed dogs and that was all right with him. Hell, bring one on and he'd fuck it now if they'd let him go afterwards.

Fat Man Number One said, "You boys running around with a jungle bunny makes me sick."

"He's just a nigger from school," Farto said. "We don't like him none. We just picked him up because some White Tree boys were beating on him and we didn't want him to get wrecked on account of he's our quarterback."

"Ah," Fat Man Number One said, "I see. Personally, me and Vinnie don't cotton to niggers in sports. They start taking showers with white boys the next thing they want is to take white girls to bed. It's just one step from one to the other."

"We don't have nothing to do with him playing," Leonard said. "We didn't integrate the schools."

"No," Fat Man Number One said, "that was ole Big Ears Johnson, but you're running around with him and drinking with him."

"His cup's been peed in," Farto said. "That was kind of a joke on him, you see. He ain't our friend, I swear it. He's just a nigger that plays football."

"Peed in his cup, huh?" said the one called Vinnie. "I like that, Pork, don't you? Peed in his fucking cup."

Pork dropped Scott's cup on the ground and smiled at him. "Come here, nigger. I got something to tell you."

Scott looked at Farto and Leonard. No help there. They had suddenly become interested in the toes of their shoes; they examined them as if they were true marvels of the world.

Scott moved toward Pork, and Pork, still smiling, put his arm around Scott's shoulders and walked him toward the big storage building. Scott said, "What are we doing?"

Pork turned Scott around so they were facing Leonard and Farto who still stood holding their drinks and contemplating their shoes. "I didn't want to get it on the new gravel drive," Pork said and pulled Scott's head in close to his own and with his free hand reached back and under his Hawaiian shirt and brought out a short, black revolver and put it to Scott's temple and pulled the trigger. There was a snap like a bad knee going out and Scott's feet lifted in unison and went to the side and something dark squirted from his head and his feet swung back toward Pork and his shoes shuffled, snapped, and twisted on the concrete in front of the building.

"Ain't that somethin'," Pork said as Scott went limp and dangled from the thick crook of his arm, "the rhythm is the last thing to go."

Leonard couldn't make a sound. His guts were in his throat. He wanted to melt and run under the car. Scott was dead and the brains that had made plays twisted as fishing worms and commanded his feet on down the football field were scrambled like breakfast eggs.

Farto said, "Holy shit."

Pork let go of Scott and Scott's legs split and he sat down and his head went forward and clapped on the cement between his knees. A dark pool formed under his face.

"He's better off, boys," Vinnie said. "Nigger was begat by Cain and the ape and he ain't quite monkey and he ain't quite man. He's got no place in this world 'cept as a beast of burden. You start trying to train them to do things like drive cars and run with footballs it ain't nothing but grief to them and the whites too. Get any on your shirt, Pork?"

"Nary a drop."

Vinnie went inside the building and said something to the men there that could be heard but not understood, then he came back with some crumpled newspapers. He went over to Scott and wrapped them around the bloody head and let it drop back on the cement. "You try hosing down that shit when it's dried, Pork, and you wouldn't worry none about that gravel. The gravel ain't nothing."

Then Vinnie said to Farto, "Open the back door of that car." Farto nearly twisted an ankle doing it. Vinnie picked Scott up by the back of the neck and the seat of his pants and threw him onto the floorboard of the Impala.

Pork used the short barrel of his revolver to scratch his nuts, then put the gun behind him, under his Hawaiian shirt. "You boys are gonna go to the river bottoms with us and help us get shed of this nigger."

"Yes, sir," Farto said. "We'll toss his ass in the Sabine for you."

"How about you?" Pork asked Leonard. "You trying to go weak sister?"

"No," Leonard croaked, "I'm with you."

"That's good," Pork said. "Vinnie, you take the truck and lead the way."

Vinnie took a key from his pocket and unlocked the building door next to the one with the light, went inside, and backed out a sharp-looking gold Dodge pickup. He backed it in front of the Impala and sat there with the motor running.

"You boys keep your place," Pork said. He went inside the lighted building for a moment. They heard him say to the men inside, "Go on and watch the movies. And save some of them beers for us. We'll be back." Then the light went out and Pork came out, shutting the door. He looked at Leonard and Farto and said, "Drink up, boys."

Leonard and Farto tossed off their warm Coke and whiskey and dropped the cups on the ground.

"Now," Pork said, "you get in the back with the nigger, I'll ride with the driver."

Farto got in the back and put his feet on Scott's knees. He tried not to look at the head wrapped in newspaper, but he couldn't help it. When Pork opened the front door and the overhead light came on Farto saw there was a split in the paper and Scott's eye was visible behind it. Across the forehead the wrapping had turned dark. Down by the mouth and chin was an ad for a fish sale.

Leonard got behind the wheel and started the car. Pork reached over and honked the horn. Vinnie rolled the pickup forward and Leonard followed him to the river bottoms. No one spoke. Leonard found himself wishing with all his heart that he had gone to the outdoor picture show to see the movie with the nigger starring in it.

The river bottoms were steamy and hot from the closeness of the trees and the under and overgrowth. As Leonard wound the Impala down the narrow, red clay roads amidst the dense foliage, he felt as if his car were a crab crawling about in a pubic thatch. He could feel from the way the steering wheel handled that the dog and the chain were catching brush and limbs here and there. He had forgotten all about the dog and now being reminded of it worried him. What if the dog got tangled and he had to stop? He didn't think Pork would take kindly to stopping, not with the dead burrhead on the floorboards and him wanting to get rid of the body.

Finally they came to where the woods cleared out a spell and they drove along the edge of the Sabine River. Leonard hated water and always had. In the moonlight the river looked like poisoned coffee flowing there. Leonard knew there were alligators and gars big as little alligators and water moccasins by the thousands swimming underneath the water, and just the thought of all those slick, darting bodies made him queasy.

They came to what was known as Broken Bridge. It was an old worn-out bridge that had fallen apart in the middle and it was connected to the land on this side only. People sometimes fished off of it. There was no one fishing tonight.

Vinnie stopped the pickup and Leonard pulled up beside it, the nose of the Chevy pointing at the mouth of the bridge. They all got out and Pork made Farto pull Scott out by the feet. Some of the newspapers came loose from Scott's head exposing an ear and part of the face. Farto patted the newspaper back into place.

"Fuck that," Vinnie said. "It don't hurt if he stains the fucking ground. You two idgits find some stuff to weight this coon down so we can sink him."

Farto and Leonard started scurrying about like squirrels, looking for rocks or big, heavy logs. Suddenly they heard Vinnie cry out. "Godamighty, fucking A. Pork. Come look at this."

Leonard looked over and saw that Vinnie had discovered Rex. He was standing looking down with his hands on his hips. Pork went over to stand by him, then Pork turned around and looked at them. "Hey, you fucks, come here."

Leonard and Farto joined them in looking at the dog. There was mostly just a head now, with a little bit of meat and fur hanging off a spine and some broken ribs.

"That's the sickest fucking thing I've ever fucking seen," Pork said.

"Godamighty," Vinnie said.

"Doing a dog like that. Shit, don't you got no heart? A dog. Man's best fucking goddamn friend and you two killed him like this."

"We didn't kill him," Farto said.

"You trying to fucking tell me he done this to himself? Had a bad fucking day and done this."

"Godamighty," Vinnie said.

"No, sir," Leonard said. "We chained him on there after he was dead."

"I believe that," Vinnie said. "That's some rich shit. You guys murdered this dog. Godamighty."

"Just thinking about him trying to keep up and you fucks driving faster and faster makes me mad as a wasp," Pork said.

"No," Farto said. "It wasn't like that. He was dead

and we were drunk and we didn't have anything to do, so we—"

"Shut the fuck up," Pork said, sticking a finger hard against Farto's forehead. "You just shut the fuck up. We can see what the fuck you fucks did. You drug this here dog around until all his goddamn hide came off . . . What kind of mothers you boys got anyhow that they didn't tell you better about animals?"

"Godamighty," Vinnie said.

Everyone grew silent, stood looking at the dog. Finally Farto said, "You want us to go back to getting some stuff to hold the nigger down?"

Pork looked at Farto as if he had just grown up whole from the ground. "You fucks are worse than niggers, doing a dog like that. Get on back over to the car."

Leonard and Farto went over to the Impala and stood looking down at Scott's body in much the same way they had stared at the dog. There, in the dim moonlight shadowed by trees, the paper wrapped around Scott's head made him look like a giant papier-mâché doll. Pork came up and kicked Scott in the face with a swift motion that sent newspapers flying and sent a thonking sound across the water that made frogs jump.

"Forget the nigger," Pork said. "Give me your car keys, ball sweat." Leonard took out his keys and gave them to Pork and Pork went around to the trunk and opened it. "Drag the nigger over here."

Leonard took one of Scott's arms and Farto took the other and they pulled him over to the back of the car.

"Put him in the trunk," Pork said.

"What for?" Leonard asked.

" 'Cause I fucking said so," Pork said.

Leonard and Farto heaved Scott into the trunk. He looked pathetic lying there next to the spare tire, his face partially covered with newspaper. Leonard thought, if only the nigger had stolen a car with a spare he might not be here tonight. He could have gotten that flat changed and driven on before the White Tree boys even came along.

"All right, you get in there with him," Pork said, gesturing to Farto.

"Me?" Farto said.

"Nah, not fucking you, the fucking elephant on your fucking shoulder. Yeah, you, get in the trunk. I ain't got all night."

"Jesus, we didn't do anything to that dog, mister. We told you that. I swear. Me and Leonard hooked him up after he was dead . . . It was Leonard's idea."

Pork didn't say a word. He just stood there with one hand on the trunk lid looking at Farto. Farto looked at Pork, then the trunk, then back to Pork. Lastly he looked at Leonard, then climbed into the trunk, his back to Scott.

"Like spoons," Pork said, and closed the lid. "Now you, whatsit, Leonard? You come over here." But Pork didn't wait for Leonard to move. He scooped the back of Leonard's neck with a chubby hand and pushed him over to where Rex lay at the end of the chain with Vinnie still looking down at him.

"What you think, Vinnie?" Pork asked. "You got what I got in mind?"

Vinnie nodded. He bent down and took the collar off the dog. He fastened it on Leonard. Leonard could smell the odor of the dead dog in his nostrils. He bent his head and puked.

"There goes my shoeshine," Vinnie said, and he hit Leonard a short one in the stomach. Leonard went to his knees and puked some more of the hot Coke and whiskey.

"You fucks are the lowest pieces of shit on this earth, doing a dog like that," Vinnie said. "A nigger ain't no lower."

Vinnie got some strong fishing line out of the back of the truck and they tied Leonard's hands behind his back. Leonard began to cry.

"Oh shut up," Pork said. "It ain't that bad. Ain't nothing that bad."

But Leonard couldn't shut up. He was caterwauling now and it was echoing through the trees. He closed his eyes and tried to pretend he had gone to the show with the nigger starring in it and had fallen asleep in his car and was having a bad dream, but he couldn't imagine that. He thought about Harry the janitor's flying saucers with the peppermint rays, and he knew if there were any saucers shooting rays down, they weren't boredom rays after all. He wasn't a bit bored.

Pork pulled off Leonard's shoes and pushed him back flat on the ground and pulled off the socks and stuck them in Leonard's mouth so tight he couldn't spit them out. It wasn't that Pork thought anyone was going to hear Leonard, he just didn't like the noise. It hurt his ears.

Leonard lay on the ground in the vomit next to the dog and cried silently. Pork and Vinnie went over to the Impala and opened the doors and stood so they could get a grip on the car to push. Vinnie reached in and moved the gear from park to neutral and he and Pork began to shove the car forward. It moved slowly at first, but as it made the slight incline that led down to the old bridge, it picked up speed. From inside the trunk, Farto hammered lightly at the lid as if he didn't really mean it. The chain took up slack and Leonard felt it jerk and pop his neck. He began to slide along the ground like a snake.

Vinnie and Pork jumped out of the way and watched the car make the bridge and go over the edge and disappear into the water with amazing quietness. Leonard, pulled by the weight of the car, rustled past them. When he hit the bridge, splinters tugged at his clothes so hard they ripped his pants and underwear down almost to his knees.

The chain swung out once toward the edge of the bridge and the rotten railing, and Leonard tried to hook a leg around an upright board there, but that proved wasted. The weight of the car just pulled his knee out of joint and jerked the board out of place with a screech of nails and lumber.

Leonard picked up speed and the chain rattled over the edge of the bridge, into the water and out of sight, pulling its connection after it like a pull toy. The last sight of Leonard was the soles of his bare feet, white as the bellies of fish.

"It's deep there," Vinnie said. "I caught an old channel cat there once, remember? Big sucker. I bet it's over fifty feet deep down there."

They got in the truck and Vinnie cranked it.

"I think we did them boys a favor," Pork said. "Them running around with niggers and what they did to that dog and all. They weren't worth a thing."

"I know it," Vinnie said. "We should have filmed this, Pork, it would have been good. Where the car and that nigger lover went off in the water was choice."

"Nah, there wasn't any women."

"Point," Vinnie said, and he backed around and drove onto the trail that wound its way out of the bottoms.

ON THE FAR SIDE OF THE CADILLAC DESERT WITH DEAD FOLKS

For David Schow, a story of the Bad Guys and the Bad Guys

1

After a month's chase, Wayne caught up with Calhoun one night at a little honky-tonk called Rosalita's. It wasn't that Calhoun had finally gotten careless, it was just that he wasn't worried. He'd killed four bounty hunters so far, and Wayne knew a fifth didn't concern him.

The last bounty hunter had been the famous Pink Lady McGuire—one mean mama—three hundred pounds of rolling, ugly meat that carried a twelve-gauge Remington pump and a bad attitude. Story was, Calhoun jumped her from behind, cut her throat, and as a joke, fucked her before she bled to death. This not only proved to Wayne that Calhoun was a dangerous sonofabitch, it also proved he had bad taste.

Wayne stepped out of his '57 Chevy reproduction, pushed his hat back on his forehead, opened the trunk, and got the sawed-off double barrel and some shells out of there. He already had a .38 revolver in the holster at his side and a bowie knife in each boot, but when you went into a place like Rosalita's it was best to have plenty of backup.

Wayne put a handful of shotgun shells in his shirt pocket, snapped the flap over them, looked up at the red-and-blue neon sign that flashed ROSALITA'S: COLD BEER

AND DEAD DANCING, found his center, as they say in Zen, and went on in.

He held the shotgun against this leg, and as it was dark in there and folks were busy with talk or drinks or dancing, no one noticed him or his artillery right off.

He spotted Calhoun's stocky, black-hatted self immediately. He was inside the dance cage with a dead buck-naked Mexican girl of about twelve. He was holding her tight around the waist with one hand and massaging her rubbery ass with the other like it was a pillow he was trying to shape. The dead girl's handless arms flailed on either side of Calhoun, and her little tits pressed to his thick chest. Her wire-muzzled face knocked repeatedly at his shoulder and drool whipped out of her mouth in thick spermy ropes, stuck to his shirt, faded and left a patch of wetness.

For all Wayne knew, the girl was Calhoun's sister or daughter. It was that kind of place. The kind that had sprung up immediately after that stuff had gotten out of a lab upstate and filled the air with bacterium that brought dead humans back to life, made their basic motor functions work and made them hungry for human flesh; made it so if a man's wife, daughter, sister, or mother went belly up and he wanted to turn a few bucks, he might think: "Damn, that's tough about ole Betty Sue, but she's dead as hoot-owl shit and ain't gonna be needing nothing from here on out, and with them germs working around in her, she's just gonna pull herself out of the ground and cause me a problem. And the ground out back of the house is harder to dig than a calculus problem is to work, so I'll just toss her cold ass in the back of the pickup next to the chain saw and the barbed-wire roll, haul her across the border to sell her to the Meat Boys to sell to the tonks for dancing.

"It's a sad thing to sell one of your own, but shit, them's the breaks. I'll just stay out of the tonks until all the meat rots off her bones and they have to throw her away. That way I won't go in some place for a drink and see her up there shaking her dead tits and end up going sentimental and dewey-eyed in front of one of my buddies or some ole two-dollar gal.''

This kind of thinking supplied the dancers. In other parts of the country, the dancers might be men or children, but here it was mostly women. Men were used for hunting and target practice.

The Meat Boys took the bodies, cut off the hands so they couldn't grab, ran screws through their jaws to fasten on wire muzzles so they couldn't bite, sold them to the honky-tonks about the time the germ started stirring.

Tonk owners put them inside wire enclosures up front of their joints, started music, and men paid five dollars to get in there and grab them and make like they were dancing when all the women wanted to do was grab and bite, which, muzzled and handless, they could not do.

If a man liked his partner enough, he could pay more money and have her tied to a cot in the back and he could get on her and do some business. Didn't have to hear no arguments or buy presents or make promises or make them come. Just fuck and hike.

As long as the establishment sprayed the dead for maggots and kept them perfumed and didn't keep them so long hunks of meat came off on a fella's dick, the customers were happy as flies on shit.

Wayne looked to see who might give him trouble, and figured everyone was a potential customer. The six foot two, two-hundred fifty pound bouncer being the most immediate concern.

But, there wasn't anything to do but to get on with things and handle problems when they came up. He went into the cage where Calhoun was dancing, shouldered through the other dancers and went for him.

Calhoun had his back to Wayne, and as the music was loud, Wayne didn't worry about going quietly. But Calhoun sensed him and turned with his hand full of a little .38.

Wayne clubbed Calhoun's arm with the barrel of the shotgun. The little gun flew out of Calhoun's hand and went skidding across the floor and clanked against the metal cage.

Calhoun wasn't outdone. He spun the dead girl in front of him and pulled a big pigsticker out of his boot and held it under the girl's armpit in a threatening manner, which with a knife that big was no feat.

Wayne shot the dead girl's left kneecap out from under her and she went down. Her armpit trapped Calhoun's knife. The other men deserted their partners and went over the wire netting like squirrels.

Before Calhoun could shake the girl loose, Wayne stepped in and hit him over the head with the barrel of the shotgun. Calhoun crumpled and the girl began to crawl about on the floor as if looking for lost contacts.

The bouncer came in behind Wayne, grabbed him under the arms and tried to slip a full nelson on him.

Wayne kicked back on the bouncer's shin and raked his boot down the man's instep and stomped his foot. The bouncer let go. Wayne turned and kicked him in the balls and hit him across the face with the shotgun.

The bouncer went down and didn't even look like he wanted up.

Wayne couldn't help but note he liked the music that was playing. When he turned he had someone to dance with.

Calhoun.

Calhoun charged him, hit Wayne in the belly with his head, knocked him over the bouncer. They tumbled to the floor and the shotgun went out of Wayne's hands and scraped across the floor and hit the crawling girl in the head. She didn't even notice, just kept snaking in circles, dragging her blasted leg behind her like a skin she was trying to shed.

The other women, partnerless, wandered about the cage. The music changed. Wayne didn't like this tune as well. Too slow. He bit Calhoun's earlobe off.

Calhoun screamed and they grappled around on the floor. Calhoun got his arm around Wayne's throat and tried to choke him to death.

Wayne coughed out the earlobe, lifted his leg and took the knife out of his boot. He brought it around and back and hit Calhoun in the temple with the hilt.

Calhoun let go of Wayne and rocked on his knees, then collapsed on top of him.

Wayne got out from under him and got up and kicked him in the head a few times. When he was finished, he put the bowie in its place, got Calhoun's .38 and the shotgun. To hell with the pig sticker.

A dead woman tried to grab him, and he shoved her away with a thrust of his palm. He got Calhoun by the collar, started pulling him toward the gate.

Faces were pressed against the wire, watching. It had been quite a show. A friendly cowboy type opened the gate for Wayne and the crowd parted as he pulled Calhoun by. One man felt helpful and chased after them and said, "Here's his hat, Mister," and dropped it on Calhoun's face and it stayed there.

Outside, a professional drunk was standing between two cars taking a leak on the ground. As Wayne pulled Calhoun past, the drunk said, "Your buddy don't look so good."

"Look worse than that when I get him to Law Town," Wayne said.

Wayne stopped by the '57, emptied Calhoun's pistol and tossed it as far as he could, then took a few minutes to kick Calhoun in the ribs and ass. Calhoun grunted and farted, but didn't come to.

When Wayne's leg got tired, he put Calhoun in the passenger seat and handcuffed him to the door.

He went over to Calhoun's '62 Impala replica with the plastic bull horns mounted on the hood—which was how he had located him in the first place, by his well known car—and kicked the glass out of the window on the driver's side and used the shotgun to shoot the bull horns off. He took out his pistol and shot all the tires flat, pissed on the driver's door, and kicked a dent in it.

By then he was too tired to shit in the back seat, so he took some deep breaths and went back to the '57 and climbed in behind the wheel.

Reaching across Calhoun, he opened the glove box and got out one of his thin, black cigars and put it in his mouth.

He pushed the lighter in, and while he waited for it to heat up, he took the shotgun out of his lap and reloaded it.

A couple of men poked their heads outside of the tonk's door, and Wayne stuck the shotgun out the window and fired above their heads. The disappeared inside so fast they might have been an optical illusion.

Wayne put the lighter to his cigar, picked up the wanted poster he had on the seat, and set fire to it. He thought about putting it in Calhoun's lap as a joke, but didn't. He tossed the flaming poster out of the window.

He drove over close to the tonk and used the remaining shotgun load to shoot at the neon Rosalita's sign. Glass tinkled onto the tonk's roof and onto the gravel drive.

Now if he only had a dog to kick.

He drove away from there, bound for the Cadillac Desert, and finally Law Town on the other side.

2

The Cadillacs stretched for miles, providing the only shade in the desert. They were buried nose down at a slant, almost to the windshields, and Wayne could see skeletons of some of the drivers in the cars, either lodged behind the steering wheels or lying on the dashboards against the glass. The roof and hood guns had long since been removed and all the windows on the cars were rolled up, except for those that had been knocked out and vandalized by travelers, or dead folks looking for goodies.

The thought of being in one of those cars with the windows rolled up in all this heat made Wayne feel even more uncomfortable than he already was. Hot as it was, he was certain even the skeletons were sweating.

He finished pissing on the tire of the Chevy, saw the piss had almost dried. He shook the drops off, watched them fall and evaporate against the burning sand. Zipping up, he thought about Calhoun, and how when he'd pulled over earlier to let the sonofabitch take a leak, he'd seen there was a little metal ring through the head of his dick and a Texas emblem dangling from that. He could understand the Texas emblem, being from there himself, but he couldn't for the life of him imagine why a fella would do that to his general. Any idiot who would put a ring through the head of his pecker deserved to die, innocent or not.

Wayne took off his cowboy hat and rubbed the back of his neck and ran his hand over the top of his head and back again. The sweat on his fingers was thick as lube oil, and the thinning part of his hairline was tender; the heat was cooking the hell out of his scalp, even through the brown felt of his hat.

Before he put his hat on, the sweat on his fingers was dry. He broke open the shotgun, put the shells in his pocket, opened the Chevy's back door and tossed the shotgun on the floorboard.

He got in the front behind the wheel and the seat was hot as a griddle on his back and ass. The sun shone through the slightly tinted windows like a polished chrome hubcap; it forced him to squint.

Glancing over at Calhoun, he studied him. The fucker was asleep with his head thrown back and his black wilted hat hung precariously on his head—it looked jaunty almost. Sweat oozed down Calhoun's red face, flowed over his eyelids and around his neck, running in riverlets down the white seat covers, drying quickly. He had his left hand between his legs, clutching his balls, and his right was on the arm rest, which was the only place it could be since he was handcuffed to the door.

Wayne thought he ought to blow the bastard's brains out and tell God he died. The shithead certainly needing shooting, but Wayne didn't want to lose a thousand dollars off his reward. He needed every penny if he was going to get that wrecking yard he wanted. The yard was the dream that went before him like a carrot before a donkey, and he didn't want any more delays. If he never made another trip across this goddamn desert, that would suit him fine.

Pop would let him buy the place with the money he had now, and he could pay the rest out later. But that wasn't what he wanted to do. The bounty business had finally gone sour, and he wanted to do different. It wasn't any goddamn fun anymore. Just met the dick cheese of the earth. And when you ran the sonofabitches to ground and put the cuffs on them, you had to watch your ass 'til you got them turned in. Had to sleep with one eye open and a hand on your gun. It wasn't any way to live.

And he wanted a chance to do right by Pop. Pop had been like a father to him. When he was a kid and his mama was screwing the Mexicans across the border for the rent money, Pop would let him hang out in the yard and climb on the rusted cars and watch him fix the better ones, tune those babies so fine they purred like dick-whipped women.

When he was older, Pop would haul him to Galveston for the whores and out to the beach to take potshots at all the ugly, fucked-up critters swimming around in the Gulf. Sometimes he'd take him to Oklahoma for the Dead Roundup. It sure seemed to do the old fart good to whack those dead fuckers with a tire iron, smash their diseased brains so they'd lay down for good. And it was a challenge. 'Cause if one of those dead buddies bit you, you could put your head between your legs and kiss your rosy ass goodbye.

Wayne pulled out of his thoughts of Pop and the wrecking yard and turned on the stereo system. One of his favorite country-and-western tunes whispered at him. It was Billy Conteegas singing, and Wayne hummed along with the music as he drove into the welcome, if mostly ineffectual, shadows provided by the Cadillacs.

> "My baby left me,
>   She left me for a cow,
>   But I don't give a flying fuck,
>   She's gone radioactive now,
>   Yeah, my baby left me,
>   Left me for a six-tittied cow."

Just when Conteegas was getting to the good part, doing the trilling sound in his throat he was famous for, Calhoun opened his eyes and spoke up.

"Ain't it bad enough I got to put up with the fucking heat and your fucking humming without having to listen to that shit? Ain't you got no Hank Williams stuff, or maybe some of that nigger music they used to make? You know, where the coons harmonize and one of 'em sings like his nuts are cut off.''

"You just don't know good music when you hear it, Calhoun.''

Calhoun moved his free hand to his hatband, found one of his few remaining cigarettes and a match there. He struck the match on his knee, lit the smoke and coughed a few rounds. Wayne couldn't imagine how Calhoun could smoke in all this heat.

"Well, I may not know good music when I hear it, capon, but I damn sure know bad music when I hear it. And that's some bad music.''

"You ain't got any kind of culture, Calhoun. You been too busy raping kids.''

"Reckon a man has to have a hobby,'' Calhoun said, blowing smoke at Wayne. "Young pussy is mine. Besides, she wasn't in diapers. Couldn't find one that young. She was thirteen. You know what they say. If they're old enough to bleed, they're old enough to breed.''

"How old they have to be for you to kill them?''

"She got loud.''

"Change channels, Calhoun.''

"Just passing the time of day, capon. Better watch yourself, bounty hunter, when you least expect it, I'll bash your head.''

"You're gonna run your mouth one time too many, Calhoun, and when you do, you're gonna finish this ride in the trunk with ants crawling on you. You ain't so priceless I won't blow you away.''

"You lucked out at the tonk, boy. But there's always tomorrow, and every day can't be like at Rosalita's.''

Wayne smiled. "Trouble is, Calhoun, you're running out of tomorrows.''

3

As they drove between the Cadillacs, the sky fading like a bad bulb, Wayne looked at the cars and tried to imagine what the Chevy-Cadillac Wars had been like, and why they had been fought in this miserable desert. He had heard it was a hell of a fight, and close, but the outcome had been Chevy's and now they were the only cars Detroit made. And as far as he was concerned, that was the only thing about Detroit that was worth a damn. Cars.

He felt that way about all cities. He'd just as soon lie down and let a diseased dog shit in his face than drive through one, let alone live in one.

Law Town being an exception. He'd go there. Not to live, but to give Calhoun to the authorities and pick up his reward. People in Law Town were always glad to see a criminal brought in. The public executions were popular and varied and supplied a steady income.

Last time he'd been to Law Town he'd bought a front-row ticket to one of the executions and watched a chronic shoplifter, a red-headed rat of a man, get pulled apart by being chained between two souped-up tractors. The execution itself was pretty brief, but there had been plenty of buildup with clowns and balloons and a big-tittied stripper who could swing her tits in either direction to boom-boom music.

Wayne had been put off by the whole thing. It wasn't organized enough and the drinks and food were expensive and the front-row seats were too close to the tractors. He had gotten to see that the red-head's insides were brighter than his hair, but some of the insides got sprinkled on his new shirt, and cold water or not, the spots hadn't come out. He had suggested to one of the management that they put up a big plastic shield so the front row wouldn't get splattered, but he doubted anything had come of it.

They drove until it was solid dark. Wayne stopped and fed Calhoun a stick of jerky and some water from his canteen. Then he handcuffed him to the front bumper of the Chevy.

"See any snakes, Gila monsters, scorpions, stuff like that," Wayne said, "yell out. Maybe I can get around here in time."

"I'd let the fuckers run up my asshole before I'd call you," Calhoun said.

Leaving Calhoun with his head resting on the bumper, Wayne climbed in the back seat of the Chevy and slept with one ear cocked and one eye open.

Before dawn Wayne got Calhoun loaded in the '57 and they started out. After a few minutes of sluicing through the early morning grayness, a wind started up. One of those weird desert winds that come out of nowhere. It carried grit through the air at the speed of bullets, hit the '57 with a sound like rabid cats scratching.

The sand tires crunched on through, and Wayne turned on the windshield blower, the sand wipers, and the headbeams, and kept on keeping on.

When it was time for the sun to come up, they couldn't see it. Too much sand. It was blowing harder than ever and the blowers and wipers couldn't handle it. It was piling up. Wayne couldn't even make out the Cadillacs anymore.

He was about to stop when a shadowy, whale-like shape crossed in front of him and he slammed on the brakes, giving the sand tires a workout. But it wasn't enough.

The '57 spun around and rammed the shape on Calhoun's side. Wayne heard Calhoun yell, then felt himself thrown against the door and his head smacked metal and the outside darkness was nothing compared to the darkness into which he descended.

4

Wayne rose out of it as quickly as he had gone down. Blood was trickling into his eyes from a slight forehead wound. He used his sleeve to wipe it away.

His first clear sight was of a face at the window on his side; a sallow, moon-terrain face with bulging eyes and an expression like an idiot contemplating Sanskrit. On the man's head was a strange, black hat with big round ears, and in the center of the hat, like a silver tumor, was the head of a large screw. Sand lashed at the face, imbedded in it, struck the unblinking eyes and made the round-eared hat flap. The man paid no attention. Though still dazed, Wayne knew why. The man was one of the dead folks.

Wayne looked in Calhoun's direction. Calhoun's door had been mashed in and the bending metal had pinched the handcuff attached to the arm rest in two. The blow had knocked Calhoun to the center of the seat. He was holding his hand in front of him, looking at the dangling cuff and chain as if it were a silver bracelet and a line of pearls.

Leaning over the hood, cleaning the sand away from the windshield with his hands, was another of the dead folks. He too was wearing one of the round-eared hats. He pressed a wrecked face to the clean spot and looked in at Calhoun. A string of snot-green saliva ran out of his mouth and onto the glass.

More sand was wiped away by others. Soon all the car's glass showed the pallid and rotting faces of the dead folks. They stared at Wayne and Calhoun as if they were two rare fish in an aquarium.

Wayne cocked back the hammer of the .38.

"What about me," Calhoun said. "What am I supposed to use?"

"Your charm," Wayne said, and at that moment, as if by signal, the dead folk faded away from the glass, leaving one man standing on the hood holding a baseball bat. He hit the glass and it went into a thousand little stars. The bat came again and the heavens fell and the stars rained down and the sand storm screamed in on Wayne and Calhoun.

The dead folks reappeared in full force. The one with the bat started though the hole in the windshield, heedless of the jags of glass that ripped his ragged clothes and tore his flesh like damp cardboard.

Wayne shot the batter through the head, and the man, finished, fell through, pinning Wayne's arm with his body.

Before Wayne could pull his gun free, a woman's hand reached through the hole and got hold of Wayne's collar. Other dead folks took to the glass and hammered it out with their feet and fist. Hands were all over Wayne; they felt dry and cool like leather seat covers. They pulled him over the steering wheel and dash and outside. The sand worked at his flesh like a cheese grater. He could hear

Calhoun yelling, "Eat me, motherfuckers, eat me and choke."

They tossed Wayne on the hood of the '57. Faces leaned over him. Yellow teeth and toothless gums were very near. A road kill odor washed through his nostrils. He thought: now the feeding frenzy begins. His only consolation was that there were so many dead folks there wouldn't be enough of him left to come back from the dead. They'd probably have his brain for dessert.

But no. They picked him up and carried him off. Next thing he knew was a clearer view of the whale-shape the '57 had hit, and its color. It was a yellow school bus.

The door to the bus hissed open. The dead folks dumped Wayne inside on his belly and tossed his hat after him. They stepped back and the door closed, just missing Wayne's foot.

Wayne looked up and saw a man in the driver's seat smiling at him. It wasn't a dead man. Just fat and ugly. He was probably five feet tall and bald except for a fringe of hair around his shiny bald head the color of a shit ring in a toilet bowl. He had a nose so long and dark and malignant looking it appeared as if it might fall off his face at any moment, like an overripe banana. He was wearing what Wayne first thought was a bathrobe, but proved to be a robe like that of a monk. It was old and tattered and moth-eaten and Wayne could see pale flesh through the holes. An odor wafted from the fat man that was somewhere between the smell of stale sweat, cheesy balls and an unwiped asshole.

"Good to see you," the fat man said.

"Charmed," Wayne said.

From the back of the bus came a strange, unidentifiable sound. Wayne poked his head around the seats for a look.

In the middle of the aisle, about halfway back, was a nun. Or sort of a nun. Her back was to him and she wore a black-and-white nun's habit. The part that covered her head was traditional, but from there down was quite a departure from the standard attire. The outfit was cut to the middle of her thighs and she wore black fishnet stockings and thick high heels. She was slim with good legs and a high little ass that even under the circumstances, Wayne couldn't help but appreciate. She was moving one hand above her head as if sewing the air.

Sitting on the seats on either side of the aisle were dead folks. They all wore the round-eared hats, and they were responsible for the sound.

They were trying to sing.

He had never known dead folks to make any noise outside of grunts and groans, but here they were singing. A toneless sort of singing to be sure, some of the words garbled and some of the dead folks just opening and closing their mouths soundlessly, but, by golly, he recognized the tune. It was "Jesus Loves Me."

Wayne looked back at the fat man, let his hand ease down to the bowie in his right boot. The fat man produced a little .32 automatic from inside his robe and pointed it at Wayne.

"It's small caliber," the fat man said, "but I'm a real fine shot, and it makes a nice, little hole."

Wayne quit reaching in his boot.

"Oh, that's all right," said the fat man. "Take the knife out and put it on the floor in front of you and slide it to me. And while you're at it, I think I see the hilt of one in your other boot."

Wayne looked back. The way he had been thrown inside the bus had caused his pants legs to hike up over his boots, and the hilts of both his bowies were revealed. They might as well have had blinking lights on them.

It was shaping up to be a shitty day.

He slid the bowies to the fat man, who scooped them up nimbly and dumped them on the other side of his seat.

The bus door opened and Calhoun was tossed in on top of Wayne. Calhoun's hat followed after.

Wayne shrugged Calhoun off, recovered his hat, and put it on. Calhoun found his hat and did the same. They were still on their knees.

"Would you gentleman mind moving to the center of the bus?"

Wayne led the way. Calhoun took note of the nun now, said, "Man, look at that ass."

The fat man called back to them. "Right there will do fine."

Wayne slid into the seat the fat man was indicating with a wave of the .32, and Calhoun slid in beside him. The dead folks entered now, filled the seats up front, leaving only a few stray seats in the middle empty.

Calhoun said, "What are those fuckers back there making that noise for?"

"They're singing," Wayne said. "Ain't you got no churchin'?"

"Say they are?" Calhoun turned to the nun and the dead folks and yelled, "Y'all know any Hank Williams?"

The nun did not turn and the dead folks did not quit their toneless singing.

"Guess not," Calhoun said. "Seems like all the good music's been forgotten."

The noise in the back of the bus ceased and the nun came over to look at Wayne and Calhoun. She was nice in front too. The outfit was cut from throat to crotch, laced with a ribbon, and it showed a lot of tit and some tight, thin, black panties that couldn't quite hold in her escaping pubic hair, which grew as thick and wild as kudzu. When Wayne managed to work his eyes up from that and look at her face, he saw she was dark-complected with eyes the color of coffee and lips made to chew on.

Calhoun never made it to the face. He didn't care about faces. He sniffed, said into her crotch, "Nice snatch."

The nun's left hand came around and smacked Calhoun on the side of the head.

He grabbed her wrist, said, "Nice arm, too."

The nun did a magic act with her right hand; it went behind her back and hiked up her outfit and came back with a double-barreled derringer. She pressed it against Calhoun's head.

Wayne bent forward, hoping she wouldn't shoot. At that range the bullet might go through Calhoun's head and hit him too.

"Can't miss," the nun said.

Calhoun smiled. "No you can't," he said, and let go of her arm.

She sat down across from them, smiled, and crossed her legs high. Wayne felt his Levis snake swell and crawl against the inside of his thigh.

"Honey," Calhoun said, "you're almost worth taking a bullet for."

The nun didn't quit smiling. The bus cranked up. The sand blowers and wipers went to work, and the windshield turned blue, and a white dot moved on it between a series of smaller white dots.

Radar. Wayne had seen that sort of thing on desert vehicles. If he lived through this and got his car back, maybe he'd rig up something like that. And maybe not, he was sick of the desert.

Whatever, at the moment, future plans seemed a little out of place.

Then something else occurred to him. Radar. That meant these bastards had known they were coming and had pulled out in front of them on purpose.

He leaned over the seat and checked where he figured the '57 hit the bus. He didn't see a single dent. Armored, most likely. Most school buses were these days, and that's what this had been. It probably had bullet-proof-glass and puncture-proof sand tires too. School buses had gone that way on account of the race riots and the sending of mutated calves to school just like they were humans. And because of the Codgers—old farts who believed kids ought to be fair game to adults for sexual purposes, or for knocking around when they wanted to let off some tension.

"How about unlocking this cuff?" Calhoun said. "It ain't for shit now anyway."

Wayne looked at the nun. "I'm going for the cuff key in my pants. Don't shoot."

Wayne fished it out, unlocked the cuff, and Calhoun let it slide to the floor. Wayne saw the nun was curious and he said, "I'm a bounty hunter. Help me get this man to Law Town and I could see you earn a little something for your troubles."

The woman shook her head.

"That's the spirit," Calhoun said. "I like a nun that minds her own business . . . You a real nun?"

She nodded.

"Always talk so much?"

Another nod.

Wayne said, "I've never seen a nun like you. Not dressed like that and with a gun."

"We are a small and special order," she said.

"You some kind of Sunday school teacher for these dead folks?"

"Sort of."

"But with them dead, ain't it kind of pointless? They ain't got no souls now, do they?"

"No, but their work adds to the glory of God."

"Their work?" Wayne looked at the dead folks sitting stiffly in their seats. He noted that one of them was about to lose a rotten ear. He sniffed. "They may be adding to the glory of God, but they don't do much for the air."

The nun reached into a pocket on her habit and took out two round objects. She tossed one to Calhoun, and one to Wayne. "Menthol lozenges. They help you stand the smell."

Wayne unwrapped the lozenge and sucked on it. It did help overpower the smell, but the menthol wasn't all that great either. It reminded him of being sick.

"What order are you?" Wayne asked.

"Jesus Loved Mary," the nun said.

"His mama?"

"Mary Magdalene. We think he fucked her. They were lovers. There's evidence in the scriptures. She was a harlot and we have modeled ourselves on her. She gave up that life and became a harlot for Jesus."

"Hate to break it to you, sister," Calhoun said, "but that do-gooder Jesus is as dead as a post. If you're waiting for him to slap the meat to you, that sweet thing of yours is going to dry up and blow away."

"Thanks for the news," the nun said. "But we don't fuck him in person. We fuck him in spirit. We let the spirit enter into men so they may take us in the fashion Jesus took Mary."

"No shit?"

"No shit."

"You know, I think I feel the old boy moving around inside me now. Why don't you shuck them drawers, honey, throw back in that seat there and let ole Calhoun give you a big load of Jesus."

Calhoun shifted in the nun's direction.

She pointed the derringer at him, said, "Stay where you are. If it were so, if you were full of Jesus, I would let you have me in a moment. But you're full of the Devil, not Jesus."

"Shit, sister, give ole Devil a break. He's a fun kind of guy. Let's you and me mount up . . . Well, be like that. But if you change your mind, I can get religion at a moment's notice. I dearly love to fuck. I've fucked everything I could get my hands on but a parakeet, and I'd have fucked that little bitch if I could have found the hole."

"I've never known any dead folks to be trained," Wayne said, trying to get the nun talking in a direction that might help, a direction that would let him know what was going on and what sort of trouble he had fallen into.

"As I said, we are a very special order. Brother Lazarus," she waved a hand at the bus driver, and without looking he lifted a hand in acknowledgement, "is the founder. I don't think he'll mind if I tell his story, explain about us, what we do and why. It's important that we spread the word to the heathens."

"Don't call me no fucking heathen," Calhoun said. "This is heathen, riding around in a fucking bus with a bunch of stinking dead folks with funny hats on. Hell, they can't even carry a tune."

The nun ignored him. "Brother Lazarus was once known by another name, but that name no longer matters. He was a research scientist, and he was one of those who worked in the laboratory where the germs escaped into the air and made it so the dead could not truly die as long as they had an undamaged brain in their heads.

"Brother Lazarus was carrying a dish of the experiment, the germs, and as a joke, one of the lab assistants pretended to trip him, and he, not knowing it was a joke, dodged the assistant's leg and dropped the dish. In a moment, the air conditioning system had blown the germs throughout the research center. Someone opened a door, and the germs were loose on the world.

"Brother Lazarus was consumed by guilt. Not only because he dropped the dish, but because he helped create it in the first place. He quit his job at the laboratory, took to wandering the country. He came out here with nothing more than basic food, water and books. Among these books was the Bible, and the lost books of the Bible: the Apocrypha and the many cast-out chapters of the New Testament. As he studied, it occurred to him that these cast-out books actually belonged. He was able to interpret their higher meaning, and an angel came to him in a dream and told him of another book, and Brother Lazarus took up his pen and recorded the angel's words, direct from God, and in this book, all the mysteries were explained."

"Like screwing Jesus," Calhoun said.

"Like screwing Jesus, and not being afraid of words that mean sex. Not being afraid of seeing Jesus as both God and man. Seeing that sex, if meant for Christ and the opening of the mind, can be a thrilling and religious experience, not just the rutting of two savage animals.

"Brother Lazaraus roamed the desert, the mountains, thinking of the things the Lord had revealed to him, and lo and behold, the Lord revealed yet another thing to him. Brother Lazarus found a great amusement park."

"Didn't know Jesus went in for rides and such," Calhoun said.

"It was long deserted. It had once been part of a place called Disneyland. Brother Lazarus knew of it. There had been several of these Disneylands built about the country, and this one had been in the midst of the Chevy-Cadillac Wars, and had been destroyed and sand had covered most of it."

The nun held out her arms. "And in this rubble, he saw a new beginning."

"Cool off, baby," Calhoun said, "before you have a stroke."

"He gathered to him men and women of a like mind

and taught the gospel to them. The Old Testament. The New Testament. The Lost Books. And his own Book of Lazarus, for he had begun to call himself Lazarus. A symbolic name signifying a new beginning, a rising from the dead and coming to life and seeing things as they really are.''

The nun moved her hands rapidly, expressively as she talked. Sweat beaded on her forehead and upper lip.

"So he returned to his skills as a scientist, but applied them to a higher purpose—God's purpose. And as Brother Lazarus, he realized the use of the dead. They could be taught to work and build a great monument to the glory of God. And this monument, this coed institution of monks and nuns would be called Jesus Land.''

At the word "Jesus," the nun gave her voice an extra trill, and the dead folks, cued, said together, "Eees num be prased.''

"How the hell did you train them dead folks?" Calhoun said. "Dog treats?''

"Science put to the use of our Lord Jesus Christ, that's how. Brother Lazarus made a special device he could insert directly into the brains of dead folks, through the tops of their heads, and the device controls certain cravings. Makes them passive and responsive—at least to simple commands. With the regulator, as Brother Lazarus calls the device, we have been able to do much positive work with the dead.''

"Where do you find these dead folks?" Wayne asked.

"We buy them from the Meat Boys. We save them from amoral purposes.''

"They ought to be shot through the head and put in the goddamn ground," Wayne said.

"If our use of the regulator and the dead folks was merely to better ourselves, I would agree. But it is not. We do the Lord's work.''

"Do the monks fuck the sisters?" Calhoun asked.

"When possessed by the Spirit of Christ. Yes.''

"And I bet they get possessed a lot. Not a bad setup. Dead folks to do the work on the amusement park—''

"It isn't an amusement park now.''

"—and plenty of free pussy. Sounds cozy. I like it. Old shithead up there's smarter than he looks."

"There is nothing selfish about our motives or those of Brother Lazarus. In fact, as penance for loosing the germ on the world in the first place, Brother Lazarus injected a virus into his nose. It is rotting slowly."

"Thought that was quite a snorkel he had on him," Wayne said.

"I take it back," Calhoun said. "He *is* as dumb as he looks."

"Why do the dead folks wear those silly hats?" Wayne asked.

"Brother Lazarus found a storeroom of them at the site of the old amusement park. They are mouse ears. They represent some cartoon animal that was popular once and part of Disneyland. Mickey Mouse, he was called. This way we know which dead folks are ours, and which ones are not controlled by our regulators. From time to time, stray dead folks wander into our area. Murder victims. Children abandoned in the desert. People crossing the desert who died of heat or illness. We've had some of the sisters and brothers attacked. The hats are a precaution."

"And what's the deal with us?" Wayne asked.

The nun smiled sweetly. "You, my children, are to add to the glory of God."

"Children?" Calhoun said. "You call an alligator a lizard, bitch?"

The nun slid back in the seat and rested the derringer in her lap. She pulled her legs into a cocked position, causing her panties to crease in the valley of her vagina; it looked like a nice place to visit, that valley.

Wayne turned from the beauty of it and put his head back and closed his eyes, pulled his hat down over them. There was nothing he could do at the moment, and since the nun was watching Calhoun for him, he'd sleep, store up and figure what to do next. If anything.

He drifted off to sleep wondering what the nun meant by, "You, my children, are to add to the glory of God."

He had a feeling that when he found out, he wasn't going to like it.

5

He awoke off and on and saw that the sunlight filtering through the storm had given everything a greenish color. Calhoun seeing he was awake, said, "Ain't that a pretty color? I had a shirt that color once and liked it lots, but I got in a fight with this Mexican whore with a wooden leg over some money and she tore it. I punched that little bean bandit good."

"Thanks for sharing that," Wayne said, and went back to sleep.

Each time he awoke it was brighter, and finally he awoke to the sun going down and the storm having died out. But he didn't stay awake. He forced himself to close his eyes and store up more energy. To help him nod off he listened to the hum of the motor and thought about the wrecking yard and Pop and all the fun they could have, just drinking beer and playing cars and fucking the border women, and maybe some of those mutated cows they had over there for sale.

Nah. Nix the cows, or any of those genetically altered critters. A man had to draw the line somewhere, and he drew it at fucking critters, even if they had been bred so that they had human traits. You had to have some standards.

'Course, those standards had a way of eroding. He remembered when he said he'd only fuck the pretty ones. His last whore had been downright scary looking. If he didn't watch himself he'd be as bad as Calhoun, trying to find the hole in the parakeet.

He awoke to Calhoun's elbow in his ribs and the nun was standing beside their seat with the derringer. Wayne knew she hadn't slept, but she looked bright-eyed and bushy-tailed. She nodded toward their window, said, "Jesus Land."

She had put that special touch in her voice again, and the dead folks responded with, "Eees num be prased."

It was good and dark now, a crisp night with a big moon the color of hammered brass. The bus sailed across the white sand like a mystical schooner with a full wind in its sails. It went up an impossible hill toward what looked like an aurora borealis, then dove into an atomic rainbow of colors that filled the bus with fairy lights.

When Wayne's eyes became accustomed to the lights, and the bus took a right turn along a precarious curve, he glanced down into the valley. An aerial view couldn't have been any better than the view from his window.

Down there was a universe of polished metal and twisted neon. In the center of the valley was a great statue of Jesus crucified that must have been twenty-five stories high. Most of the body was made of bright metals and multi-colored neon, and much of the light was coming from that. There was a crown of barbed wire wound several times around a chromium plate of a forehead and some rust-colored strands of neon hair. The savior's eyes were huge, green strobes that swung left and right with the precision of an oscillating fan. There was an ear to ear smile on the savior's face and the teeth were slats of sparkling metal with wide cavity-black gaps between them. The statue was equipped with a massive dick of polished, interwoven cables and coils of neon, the dick was thicker and more solid looking than the arthritic steel-tube legs on either side of it; the head of it was made of an enormous spotlight that pulsed the color of irritation.

The bus went around and around the valley, descending like a dead roach going down a slow drain, and finally the road rolled out straight and took them into Jesus Land.

They passed through the legs of Jesus, under the throbbing head of his cock, toward what looked like a small castle of polished gold bricks with an upright drawbridge interlayed with jewels.

The castle was only one of several tall structures that appeared to be made of rare metals and precious stones: gold, silver, emeralds, rubies and sapphires. But the closer they got to the buildings, the less fine they looked and the more they looked like what they were: stucco, cardboard, phosphorescent paint, colored spotlights, and bands of neon.

Off to the left Wayne could see a long, open shed full of vehicles, most of them old school buses. And there were unlighted hovels made of tin and tar paper; homes for the dead, perhaps. Behind the shacks and the bus barn rose skeletal shapes that stretched tall and bleak against the sky and the candy-gem lights; shapes that looked like the bony remains of beached whales.

On the right, Wayne glimpsed a building with an open front that served as a stage. In front of the stage were chairs filled with monks and nuns. On the stage, six monks—one behind a drum set, one with a saxophone, the others with guitars—were blasting out a loud, rocking rhythm that made the bus shake. A nun with the front of her habit thrown open, her headpiece discarded, sang into a microphone with a voice like a suffering angel. The voice screeched out of the amplifiers and came in through the windows of the bus, crushing the sound of the engine. The nun crowed ''Jesus'' so long and hard it sounded like a plea from hell. Then she leapt up and came down doing the splits, the impact driving her back to her feet as if her ass had been loaded with springs.

''Bet that bitch can pick up a quarter with that thing,'' Calhoun said.

Brother Lazarus touched a button, the pseudo-jeweled drawbridge lowered over a narrow moat, and he drove them inside.

It wasn't as well lighted in there. The walls were bleak and gray. Brother Lazarus stopped the bus and got off, and another monk came on board. He was tall and thin and had crooked buck teeth that dented his bottom lip. He also had a twelve-gauge pump shotgun.

''This is Brother Fred,'' the nun said. ''He'll be your tour guide.''

Brother Fred forced Wayne and Calhoun off the bus, away from the dead folks in their mouse-ear hats and the nun in her tight, black panties, jabbed them along a dark corridor, up a swirl of stairs and down a longer corridor with open doors on either side and rooms filled with dark and light and spoiled meat and guts on hooks and skulls and bones lying about like discarded walnut shells and broken sticks; rooms full of dead folks (truly dead) stacked neat as firewood, and rooms full of stone shelves stuffed with beakers of fiery-red and sewer-green and sky-blue and piss-yellow liquids, as well as glass coils through which other colored fluids fled as if chased, smoked as if nervous, and ran into big flasks as if relieved; rooms with platforms and tables and boxes and stools and chairs covered with instruments or dead folks or dead-folk pieces or the asses of monks and nuns as they sat and held charts or tubes or body parts and frowned at them with concentration, lips pursed as if about to explode with some earth-shattering pronouncement; and finally they came to a little room with a tall, glassless window that looked out upon the bright, shiny mess that was Jesus Land.

The room was simple. Table, two chairs, two beds—one on either side of the room. The walls were stone and unadorned. To the right was a little bathroom without a door.

Wayne walked to the window and looked out at Jesus Land pulsing and thumping like a desperate heart. He listened to the music a moment, leaned over and stuck his head outside.

They were high up and there was nothing but a straight drop. If you jumped, you'd wind up with the heels of your boots under your tonsils.

Wayne let out a whistle in appreciation of the drop. Brother Fred thought it was a compliment for Jesus Land. He said, "It's a miracle, isn't it?"

"Miracle?" Calhoun said. "This goony light show? This ain't no miracle. This is for shit. Get that nun on the bus back there to bend over and shit a perfectly round turd through a hoop at twenty paces, and I'll call that a miracle, Mr. Fucked-up Teeth. But this Jesus Land crap is the dumbest, fucking idea since dog sweaters.

"And look at this place. You could use some knick-knacks or something in here. A picture of some ole naked gal doing a donkey, couple of pigs fucking. Anything. And a door on the shitter would be nice. I hate to be straining out a big one and know someone can look in on me. It ain't decent. A man ought to have his fucking grunts in private. This place reminds me of a motel I stayed at in Waco one night, and I made the goddamn manager give me my money back. The roaches in that shit hole were big enough to use the shower.''

Brother Fred listened to all this without blinking an eye, as if seeing Calhoun talk was as amazing as seeing a frog sing. He said. ''Sleep tight, don't let the bed bugs bite. Tomorrow you start to work.''

''I don't want no fucking job,'' Calhoun said.

''Goodnight, children,'' Brother Fred said, and with that he closed the door and they heard it lock, loud and final as the clicking of the drop board on a gallows.

6

At dawn, Wayne got up and took a leak, went to the window to look out. The stage where the monks had played and the nun had jumped was empty. The skeletal shapes he had seen last night were tracks and frames from rides long abandoned. He had a sudden vision of Jesus and his disciples riding a roller coaster, their long hair and robes flapping in the wind.

The large crucified Jesus looked unimpressive without its lights and night's mystery, like a whore in harsh sunlight with makeup gone and wig askew.

''Got any ideas how we're gonna get out of here?'' Calhoun asked.

Wayne looked at Calhoun. He was sitting on the bed, pulling on his boots.

Wayne shook his head.

''I could use a smoke. You know, I think we ought to work together. Then we can try to kill each other.''

Unconsciously, Calhoun touched his ear where Wayne had bitten off the lobe.

''Wouldn't trust you as far as I could kick you,'' Wayne said.

''I hear that. But I give my word. And my word's something you can count on. I won't twist it.''

Wayne studied Calhoun, thought: Well, there wasn't anything to lose. He'd just watch his ass.

''All right,'' Wayne said. ''Give me your word you'll work with me on getting us out of this mess, and when we're good and free, and you say your word has gone far enough, we can settle up.''

"Deal," Calhoun said, and offered his hand.

Wayne looked at it.

"This seals it," Calhoun said.

Wayne took Calhoun's hand and they shook.

7

Moments later the door unlocked and a smiling monk with hair the color and texture of mold fuzz came in with Brother Fred, who still had his pump shotgun. There were two dead folks with them. A man and a woman. They wore torn clothes and the mouse-ear hats. Neither looked long dead or smelled particularly bad. Actually, the monks smelled worse.

Using the barrel of the shotgun, Brother Fred poked them down the hall to a room with metal tables and medical instruments.

Brother Lazarus was on the far side of one of the tables. He was smiling. His nose looked especially cancerous this morning. A white pustule the size of a thumb tip had taken up residence on the left side of his snout, and it looked like a pearl onion in a turd.

Nearby stood a nun. She was short with good, if skinny, legs, and she wore the same outfit as the nun on the bus. It looked more girlish on her, perhaps because she was thin and small-breasted. She had a nice face and eyes that were all pupil. Wisps of blond hair crawled out around the edges of her headgear. She looked pale and weak, as if wearied to the bone. There was a birthmark on her right cheek that looked like a distant view of a small bird in flight.

"Good morning," Brother Lazarus said. "I hope you gentlemen slept well."

"What's this about work?" Wayne said.

"Work?" Brother Lazarus said.

"I described it to them that way," Brother Fred said. "Perhaps an impulsive description."

"I'll say," Brother Lazarus said. "No work here, gentlemen. You have my word on that. We do all the work. Lie on these tables and we'll take a sampling of your blood.''

''Why?'' Wayne said.

''Science,'' Brother Lazarus said. ''I intend to find a cure for this germ that makes the dead come back to life, and to do that, I need living human beings to study. Sounds kind of mad scientist, doesn't it? But I assure you, you've nothing to lose but a few drops of blood. Well, maybe more than a few drops, but nothing serious.''

''Use your own goddamn blood,'' Calhoun said.

''We do. But we're always looking for fresh specimens. Little here, little there. And if you don't do it, we'll kill you.''

Calhoun spun and hit Brother Fred on the nose. It was a solid punch and Brother Fred hit the floor on his butt, but he hung onto the shotgun and pointed it up at Calhoun. ''Go on,'' he said, his nose streaming blood. ''Try that again.''

Wayne flexed to help, but hesitated. He could kick Brother Fred in the head from where he was, but that might not keep him from shooting Calhoun, and there would go the extra reward money. And besides, he'd given his word to the bastard that they'd try to help each other survive until they got out of this.

The other monk clasped his hands and swung them into the side of Calhoun's head, knocking him down. Brother Fred got up, and while Calhoun was trying to rise, he hit him with the stock of the shotgun in the back of the head, hit him so hard it drove Calhoun's forehead into the floor. Calhoun rolled over on his side and lay there, his eyes fluttering like moth wings.

''Brother Fred, you must learn to turn the other cheek,'' Brother Lazarus said. ''Now put this sack of shit on the table.''

Brother Fred checked Wayne to see if he looked like trouble. Wayne put his hands in his pockets and smiled.

Brother Fred called the two dead folks over and had them put Calhoun on the table. Brother Lazarus strapped him down.

The nun brought a tray of needles, syringes, cotton and bottles over, put it down on the table next to Calhoun's head. Brother Lazarus rolled up Calhoun's sleeve and fixed up a needle and stuck it in Calhoun's arm, drew it full of blood. He stuck the needle through the rubber top of one of the bottles and shot the blood into that.

He looked at Wayne and said, "I hope you'll be less trouble."

"Do I get some orange juice and a little cracker afterwards?" Wayne said.

"You get to walk out without a knot on your head," Brother Lazarus said.

"Guess that'll have to do."

Wayne got on the table next to Calhoun and Brother Lazarus strapped him down. The nun brought the tray over and Brother Lazarus did to him what he had done to Calhoun. The nun stood over Wayne and looked down at his face. Wayne tried to read something in her features but couldn't find a clue.

When Brother Lazarus was finished he took hold of Wayne's chin and shook it. "My, but you two boys look healthy. But you can never be sure. We'll have to run the blood through some tests. Meantime, Sister Worth will run a few additional tests on you, and," he nodded at the unconscious Calhoun, "I'll see to your friend here."

"He's no friend of mine," Wayne said.

They took Wayne off the table, and Sister Worth and Brother Fred and his shotgun, directed him down the hall into another room.

The room was lined with shelves that were lined with instruments and bottles. The lighting was poor, most of it coming through a slatted window, though there was an anemic yellow bulb overhead. Dust motes swam in the air.

In the center of the room on its rim was a great, spoked wheel. It had two straps well spaced at the top, and two more at the bottom. Beneath the bottom straps were blocks of wood. The wheel was attached in back to an upright metal bar that had switches and buttons all over it.

Brother Fred made Wayne strip and get on the wheel with his back to the hub and his feet on the blocks. Sister

Worth strapped his ankles down tight, then he was made to put his hands up, and she strapped his wrists to the upper part of the wheel.

"I hope this hurts a lot," Brother Fred said.

"Wipe the blood off your face," Wayne said. "It makes you look silly."

Brother Fred made a gesture with his middle finger that wasn't religious and left the room.

8

Sister Worth touched a switch and the wheel began to spin, slowly at first, and the bad light came through the windows and poked through the rungs and the dust swam before his eyes and the wheel and its spokes threw twisting shadows on the wall.

As he went around, Wayne closed his eyes. It kept him from feeling so dizzy, especially on the down swings.

On a turn up, he opened his eyes and caught sight of Sister Worth standing in front of the wheel staring at him. He said, "Why?" and closed his eyes as the wheel dipped.

"Because Brother Lazarus says so," came the answer after such a long time Wayne had almost forgotten the question. Actually, he hadn't expected a response. He was surprised that such a thing had come out of his mouth, and he felt a little diminished for having asked.

He opened his eyes on another swing up, and she was moving behind the wheel, out of his line of vision. He heard a snick like a switch being flipped and lightning jumped through him and he screamed in spite of himself. A little fork of electricity licked out of his mouth like a reptile tongue tasting air.

Faster spun the wheel and the jolts came more often and he screamed less loud, and finally not at all. He was too numb. He was adrift in space wearing only his cowboy hat and boots, moving away from earth very fast. Floating all around him were wrecked cars. He looked and saw that one of them was his '57, and behind the steering wheel was Pop. Sitting beside the old man was a Mexican whore. Two more were in the back seat. They looked a little drunk.

One of the whores in back pulled up her dress and cocked it high up so he could see her pussy. It looked like a taco that needed a shave.

He smiled and tried to go for it, but the '57 was moving away, swinging wide and turning its tail to him. He could see a face at the back window. Pop's face. He had crawled back there and was waving slowly and sadly. A whore pulled Pop from view.

The wrecked cars moved away too, as if caught in the vacuum of the '57's retreat. Wayne swam with his arms, kicked with his legs, trying to pursue the '57 and the wrecks. But he dangled where he was, like a moth pinned to a board. The cars moved out of sight and left him there with his arms and legs stretched out, spinning amidst an infinity of cold, uncaring stars.

". . . how the tests are run . . . marks everything about you . . . charts it . . . EKG, brain waves, liver . . . everything . . . it hurts because Brother Lazarus wants it to . . . thinks I don't know these things . . . that I'm slow . . . I'm slow, not stupid . . . smart really . . . used to be scientist . . . before the accident . . . Brother Lazarus is not holy . . . he's mad . . . made the wheel because of the Holy Inquisition . . . knows a lot about the Inquisition . . . thinks we need it again . . . for the likes of men like you . . . the unholy, he says . . . But he just likes to hurt . . . I know."

Wayne opened his eyes. The wheel had stopped. Sister Worth was talking in her monotone, explaining the wheel. He remembered asking her, "Why" about three thousand years ago.

Sister Worth was staring at him again. She went away and he expected the wheel to start up, but when she returned, she had a long, narrow mirror under her arm. She put it against the wall across from him. She got on the wheel with him, her little feet on the wooden platforms beside his. She hiked up the bottom of her habit and pulled down her black panties. She put her face close to his, as if searching for something.

"He plans to take your body . . . piece by piece . . . blood, cells, brain, your cock . . . all of it . . . He wants to live forever."

She had her panties in her hand, and she tossed them. Wayne watched them fly up and flutter to the floor like a dying bat.

She took hold of his dick and pulled on it. Her palm was cold and he didn't feel his best, but he began to get hard. She put him between her legs and rubbed his dick between her thighs. They were as cold as her hands, and dry.

"I know him now . . . know what he's doing . . . the dead germ virus . . . he was trying to make something that would make him live forever . . . it made the dead come back . . . didn't keep the living alive, free of old age . . ."

His dick was throbbing now, in spite of the coolness of her body.

"He cuts up dead folks to learn . . . experiments on them . . . but the secret of eternal life is with the living . . . that's why he wants you . . . you're an outsider . . . those who live here he can test . . . but he must keep them alive to do his bidding . . . not let them know how he really is . . . needs your insides and the other man's . . . he wants to be a God . . . flies high above us in a little plane and looks down . . . Likes to think he is the creator, I bet . . ."

"Plane?"

"Ultralight."

She pushed his cock inside her, and it was cold and dry in there, like liver left overnight on a drainboard. Still, he found himself ready. At this point, he would have gouged a hole in a turnip.

She kissed him on the ear and alongside the neck; cold little kisses, dry as toast.

". . . thinks I don't know . . . But I know he doesn't love Jesus . . . He loves himself, and power . . . He's sad about his nose . . ."

"I bet."

"Did it in a moment of religious fervor . . . before he

lost the belief . . . Now he wants to be what he was . . .
A scientist. He wants to grow a new nose . . . know how
. . . saw him grow a finger in a dish once . . . grew it
from the skin off a knuckle of one of the brothers . . . He
can do all kinds of things.''

She was moving her hips now. He could see over her
shoulder into the mirror against the wall. Could see her
white ass rolling, the black habit hiked up above it, threatening to drop like a curtain. He began to thrust back,
slowly, firmly.

She looked over her shoulder into the mirror, watching
herself fuck him. There was a look more of study than
rapture on her face.

''Want to feel alive,'' she said. ''Feel a good, hard
dick . . . Been too long.''

''I'm doing the best I can,'' Wayne said. ''This ain't
the most romantic of spots.''

''Push so I can feel it.''

''Nice,'' Wayne said. He gave it everything he had. He
was beginning to lose his erection. He felt as if he were
auditioning for a job and not making the best of impres-
sions. He felt like a knothole would be dissatisfied with
him.

She got off of him and climbed down.

''Don't blame you,'' he said.

She went behind the wheel and touched some things on
the upright. She mounted him again, hooked her ankles
behind his. The wheel began to turn. Short electrical
shocks leaped through him. They weren't as powerful as
before. They were invigorating. When he kissed her it was
like touching his tongue to a battery. It felt as if electricity
was racing through his veins and flying out the head of his
dick; he felt as if he might fill her with lightning instead
of come.

The wheel creaked to a stop; it must have had a timer
on it. They were upside down and Wayne could see their
reflection in the mirror; they looked like two lizards fucking on a window pane.

He couldn't tell if she had finished or not, so he went
ahead and got it over with. Without the electricity he was

losing his desire. It hadn't been an A-one piece of ass, but hell, as Pop always said, "Worse pussy I ever had was good."

"They'll be coming back," she said. "Soon . . . Don't want them to find us like this . . . Other tests to do yet."

"Why did you do this?"

"I want out of the order . . . Want out of this desert . . . I want to live . . . And I want you to help me."

"I'm game, but the blood is rushing to my head and I'm getting dizzy. Maybe you ought to get off me."

After an eon she said, "I have a plan."

She untwined from him and went behind the wheel and hit a switch that turned Wayne upright. She touched another switch and he began to spin slowly, and while he spun and while lightning played inside him, she told him her plan.

9

"I think ole Brother Fred wants to fuck me," Calhoun said. "He keeps trying to get his finger up my asshole."

They were back in their room. Brother Fred had brought them back, making them carry their clothes, and now they were alone again, dressing.

"We're getting out of here," Wayne said. "The nun, Sister Worth, she's going to help."

"What's her angle?"

"She hates this place and wants my dick. Mostly, she hates this place."

"What's the plan?"

Wayne told him first what Brother Lazarus had planned. On the morrow he would have them brought to the room with the steel tables, and they would go on the tables, and if the tests had turned out good, they would be pronounced fit as fiddles and Brother Lazarus would strip the skin from their bodies, slowly, because according to Sister Worth he liked to do it that way, and he would drain their blood and percolate it into his formulas like coffee, cut their brains out and put them in vats and store their veins and organs in freezers.

All of this would be done in the name of God and Jesus Christ (Eees num be prased) under the guise of finding a cure for the dead folks germ. But it would all instead be for Brother Lazarus who wanted to have a new nose, fly his ultralight above Jesus Land and live forever.

Sister Worth's plan was this:

She would be in the dissecting room. She would have guns hidden. She would make the first move, a distraction, then it was up to them.

"This time," Wayne said, "one of us has to get on top of that shotgun."

"You had your finger up your ass in there today, or we'd have had them."

"We're going to have surprise on our side this time. Real surprise. They won't be expecting Sister Worth. We can get up there on the roof and take off in that ultralight. When it runs out of gas we can walk, maybe get back to the '57 and hope it runs."

"We'll settle our score then. Whoever wins keeps the car and the split tail. As for tomorrow, I've got a little ace."

Calhoun pulled on his boots. He twisted the heel of one of them. It swung out and a little knife dropped into his hand. "It's sharp," Calhoun said. "I cut a Chinaman from gut to gill with it. It was easy as sliding a stick through fresh shit."

"Been nice if you'd had that ready today."

"I wanted to scout things out first. And to tell the truth, I thought one pop to Brother Fred's mouth and he'd be out of the picture."

"You hit him in the nose."

"Yeah, goddamn it, but I was aiming for his mouth."

10

Dawn and the room with the metal tables looked the same. No one had brought in a vase of flowers to brighten the place.

Brother Lazarus's nose had changed however; there were two pearl onions nestled in it now.

Sister Worth, looking only a little more animated than yesterday, stood nearby. She was holding the tray with the instruments. This time the tray was full of scalpels. The light caught their edges and made them wink.

Brother Fred was standing behind Calhoun, and Brother Mold Fuzz was behind Wayne. They must have felt pretty confident today. They had dispensed with the dead folks.

Wayne looked at Sister Worth and thought maybe things were not good. Maybe she had lied to him in her slow talking way. Only wanted a little dick and wanted to keep it quiet. To do that, she might have promised anything. She might not care what Brother Lazarus did to them.

If it looked like a double cross, Wayne was going to go for it. If he had to jump right into the mouth of Brother Fred's shotgun. That was a better way to go than having the hide peeled from your body. The idea of Brother Lazarus and his ugly nose leaning over him did not appeal at all.

"It's so nice to see you," Brother Lazarus said. "I hope we'll have none of the unpleasantness of yesterday. Now, on the tables."

Wayne looked at Sister Worth. Her expression showed nothing. The only thing about her that looked alive was the bent wings of the bird birthmark on her cheek.

All right, Wayne thought, I'll go as far as the table, then I'm going to do something. Even if it's wrong.

He look a step forward, and Sister Worth flipped the contents of the tray into Brother Lazarus's face. A scalpel went into his nose and hung there. The tray and the rest of its contents hit the floor.

Before Brother Lazarus could yelp, Calhoun dropped and wheeled. He was under Brother Fred's shotgun and he used his forearm to drive the barrel upwards. The gun went off and peppered the ceiling. Plaster sprinkled down.

Calhoun had concealed the little knife in the palm of his hand and he brought it up and into Brother Fred's groin. The blade went through the robe and buried to the hilt.

The instant Calhoun made his move, Wayne brought his forearm back and around into Brother Mold Fuzz's throat, then turned and caught his head and jerked that down and kneed him a couple of times. He floored him by driving an elbow into the back of his neck.

Calhoun had the shotgun now, and Brother Fred was on the floor trying to pull the knife out of his balls. Calhoun blew Brother Fred's head off, then did the same for Brother Mold Fuzz.

Brother Lazarus, the scalpel hanging from his nose, tried to run for it, but he stepped on the tray and that sent him flying. He landed on his stomach. Calhoun took two deep steps and kicked him in the throat. Brother Lazarus made a sound like he was gargling and tried to get up.

Wayne helped him. He grabbed Brother Lazarus by the back of his robe and pulled him up, slammed him back against a table. The scalpel still dangled from the monk's nose. Wayne grabbed it and jerked, taking away a chunk of nose as he did. Brother Lazarus screamed.

Calhoun put the shotgun in Brother Lazarus's mouth and that made him stop screaming. Calhoun pumped the shotgun. He said, "Eat it," and pulled the trigger. Brother Lazarus's brains went out the back of his head riding on a chunk of skull. The brains and skull hit the table and sailed on to the floor like a plate of scrambled eggs pushed the length of a cafe counter.

Sister Worth had not moved. Wayne figured she had used all of her concentration to hit Brother Lazarus with the tray.

"You said you'd have guns," Wayne said to her.

She turned her back to him and lifted her habit. In a belt above her panties were two .38 revolvers. Wayne pulled them out and held one in each hand. "Two-Gun Wayne," he said.

"What about the ultralight?" Calhoun said. "We've made enough noise for a prison riot. We need to move."

Sister Worth turned to the door at the back of the room, and before she could say anything or lead, Wayne and Calhoun snapped to it and grabbed her and pushed her toward it.

There were stairs on the other side of the door and they took them two at a time. They went through a trap door and onto the roof and there, tied down with bungie straps to metal hoops, was the ultralight. It was blue-and-white canvas and metal rods, and strapped to either side of it was a twelve gauge pump and a bag of food and a canteen of water.

They unsnapped the roof straps and got in the two seater and used the straps to fasten Sister Worth between them. It wasn't comfortable, but it was a ride.

They sat there. After a moment, Calhoun said, "Well?"

"Shit," Wayne said. "I can't fly this thing."

They looked at Sister Worth. She was staring at the controls.

"Say something, damn it," Wayne said.

"That's the switch," she said. "That stick . . . forward is up, back brings the nose down . . . side to side . . ."

"Got it."

"Well, shoot this bastard over the side," Calhoun said.

Wayne cranked it, gave it the throttle. The machine rolled forward, wobbled.

"Too much weight," Wayne said.

"Throw the cunt over the side," Calhoun said.

"It's all or nothing," Wayne said. The ultralight continued to swing its tail left and right, but leveled off as they went over the edge.

They sailed for a hundred yards, made a mean curve Wayne couldn't fight, and fell straight away into the statue of Jesus, striking it in the head, right in the midst of the barbed wire crown. Spot lights shattered, metal groaned, the wire tangled in the nylon wings of the craft and held it. The head of Jesus nodded forward, popped off and shot out on the electric cables inside like a jack-in-the-box. The cables pulled tight a hundred feet from the ground and worked the head and the craft like a yoyo. Then the barbed wire crown unraveled and dropped the craft the rest of the way. It hit the ground with a crunch and a rip and a cloud of dust.

The head of Jesus bobbed above the shattered ultralight like a bird preparing to peck a worm.

11

Wayne crawled out of the wreckage and tried his legs. They worked.

Calhoun was on his feet cussing, unstrapping the shotguns and supplies.

Sister Worth lay in the midst of the wreck, the nylon and aluminum supports folded around her like butterfly wings.

Wayne started pulling the mess off of her. He saw that her leg was broken. A bone punched out of her thigh like a sharpened stick. There was no blood.

"Here comes the church social," Calhoun said.

The word was out about Brother Lazarus and the others. A horde of monks, nuns and dead folks, were rushing over the drawbridge. Some of the nuns and monks had guns. All of the dead folks had clubs. The clergy was yelling.

Wayne nodded toward the bus barn, "Let's get a bus."

Wayne picked up Sister Worth, cradled her in his arms, and made a run for it. Calhoun, carrying the guns and the supplies, passed them. He jumped through the open doorway of a bus and dropped out of sight. Wayne knew he was jerking wires loose, trying to hotwire them a ride. Wayne hoped he was good at it and fast.

When Wayne got to the bus, he laid Sister Worth down beside it and pulled the .38's and stood in front of her. If he was going down he wanted to go like Wild Bill Hickock. A blazing gun in either fist and a woman to protect.

Actually, he'd prefer the bus to start.

It did.

Calhoun jerked it in gear, backed it out and around in front of Wayne and Sister Worth. The monks and nuns had started firing and their rounds bounced off the side of the armored bus.

From inside Calhoun yelled, "Get the hell on."

Wayne stuck the guns in his belt, grabbed up Sister Worth and leapt inside. Calhoun jerked the bus forward and Wayne and Sister Worth went flying over a seat and into another.

"I thought you were leaving," Wayne said.

"I wanted to. But I gave my word."

Wayne stretched Sister Worth out on the seat and looked at her leg. After that tossing Calhoun had given them, the break was sticking out even more.

Calhoun closed the bus door and checked his wing-mirror. Nuns and monks and dead folks had piled into a couple of buses, and now the buses were pursuing them. One of them moved very fast, as if souped up.

"I probably got the granny of the bunch," Calhoun said.

They climbed over a ridge of sand, then they were on the narrow road that wound itself upwards. Behind them, one of the buses had fallen back, maybe some kind of mechanical trouble. The other was gaining.

The road widened and Calhoun yelled, "I think this is what the fucker's been waiting for."

Even as Calhoun spoke, their pursuer put on a burst of speed and swung left and came up beside them, tried to swerve over and push them off the road, down into the deepening valley. But Calhoun fought the curves and didn't budge.

The other bus swung its door open and a nun, the very one who had been on the bus that brought them to Jesus Land, stood there with her legs spread wide, showing the black-pantied mound of her crotch. She had one arm bent around a seat post and was holding in both hands the ever-popular clergy tool, the twelve-gauge pump.

As they made a curve, the nun fired a round into the window next to Calhoun. The window made a cracking noise and thin crooked lines spread in all directions, but the glass held.

She pumped a round into the chamber and fired again. Bullet proof or not, this time the front sheet of glass fell away. Another well-placed round and the rest of the glass would go and Calhoun could wave his head goodbye.

Wayne put his knees in a seat and got the window down. The nun saw him, whirled and fired. The shot was low and hit the bottom part of the window and starred it and pelleted the chassis.

Wayne stuck a .38 out of the window and fired as the nun was jacking another load into position. His shot hit her in the head and her right eye went big and wet, and she swung around on the pole and lost the shotgun. It went out the door. She clung there by the bend of her elbow for a moment, then her arm straightened and she fell outside. The bus ran over her and she popped red and juicy at both ends like a stomped jelly roll.

"Waste of good pussy," Calhoun said. He edged into the other bus, and it pushed back. But Calhoun pushed harder and made it hit the wall with a screech like a panther.

The bus came back and shoved Calhoun to the side of the cliff and honked twice for Jesus.

Calhoun down-shifted, let off the gas, allowed the other bus to soar past by half a length. Then he jerked the wheel so that he caught the rear of it and knocked it across the road. He speared it in the side with the nose of his bus and the other started to spin. It clipped the front of Calhoun's bus and peeled the bumper back. Calhoun braked and the other bus kept spinning. It spun off the road and down into the valley amidst a chorus of cries.

Thirty minutes later they reached the top of the canyon and were in the desert. The bus began to throw up smoke from the front and make a noise like a dog strangling on a chicken bone. Calhoun pulled over.

12

"Goddamn bumper got twisted under there and it's shredded the tire some," Calhoun said. "I think if we can peel the bumper off, there's enough of that tire to run on."

Wayne and Calhoun got hold of the bumper and pulled but it wouldn't come off. Not completely. Part of it had been creased, and that part finally gave way and broke off from the rest of it.

"That ought to be enough to keep from rubbing the tire," Calhoun said.

Sister Worth called from inside the bus. Wayne went to check on her. "Take me off the bus," she said. ". . . I want to feel free air and sun."

"There doesn't feel like there's any air out there,"

Wayne said. "And the sun feels just like it always does. Hot."

"Please."

He picked her up and carried her outside and found a ridge of sand and laid her down so her head was propped against it.

"I . . . I need batteries," she said.

"Say what?" Wayne said.

She lay looking straight into the sun. "Brother Lazarus's greatest work . . . a dead folk that can think . . . has memory of the past . . . Was a scientist too . . ." Her hand came up in stages, finally got hold of her head gear and pushed it off.

Gleaming from the center to her tangled blond hair was a silver knob.

"He . . . was not a good man . . . I am a good woman . . . I want to feel alive . . . like before . . . batteries going . . . brought others."

Her hand fumbled at a snap pocket on her habit. Wayne opened it for her and got out what was inside. Four batteries.

"Uses two . . . simple."

Calhoun was standing over them now. "That explains some things," he said.

"Don't look at me like that . . ." Sister Worth said, and Wayne realized he had never told her his name and she had never asked. "Unscrew . . . put the batteries in . . . Without them I'll be an eater . . . Can't wait too long."

"All right," Wayne said. He went behind her and propped her up on the sand drift and unscrewed the metal shaft from her skull. He thought about when she had fucked him on the wheel and how desperate she had been to feel something, and how she had been cold as flint and lustless. He remembered how she had looked in the mirror hoping to see something that wasn't there.

He dropped the batteries in the sand and took out one of the revolvers and put it close to the back of her head and pulled the trigger. Her body jerked slightly and fell over, her face turning toward him.

The bullet had come out where the bird had been on her cheek and had taken it completely away, leaving a bloodless hole.

"Best thing," Calhoun said. "There's enough live pussy in the world without you pulling this broken-legged dead thing around after you on a board."

"Shut up," Wayne said.

"When a man gets sentimental over women and kids, he can count himself out."

Wayne stood up.

"Well boy," Calhoun said. "I reckon it's time."

"Reckon so," Wayne said.

"How about we do this with some class? Give me one of your pistols and we'll get back-to-back and I'll count to ten, and when I get there, we'll turn and shoot."

Wayne gave Calhoun one of the pistols. Calhoun checked the chambers, said, "I've got four loads."

Wayne took two out of his pistol and tossed them on the ground. "Even Steven," he said.

They got back-to-back and held the guns by their legs.

"Guess if you kill me you'll take me in," Calhoun said. "So that means you'll put a bullet through my head if I need it. I don't want to come back as one of the dead folks. Got your word on that?"

"Yep."

"I'll do the same for you. Give my word. You know that's worth something."

"We gonna shoot or talk?"

"You know, boy, under different circumstances, I could have liked you. We might have been friends."

"Not likely."

Calhoun started counting, and they started stepping. When he got to ten, they turned.

Calhoun's pistol barked first, and Wayne felt the bullet punch him low in the right side of his chest, spinning him slightly. He lifted his revolver and took his time and shot just as Calhoun fired again.

Calhoun's second bullet whizzed by Wayne's head. Wayne's shot hit Calhoun in the stomach.

Calhoun went to his knees and had trouble drawing a

breath. He tried to lift his revolver but couldn't; it was as if it had turned into an anvil.

Wayne shot him again. Hitting him in the middle of the chest this time and knocking him back so that his legs were curled beneath him.

Wayne walked over to Calhoun, dropped to one knee and took the revolver from him.

"Shit," Calhoun said. "I wouldn't have thought that for nothing. You hit?"

"Scratched."

"Shit."

Wayne put the revolver to Calhoun's forehead and Calhoun closed his eyes and Wayne pulled the trigger.

13

The wound wasn't a scratch. Wayne knew he should leave Sister Worth where she was and load Calhoun on the bus and haul him in for bounty. But he didn't care about the bounty anymore.

He used the ragged piece of bumper to dig them a shallow side-by-side grave. When he finished, he stuck the fender fragment up between them and used the sight of one of the revolvers to scratch into it: HERE LIES SISTER WORTH AND CALHOUN WHO KEPT HIS WORD.

You couldn't really read it good and he knew the first real wind would keel it over, but it made him feel better about something, even if he couldn't put his finger on it.

His wound had opened up and the sun was very hot now, and since he had lost his hat he could feel his brain cooking in his skull like meat boiling in a pot.

He got on the bus, started it and drove through the day and the night and it was near morning when he came to the Cadillacs and turned down between them and drove until he came to the '57.

When he stopped and tried to get off the bus, he found he could hardly move. The revolvers in his belt were stuck to his shirt and stomach because of the blood from his wound.

He pulled himself up with the steering wheel, got one

of the shotguns and used it for a crutch. He got the food
and water and went out to inspect the '57.

It was for shit. It had not only lost its windshield, the
front end was mashed way back and one of the big sand
tires was twisted at such an angle he knew the axle was
shot.

He leaned against the Chevy and tried to think. The bus
was okay and there was still some gas in it, and he could
get the hose out of the trunk of the '57 and siphon gas out
of its tanks and put it in the bus. That would give him a
few miles.

Miles.

He didn't feel as if he could walk twenty feet, let alone
concentrate on driving.

He let go of the shotgun, the food and water. He scooted
onto the hood of the Chevy and managed himself to the
roof. He lay there on his back and looked at the sky.

It was a clear night and the stars were sharp with no
fuzz around them. He felt cold. In a couple of hours the
stars would fade and the sun would come up and the cool
would give way to heat.

He turned his head and looked at one of the Cadillacs
and a skeleton face pressed to its windshield, forever looking down at the sand.

That was no way to end, looking down.

He crossed his legs and stretched out his arms and studied the sky. It didn't feel so cold now, and the pain had
almost stopped. He was more numb than anything else.

He pulled one of the revolvers and cocked it and put it
to his temple and continued to look at the stars. Then he
closed his eyes and found that he could still see them. He
was once again hanging in the void between the stars
wearing only his hat and cowboy boots, and floating about
him were the junk cars and the '57, undamaged.

The cars were moving toward him this time, not away.
The '57 was in the lead, and as it grew closer he saw Pop
behind the wheel and beside him was a Mexican puta, and
in the back, two more. They were all smiling and Pop
honked the horn and waved.

The '57 came alongside him and the back door opened.

Sitting between the whores was Sister Worth. She had not been there a moment ago, but now she was. And he had never noticed how big the back seat of the '57 was.

Sister Worth smiled at him and the bird on her cheek lifted higher. Her hair was combed out long and straight and she looked pink-skinned and happy. On the floorboard at her feet was a chest of iced-beer. Lone Star, by God.

Pop was leaning over the front seat, holding out his hand and Sister Worth and the whores were beckoning him inside.

Wayne worked his hands and feet, found this time that he could move. He swam through the open door, touched Pop's hand, and Pop said, "It's good to see you, son," and at the moment Wayne pulled the trigger, Pop pulled him inside.